"*Christmas in Vermont* is a Hallmark movie dunked in a cup of hot cocoa wrapped in a tartan scarf. . . With a Stars Hollow–worthy ensemble of supporting characters and a preciously precocious young-girl character, it will charm fans of Mary Kay Andrews and Debbie Macomber." —*Booklist*

"A fun, romantic novel set at a beautiful location at an inn in Vermont makes for a heartfelt story of two people who may find love again." —Redcarpetcrash.com

"*Christmas in Vermont* is a sweet, holiday treat of a holiday novel." —Freshfiction.com

"Filled with charming characters, sweet romance, and second chances set at a picturesque Vermont inn, *Christmas in Vermont* is Anita Hughes at her finest. You'll find yourself filled with holiday spirit after reading this enchanting love story."
—Lucy Sykes, bestselling co-author of *The Knockoff*

"A charming tale of missed opportunities and second chances that is guaranteed to leave readers with a sigh of satisfaction. With a picturesque setting and cast of genuinely likeable characters, Anita Hughes has crafted a holiday romance that is sure to become an annual favorite."
—Bette Lee Crosby, *USA Today* bestselling author

"*Christmas in Vermont* is a charming romance that sparks with holiday magic. Set in the quaint village in Snowberry, Vermont, it is an enchanting story about a second chance at first love. Filled with endearing characters and dazzling backdrops, it's the kind of story that makes you want to curl up in front of a blazing fire with a cup of hot chocolate and read."

—Suzanne Redfearn, author of *Hush Little Baby*

"*Christmas in Vermont* is such a cozy, feel-good book. Set in a picturesque Vermont town at a quaint inn struggling to make ends meet, the story is reminiscent of the holiday classic *White Christmas*."

—Bookishwayfarer.com

"If you love holiday romances then you do not want to miss Anita Hughes."

—Thelitbitch.com

Also by Anita Hughes

CHRISTMAS IN VERMONT

ANITA HUGHES

St. Martin's Paperbacks

Published in the United States by St. Martin's Paperbacks, an imprint of St. Martin's Publishing Group.

CHRISTMAS IN VERMONT

Copyright © 2019 by Anita Hughes.
Excerpt from *A Magical New York Christmas* copyright © 2021 by Anita Hughes.

For information, address St. Martin's Publishing Group, 120 Broadway, New York, NY 10271.

www.stmartins.com

ISBN: 978-1-250-80183-8

Our books may be purchased in bulk for promotional, educational, or business use. Please contact your local bookseller or the Macmillan Corporate and Premium Sales Department at 1-800-221-7945, ext. 5442, or by email at MacmillanSpecialMarkets@macmillan.com.

Printed in the United States of America

St. Martin's Griffin edition / October 2019
St. Martin's Paperbacks edition / November 2021

10 9 8 7 6 5 4 3 2 1

To my mother

CHRISTMAS IN VERMONT

One

EMMA STROLLED THROUGH THE EAST Village and admired the lampposts wrapped in red bows and the shop windows littered with fake snow and tinsel. Most of her friends fled New York City during Christmas, but Emma adored Manhattan during the holidays. Fifth Avenue flooded in lights was so romantic, and she could stare at the cashmere sweaters in the windows of Barney's for hours.

A small part of her knew she was trying to make herself feel better because right this minute her ex-boyfriend, Scott, was walking through the arrivals lounge in Maui and letting one of those pretty Hawaiian women place a lei around his neck. It didn't help that they'd only broken up five days ago; she should have been beside him, deciding whether to watch the sunset at the beach or drink banana daiquiris in the hotel bar.

Instead, she would watch the ball drop at Times Square, and go with her best friend, Bronwyn, and her two young girls to see the Nutcracker. It wouldn't have been fair to wait to break up with Scott until after they'd returned from Hawaii, no matter how tempting the feasts of roasted pig and moonlight boat rides had sounded in the brochure.

She looked at the scrap of paper in her hand and checked the sign above the storefront. A bell tinkled when she opened the door, and she found herself in a small shop. There was a plastic Christmas tree and a tray with stale-looking Christmas cookies.

"Merry Christmas," a male voice said. "Can I help you?"

Emma looked up and noticed a man in his early sixties, wearing a rumpled shirt and round glasses.

"I didn't think anyone would be open this close to Christmas, but I saw your ad online. I'd like to sell this bracelet." She took a case out of her purse and snapped it open. Inside was a gold bracelet with an emerald clasp.

"I like being open this late; people often need last-minute presents. That's a beautiful piece." He glanced from the bracelet to Emma's Burberry coat and leather boots. "It's none of my business, but you don't look like you need the money, and I can't afford to give you nearly what it's worth. Most of my customers are behind on their rent or maxed out on their credit cards and just want me to take an item off their hands."

The man looked so kind, a bit like the basset hound she'd had as a child, and she had a sudden urge to tell him everything: how Scott had given it to her a week before Christmas because it matched the green dress she was wearing to his company's Christmas party, and how she'd felt so bad accepting it when she was certain their relationship was over. She'd thought it would be mean to make him attend the party alone, but she'd known it was a bad idea as soon as they arrived. Other guests kept clapping Scott on the back and saying he hadn't exaggerated, Emma was beautiful and they were a perfect couple.

"It *is* gorgeous," Emma agreed, turning it over. "My boyfriend gave it to me for Christmas. You see, it's engraved, so I can't return it."

"*To Emma, the light of my life,*" the man read out loud. He whistled. "Don't tell me he cheated on you. I told my son, if he ever cheats on his girlfriend, I'll put him across my knee like my father did when I was a child. All these dating apps make young people think there's something better out there, but when you find the person you love, you should stick to them like toffee on a candy apple. My wife and I were married for thirty-two years before she died."

"Scott would never cheat on me." Emma shook her head.

"Why else would you sell a bracelet from Harry Winston?" he inquired, waving at the box.

"I broke up with him," she said, wondering why she was telling a complete stranger. Bronwyn would say it was because Emma felt slightly guilty, and she'd be right. For the last ten years, she hadn't been able to make a relationship last more than a year. At almost exactly 365 days, she broke up with the guy; or, every so often, he broke up with her. How many New Year's Eves had she spent sitting in front of her television with a bowl of popcorn, wishing things had been different, while knowing she couldn't have done anything else?

"Let me guess," he said, peering at Emma's salon-cut hair. "You're in your early thirties and you're both professionals. You started stopping by Tiffany's after work just to look, and he's spending more nights out with the boys. The last straw was when your best friend got engaged and your boyfriend claimed he had a business trip and couldn't make the wedding."

"Just the reverse. I think Scott was going to ask me to marry him, and I had to stop him," she said, wondering again why she wanted this stranger to understand. "I couldn't marry him. I wasn't in love with him."

"Well, that's different." He examined the bracelet. "Marriage is nothing without love; it's better to end it now."

What Emma didn't say was that she was afraid she couldn't love someone deeply, and that she'd never get married at all. She wanted someone to share things with, and a kitchen like Bronwyn's that overflowed with lunchboxes and the stray pair of mittens that never made it to the mudroom. And she wanted that giddy sensation of not being able to wait to see that person at the end of the day—the thought that just looking at him was like being bathed in sunshine. And what was Christmas without someone to roast marshmallows by the fire and open presents with?

"I can give you two hundred dollars." He put the bracelet down and looked at Emma.

"That's fine. I'm going to donate the money to the Salvation Army. It's my favorite Christmas charity," she said, nodding. "I offered to give it back, but he refused."

The man went to the cash register, and Emma glanced at the jewelry cases. Suddenly she saw a familiar-looking watch. It couldn't be! She looked more closely and was sure it was the watch she'd given Fletcher before they graduated from college eleven years ago. It had been expensive, but she hadn't been able to resist the leather band and white face with roman numerals.

It was just before Fletcher had left to work at the Old Vic in London, and Emma moved to New York to be an assistant copy-writer at Ogilvy & Mather. She'd spent two weeks watching *Mad Men,* even though Madison Avenue in the 1960s was nothing like advertising agencies today. It was all so glamorous and exciting:

light-years away from Colby College, snuggled in Maine, or her hometown of Madison, Wisconsin.

How had the watch ended up in a secondhand jewelry store in Manhattan?

"Excuse me?" She had to know if it was Fletcher's watch. "Could I see that watch, please?"

The man took it out of the case and laid it on a strip of velvet. Emma turned it over and read: TO FLETCHER, YOU HAVE MY HEART. EMMA

"It would be a nice gift for a father," the man suggested.

"How much is it?" she asked before she could stop herself. There was no reason in the world she wanted the watch; she and Fletcher had lost touch years ago. Had he been living in New York? She had deliberately not followed his career, but she was positive he was a famous director. He'd been the most talented student in the drama department.

"I'll tell you what," the man was saying. "Why don't we call it an even trade?"

"Yes, thank you." Emma slipped the watch into her purse. "Merry Christmas and happy New Year."

"Merry Christmas." The man smiled at Emma. "And I hope you find love. I treasured every Christmas I spent with my wife, Louise."

Emma entered Bronwyn's apartment building and nodded at Owen, the doorman. Bronwyn's doorman was another thing that Emma couldn't help but envy about Bronwyn's life. Owen was the kind of doorman who would perform a quick magic show for

Bronwyn's daughters, Sarah and Liv, and give their cocker spaniel a biscuit.

It was hard not to be a little envious of Bronwyn, even though Emma loved her own job as a senior copywriter and was happy in her Upper West Side one-bedroom apartment. Bronwyn's life had all the pieces filled in, while Emma's life felt more like the puzzles scattered over her playroom floor.

Emma and Bronwyn had first met at a Christmas party a year after Emma moved to New York. Bronwyn was only twenty-four, but she was already engaged to Carlton, a junior analyst at Morgan Stanley, and the owner of dreamy blue eyes and broad shoulders like Tom Brady. Emma had just broken up with her current boyfriend and was puzzled how Bronwyn could be engaged so young. Bronwyn pointed from her respectable diamond ring to Carlton's warm smile and said that there was no reason to wait if she knew Carlton was the one.

Bronwyn had been right. Carlton supported her career as a dermatologist, and loved taking the girls out on weekends so Bronwyn could sit in a bath and read. Bronwyn learned everything about the New England Patriots, and they both loved cooking and volunteering in the local food kitchen.

Emma rang the doorbell and waited for Bronwyn to answer.

"There you are." Bronwyn appeared at the door in sweatpants and a beige sweater. "I refused to get dressed because that would mean I might leave the house, and I'm still digesting our holiday lunch. Carlton wanted to try the baked ham and pecan pie with hazelnut-flavored whipped cream before he got on the plane."

"I don't know where you put it," Emma said, following Bronwyn into the playroom. "You're as thin as the day we met."

"These are the sweatpants I bought after Liv was born." Bronwyn chuckled. "I gained forty pounds, and she came out weighing six pounds, five ounces. The rest of the weight lingered in these sweatpants for months."

Emma stepped on something sharp and picked it up. It was a My Little Pony with a blond mane.

"Tell me again why Carlton had to go to Philadelphia, and why you and the girls didn't go with him?" Emma asked, taking off her coat.

"Carlton's mother slipped in her kitchen when she was slicing carrots and ended up in the hospital with a broken leg," Bronwyn explained. "She begged him to fly home for Christmas, but Carlton put his foot down about us tagging along. We didn't think the girls should spend Christmas eating hospital cafeteria turkey and brown goop passing for gravy. I'll miss Carlton, but I don't feel too bad for him. He's going skiing in the Adirondacks with his fraternity brothers and we'll be stuck at home." Bronwyn flopped onto the sofa. "We're going to take bubble baths and watch Disney movies and try on our Christmas clothes. I still don't understand why you're subjecting yourself to sludge and leftover brussels sprouts when you could be in Hawaii, having your shoulders rubbed with coconut milk."

"I couldn't go to Hawaii when I already broke up with Scott, even if I paid for my ticket," Emma replied. "And I like New York after Christmas; it's wintery and festive at the same time."

"You'll think differently when the heat goes out in your apartment, or you try to get an Uber at rush hour." Bronwyn shook her head. "If I wasn't on call, I would have persuaded Carlton to go somewhere where you drink margaritas at lunchtime." She looked at Emma, curious. "I still don't know why you broke up with Scott. He was sweet and had a successful career and was in love with you." She smiled. "I bet Carlton that he would break the curse."

"You did not bet on my relationship!" Emma laughed in spite of herself.

"Of course I did." Bronwyn nodded. "Every year you break up with the guy right after our open house. I couldn't even bring myself to ask Scott about his promotion at Salesforce; I knew we wouldn't be seeing him again."

"You make it sound as if I wanted to break up with him," Emma said, her voice faltering. "I'd give anything for it to have worked out."

"Then why do you break up with every guy after a year?" Bronwyn wanted to know. "It doesn't make sense."

Every year Emma and Bronwyn had this conversation, and Emma found it so hard to put her reasons into words. Often she didn't know herself, except for a gut feeling that the relationship wasn't working.

"I'm thirty-three. If we're not going to spend the rest of our lives together, it's kinder to get out now," Emma offered.

"You sound like the vet when we had to put down our cat, Whistles," Bronwyn answered. "If you think the guy is right in the beginning, what goes wrong?"

Emma was about to answer when a cocker spaniel bounded onto the sofa. Emma's purse fell to the floor and its contents spilled out.

"The only problem with Carlton being away is Trixie expects me to walk her all the time." Bronwyn patted the dog. "I told her we'll go out after the girls and I make cinnamon cookies, but she's not interested in baking." Bronwyn glanced down and pointed at the jewelry case. "What's that?"

Emma had almost forgotten about the watch. She snapped open the case and rubbed the watch's white face.

"The strangest thing happened. I took the bracelet that Scott gave me to a secondhand jeweler in the East Village," she began, feeling guilty all over again. "This was inside one of the cases."

"You bought a man's watch when you just broke up with your boyfriend?" Bronwyn asked quizzically.

"It's not any watch," Emma said, handing it to Bronwyn. "It's the watch I gave Fletcher before we graduated."

"The only guy you ever regretted breaking up with? The guy who left for London to become an assistant director? You mooned around eating cookies and drinking weak tea for weeks."

"I didn't moon around," Emma corrected her. "I got a summer cold after graduation, and tea and cookies was all I could manage. And it was a mutual decision to break up. We were both starting careers on different continents; it would have been silly to stay together."

"*To Fletcher, you have my heart,*" Bronwyn read, and looked up excitedly. "Finding this watch isn't strange at all—it's synchronicity."

"What do you mean?" Emma asked.

"I took an undergraduate psych class on synchronicity at NYU," Bronwyn answered. "It means a meaningful coincidence that plays an important role in our lives," she finished triumphantly. "You were meant to find this watch."

"It was crazy finding it there, out of all the jewelry stores in the city," Emma said, nodding. "But that's what a coincidence is."

"Synchronicity is different. You have to act on it, or you lose the possibility of the greatest occurrence in your life. Synchronicity at Christmas is even more special; it's the season of miracles."

Emma wondered again why she'd had the impulse to buy

Fletcher's watch. But she couldn't let it sit there with all those rejected pieces, like the toy soldiers in the Nutcracker ballet.

"We're going to find Fletcher and get in touch with him." Bronwyn was already walking toward the computer.

"Wait!" Emma said frantically. Suddenly it all came back to her: the hours they spent in the campus coffee shop talking about their dreams; the way Fletcher used to hold her hand when they walked in the snow, so she felt safe; his mouth on hers, his fingers moving down her spine. "We haven't spoken in eleven years. He's probably married, with a family."

"Like you?" Bronwyn raised an eyebrow. "You're the one who said he was the only boy you truly loved. What if he felt the same, and he's been pining after you for all these years?"

For a moment she was tempted. But there was a reason they had broken up, and it wasn't just the physical distance between them. There was something she had never told Bronwyn and had tried to forget herself.

"I'm sure he's a successful director surrounded by actresses," she said firmly. "And, I don't believe in meaningful coincidences. It was a fluke; it didn't mean anything."

"Suit yourself." Bronwyn shrugged. "But you're missing a cosmic event that could change your life forever."

Liv and Sarah came hurtling into the playroom, and Bronwyn scooped Liv into her lap. The girls were five and three, with Carlton's blue eyes and Bronwyn's rounded cheeks and blond hair. Christmas music filtered through the sound system, and there was a Christmas tree decorated with ornaments made out of hard pasta and pipe cleaners.

Of course Emma wanted a family. When the escalator at Bloomingdale's passed the children's department, she couldn't help drooling over the tiny Christmas sweaters and velvet party dresses. And there was nothing better than being in love. But Fletcher was part of her past, and rekindling an old flame could be as unhealthy as going outside in December without a jacket.

Synchronicity was a definition in a college course; it didn't have anything to do with her life. And fate only happened in the movies. Like in her favorite Christmas movie, *Sleepless in Seattle*. In the final scene, Meg Ryan pulls the teddy bear out of the backpack just as Tom Hanks and his son return to the observation deck to find it. Emma went through a box of tissues every time it was on cable, and she always wondered what would have happened if Meg hadn't lingered over the backpack or if Tom Hanks had decided to go home instead.

But Emma's life wasn't a movie, and she was spending the evening with her best friend and her daughters. She slipped the watch back into her purse and followed Bronwyn and the girls into the kitchen to bake cinnamon cookies.

Two

Seven Days Before New Year's Eve
New York

IT WAS CHRISTMAS EVE MORNING, and Emma was sitting in her living room having a staring match with the space heater. She often did this with things in the apartment the landlord took too long to fix: the showerhead that delivered hot water in a slow trickle, the toaster oven that burned one side of a bagel while leaving the other soft and soggy. Sometimes it worked, and she got one perfectly toasted bagel that she ate with butter and jam before it went on the blink again. Today the space heater's red light refused to turn on, and she was forced to put on a wool coat and three pairs of socks.

She didn't know how to fill the long hours of Christmas Eve until she wouldn't feel guilty about climbing back in bed with a cup of hot chocolate and whatever was on Netflix. It didn't help her mood that Scott was posting pictures on Instagram of a Hawaiian sunset with pink skies and blue water you knew was warm just by looking at it. She told herself she wasn't going to look at social media while her friends were off in Aspen or the Bahamas. But this morning it was too cold to get out of bed, and she left her book in the living room and ended up scrolling through her phone.

She couldn't even be mad at Scott for posting pictures of a luau with platters of pineapples and melons. He wasn't doing it to make her jealous or show her what she was missing. When he was having a bad day at the office, it made him happy to see friends' photos of rooftop sunsets or juicy burgers accompanied by a foamy beer.

Bronwyn was right; Scott had been the perfect boyfriend. On Valentine's Day he had polled Emma's mother and Bronwyn to find out what kind of chocolates Emma preferred. He instigated "you days" once a month, where they each planned a day of activities the other would enjoy. Emma ran out of ideas after two months, but Scott surprised her with wine tasting in the Hudson Valley and tickets to a photographic retrospective on fifty years in advertising.

So why had that familiar empty feeling started a month before Christmas? When they'd picked out a Christmas tree for her apartment, Scott told the tree guy that it was their first Christmas together, as if implying there would be many more. At his company's Christmas party, Scott had kept his hand so firmly on the small of her back, she'd felt like a remote-controlled toy car.

Other women would have loved that all their milestones as a couple were input into his phone, like the day they'd first met: it had been last January, in the women's department of Saks. She was returning a sweater her previous boyfriend, Ian, had given her for Christmas, and he was buying a birthday present for his mother. She felt like a heel when she accepted his invitation to coffee: the breakup with Ian had involved angry words and a few slammed doors, and she wasn't going to start a relationship so soon. But Scott's clean-cut good looks were the opposite of Ian's brooding Irish charm, and anyway, she had to believe in love.

Except it wasn't love. The sex was consistent and satisfying, and they both were passionate about health care reform. Scott had even said she looked beautiful when she'd had the worst cold in years, but it still wasn't love.

Fletcher's watch sat on the coffee table, and she picked it up. How had the watch ended up in a secondhand jewelry store in the East Village?

Bronwyn said it was synchronicity, but Emma didn't believe the watch had skipped over the Atlantic and taken the subway to the East Village to end up in her hands. And Bronwyn's suggestion of finding Fletcher was a terrible idea. Emma and Fletcher had been together in another lifetime, and they hadn't seen each other in eleven years.

Emma picked at a slice of pumpkin bread that would double as lunch as well as breakfast, because she had expected to be in Hawaii and the fridge was empty. The space heater gurgled theatrically, and she remembered when she and Fletcher had first met.

September, 2007
Waterville, Maine

It was fall semester, senior year, and the whole campus was bathed in that multicolored fall light that made the idea of months marked by darkness seem impossible. All the students were taking advantage of the Indian summer and playing Frisbee in front of Williams Library except Emma. Emma was doing the one thing that calmed her nerves before an important paper was due: she was sitting at the piano in her residence hall and playing a medley of 90s pop songs.

"Excuse me," a tall guy said as he rushed inside. A scarf was wrapped around his neck, and he was wearing jeans and a button-down shirt. "I'm looking for Aubrey."

Aubrey was the only other resident of Alfond Hall who loved the piano. They took turns playing, and there were many nights that Emma and the whole floor went to bed listening to Aubrey's rendition of Billy Joel songs.

"Aubrey went home for the weekend. His father had an emergency appendectomy," Emma said. "He'll be back on Tuesday."

"He couldn't have left," the man said, tugging at his scarf. "He didn't say anything."

"It was an emergency," Emma repeated. "He grabbed a bag and sprinted for the train."

"Oh god, oh no." The man sank onto a lumpy sofa. "He couldn't have. Not today. Not this weekend."

Emma had never seen him before, but she guessed he was a theater major. It was too warm to be wearing a scarf, and he wasn't lugging around a heavy backpack like other students.

"I'm afraid he did." She turned back to the piano. The first draft of her senior thesis was due on Monday, and she still didn't have a clue what to write. Usually an idea came to her when she was playing, but today all she could think about was bicycling into Waterville for ice cream or shopping at the farmer's market.

"You're very good," the man said. "Play more of that."

Emma finished the chorus of "Fields of Gold" by Sting and started on the theme from *Arthur*.

"Where did you learn to play?" he asked.

"My mother was a piano teacher. She and my father were

hoping for a piano prodigy, but I never achieved more than runner-up in the middle school talent contest," she explained. "I play to relieve stress. Other people run five miles; I play Christopher Cross."

"What are you doing tonight?" He glanced at the clock above the brick fireplace. "In exactly six and a half hours?"

"I'll be putting the finishing touches on the first draft of the most brilliant senior thesis the English department ever saw," she sighed. "That is, if I come up with a topic and the first twenty pages in the next six hours and twenty-nine minutes."

"Could you possibly do that tomorrow? Please? I'm not above begging if I have to." He gulped. "I need you at the Strider Theater. Aubrey was supposed to accompany tonight's play, and there won't be any show without a pianist."

"Why would I do that?" Emma looked up. "I don't even know your name. And I can't leave a paper until the day before it's due. I'll get writer's block and end up staying up all night to get it done."

"I'm Fletcher, and I'll write a note to your professor," he pleaded. "It's so important. The whole performance depends on it."

"Are you saying your grade is more important than mine?" Emma asked. "Everyone says theater students are arrogant, and they're right. You're wearing a scarf like some character in a Fitzgerald novel, and you want me to give up a whole evening to be in some silly play."

"The scarf is a prop; if I don't wear it I might forget it. And plays are never stupid. Drama is one of the most noble forms of expression." He looked at Emma expectantly. "I can't afford to pay you, but I *can* get you and a date tickets to *The Book of Mormon* at the Waterville Opera House. I'll even throw in pre-theater cocktails. I have coupons for two free drinks."

"I don't have anyone to take," Emma said, and bit her lip. Was she giving him that piece of information because he was good-looking in an artsy way with blue eyes and dark, curly hair?

"There must be some way to convince you," he pleaded. "I have access to a car. We can drive to Kennebunkport and eat clam chowder at The Clam Shack. I washed dishes there over break, and I get free food."

Emma didn't own a car, and trips to the seashore were as tantalizing as real maple syrup in her morning oatmeal.

"I don't have time for that either." She shook her head. "I'm sorry, you'll have to find someone else."

"There is no one else." He touched her hand. "Please—the cast and the director and the technical crew are depending on it. Not to mention the audience, who will be waiting anxiously when the lights go down."

Emma wanted to tell herself she said yes because she couldn't let down so many people, but she would be lying. She agreed because his fingers against her skin made her feel completely different than she'd ever felt before.

Seven Days Before New Year's Eve
New York

Fletcher's watch was smooth in her palm, and she remembered her surprise when she'd arrived at the theater and discovered it was a one-man show. Fletcher was the actor and director and had even set up the lights and clipped on his own microphone. She recalled their drive to Kennebunkport a week later and their first kiss, their mouths sweet and salty from caramel toffees.

Her phone buzzed and Bronwyn's number popped up.

"Merry Christmas. What are you doing?" Bronwyn asked when Emma picked up.

Emma debated telling the truth: she was eating two-day-old pumpkin bread, having a battle of wills with the space heater, and reminiscing about Fletcher. But that would prompt Bronwyn to say she shouldn't have broken up with Scott or she'd be swimming with dolphins, so instead she told a little white lie.

"Working on copy for the Lancôme account. You can't imagine how difficult lipstick ads can be. All the good adjectives are overused: full-bodied, plump, luscious."

"You shouldn't work on Christmas Eve, it's unhealthy," Bronwyn rejoined. "I need you to come over. It's an emergency with the girls."

"The 'we're in the ER because Sarah got my wedding ring stuck on her thumb' kind of emergency?" Emma asked warily. "Or, the girls can't agree on which Disney DVD to watch and you have to cast the deciding vote?"

"It doesn't matter what kind. You're their godmother, and I need you," Bronwyn huffed. "Call an Uber and I'll pay when you get here."

Bronwyn's apartment had central heating that worked and her leftovers contained turkey and some vegetables instead of just flour and sugar.

"Fine, I'm coming." Emma gave the space heater a triumphant glance and walked to the closet for her boots.

"Merry Christmas, Miss Logan," Owen said when she entered Bronwyn's building. "You look lovely today."

"Merry Christmas. Can I hire you to trail after me and say that?" Emma joked. "It's too cold in my apartment to change, so I just layer on more clothes."

"If I was thirty years younger and twenty pounds lighter, I'd trail after you at no charge." Owen sucked in his gut. "I delivered cinnamon rolls to Mrs. Tucker's apartment—there are a couple of extras for you."

"Thank you, Owen." Emma headed to the elevator and the circulated air warmed her shoulders. "I knew I came to the right place."

"You ordered cinnamon rolls," Emma said to Bronwyn as they entered the playroom. The floor was harder to find than it had been yesterday, with a fort consisting of pink blankets stretched over Trixie's puppy gates. "I thought you and the girls were going to bake."

"Sarah thought waiting for the cookies to come out of the oven was the perfect time to paint the counter with nail polish, so we gave up." She pointed to the two sets of stocking feet peeking out from the fort. "They're giving Trixie a pretend bath in the doggie beauty salon."

"You said it was an emergency." Emma removed a doll's hairbrush from the sofa and sat down.

"It is." Bronwyn handed her an envelope. "This is for you."

Emma opened the envelope and a sheet of computer paper fell out. There was a photo of an inn with snow-covered turrets perched on the edge of a village square. There was a skating rink and a Christmas tree lit with multicolored lights.

"What kind of emergency involves a bed and breakfast in Vermont?" Emma read the description of The Smuggler's Inn in Snowberry, Vermont.

"The kind where you have a reservation starting this evening, and it will take you four hours to drive there," Bronwyn answered as a yelping sound came from the fort. "It's your Christmas present. Eight nights at a charming inn nestled at the base of Vermont's Green Mountains. With only one little catch."

"You already gave me a Christmas present," Emma reminded her. "And what do you mean, one little catch?"

"A beach caftan and matching tote bag aren't going to come in handy in New York," Bronwyn said. "Trust me, you need to get away. Even I'm thinking of taking the girls somewhere. Sarah gave Trixie a haircut—she only used plastic scissors, but now Trixie has bangs."

"It's really nice of you to think of me, but I don't mind staying home," Emma said. "I have work to catch up on, and there's half a dozen Netflix series I've been meaning to watch."

"There's so much to do in Snowberry," Bronwyn read from the computer paper. "You can go sled dog racing, and there's a sugarhouse and antique stores and Fletcher."

"What did you say?" Emma gasped. Her cheeks paled and she snatched at the paper.

"You didn't want to look up Fletcher on social media, but you didn't say I couldn't." Bronwyn took out her phone. "He spent ten years at the Old Vic in London directing actors like Jude Law and Emma Roberts. He moved to New York last summer, and he's directing a play on Broadway," Bronwyn finished in a rush. "He has an ex-wife in Connecticut and according to Facebook, he's spending the week between Christmas and New Year's at The Smuggler's Inn in Snowberry, Vermont."

For a moment Bronwyn's apartment, with its crown molding and Oriental rugs, receded like a landscape outside a train window. Emma was standing on the Colby Green clutching her diploma and searching the throng of graduating seniors for Fletcher. When she spotted him, wearing his father's tie and talking animatedly to the drama professor, her heart was brighter than the May sun and all she wanted was to wrap her arms around him.

"So you have to go," Bronwyn said, interrupting her thoughts. "It's synchronicity. It could change your whole future."

"That's very generous, but it's out of the question." Emma's heart pounded. "I have to work on the Lancôme campaign. And I'm planning to use the gift voucher for the Red Door spa my parents sent for Christmas."

"You don't like massages, they make you fidgety." Bronwyn picked up a hair ribbon that had been tossed out of the fort. "And the inn has a library—perfect for guests to curl up with a book or catch up on paperwork."

"I'm still not going," Emma said. "What if I do see Fletcher? How do I explain bumping into him in the middle of Vermont?"

"The same way you told me about finding his watch in the East Village. It's a crazy coincidence," Bronwyn said. "You have nothing to lose. At worst, you'll enjoy a week in the maple syrup capital of New England. And you might come home with the guy who will break the three-hundred-and-sixty-five-day curse."

"You still haven't told me what the catch is," Emma said, feeling her resolve wavering.

"Well, the funniest thing happened. When I called to make the reservation, the innkeeper said The Smuggler's Inn was fully booked," Bronwyn replied. "So I called every bed and breakfast in Snowberry, but they were all full. I was going to give up, when the owner of The Smuggler's Inn called me back."

"What did she say?" Emma couldn't help being curious.

"The woman who runs her kids' club came down with the flu. If you'd be willing to pitch in for a few hours every day, the lodging and food would be free."

"You want me to run the kids' club?" Emma asked incredulously.

"You're amazing with children—Sarah and Liv love being with you," Bronwyn returned. "And don't you see? If there was any doubt that you were supposed to spend Christmas week at the same inn in Vermont as Fletcher, this proves it was meant to be. What are the chances the only room in Snowberry became available at the exact time you want to go?"

"This is your idea," Emma grunted. "I didn't want anything."

"Only because you're my best friend and I want you to be happy," Bronwyn said. "Fate is working in your favor, and you can't ignore it."

"You're not going to take no for an answer," Emma said, sighing.

"Of course not; I'm a mother," Bronwyn agreed. "It's the only word I hear from when I come home from work until bedtime."

There were more yelping sounds and the fort collapsed. Sarah emerged, holding a dog as big as she was, and Liv climbed into Bronwyn's lap.

"Thank you; it's a wonderful gift. All right, I'll go." Emma nodded. "But first Owen promised me a cinnamon roll. It's a long drive, and I haven't had lunch."

———

Emma stood on a chair and pulled down the suitcase in her closet. It was supposed to be filled with sundresses and bikinis, with an Aloha Airlines sticker on the canvas. Was she really going to stuff it with long underwear and throw it in her trunk? And would her car even make it to Vermont?

Fletcher! Working and living in New York. She closed her eyes and tried to conjure him up. Would his blue eyes still give her that melting feeling, like looking into a candle? And would he still have the flat stomach he got from cross-country skiing, or would it have gone soft from years spent in the theater?

She didn't even want to think about his ex-wife. Maybe he'd married some stunning British actress, but what would she be doing in Connecticut? It was none of her business; she hadn't seen Fletcher in eleven years.

The practical side of her brain knew that driving to New England to spend seven days at the same inn as her first love was a bad idea. But the other side—the one that started each relationship filled with hope, the one that dreamed of a home with a dog and giggling children and a loving husband—packed the suitcase with sweaters and thick tights and headed to the front door.

Three

THE FIRST THREE HOURS OF the drive, Emma thought of every reason to turn back to New York. She had an overdue library book; she'd promised to volunteer at the local animal shelter; a package was arriving, and she wouldn't be around to sign for it.

But the New York Public Library was lenient in their fines over Christmas week, and the last time she volunteered at the animal shelter, she'd almost brought home a sweet mixed-breed beagle. It was only picturing having to walk the dog in the freezing slush that convinced her owning a dog in an apartment was a terrible idea.

Then she turned onto Route 100 and was reminded of the beauty of winter in Vermont. Every town was more picturesque than the last, with covered bridges and main streets that called out to her to stop for waffles with butter that came in half-scoops.

The exit to Snowberry had one of those roadside historic markers that told visitors interesting facts about Vermont: home of the first ski tow, birthplace of Norman Rockwell. There was a church nestled in a cluster of fir trees, and a creek that Emma was sure would be gurgling water during the summer but now was a sheet of ice.

How had Bronwyn talked her into this? Vermont was for couples taking romantic sleigh rides, or for families spending all day on the slopes. Her GPS announced she had reached her destination; it was her last chance to turn around. Emma could spend the next seven days huddled under her bedspread in her apartment, watching Christmas movies, and Bronwyn wouldn't have to know.

But Emma didn't like to lie to her best friend, and she was too tired and hungry to drive all the way home. She turned onto Main Street, and her doubts dissolved like ice cream on a hot apple pie. Every store window was strung with fairy lights, and there was a proper village green blanketed with snow. Christmas music was playing, and Emma counted three antique shops and one of those general stores you only find in Vermont that sold deli meats and toys and party dresses all in one place.

She scanned the buildings for The Smuggler's Inn and noticed an iron sign. There was a short driveway and a white clapboard house with green shutters and a red front door. In front was a fir tree decorated with Christmas ornaments, and a porch holding a sled and ice skates. The roof was the best part: it was gray shingled, and perched near the chimney were six life-sized reindeer pulling a sleigh.

"Do you think it's too much?" said a woman in her fifties, standing on the steps. Her ash-blond hair was knotted in a bun, and she was wearing an LL Bean sweater and boots. "I'm always worried I'll scare off the more sophisticated guests," she said, glancing at Emma's New York license plate. "My late husband used to put them up when our children were small, and I think he'd like to know that Rudolph and the gang were watching over us."

"It's not something you see on the Upper West Side," Emma laughed, taking her suitcase out of the trunk. "But it's perfect for a country inn in Vermont."

"I've told you that my husband died and accused you of being a typical New Yorker," the woman said worriedly. "You can tell it's my first season as an innkeeper." She held out her hand. "Merry Christmas. I'm Betty Traiser; welcome to The Smuggler's Inn.

"When you come back from ice skating or sledding, just throw your things in here," Betty said as they entered the mudroom. "Breakfast is served in the dining room. I make it myself; I hope you like chocolate muffins. And afternoon tea is available in the parlor. It's my favorite room of the house."

They entered a parlor that looked like it was straight out of the gift catalogs that crowded Emma's mailbox each December. The fireplace mantel was hung with stockings, and a toy train set wrapped around the base of a Christmas tree. The tree itself touched the ceiling, and every branch was covered with ornaments. Even the sofas had Christmas-themed cushions, and there was a sideboard set with bottles of brandy.

"My husband, John, laughed at me when I overdid Christmas, because I grew up in Texas and there wasn't a snowflake or pine tree in sight," she said, noticing Emma's wide-eyed expression. "It's my first Christmas without him. He was a brain surgeon and died from pancreatic cancer. Everyone said I should sell this house and buy a condo in Palm Beach. Why would I do that? I'd rather live where we used to spend every summer and Christmas. And long ago, I was an actress. I quite like the role of country innkeeper. Who knows, maybe I'll help start a romance between guests, or save a failing marriage. The Smuggler's Inn has a romantic history; love is in the house's bones."

"What kind of romantic history?" Emma asked.

"It was built by a bootlegger for his bride during Prohibition. He was almost caught smuggling gin to Canada, and disappeared. Everyone told her to give up on him, but ten years later he returned and she was waiting for him." She handed Emma a tray of short-bread. "You've just arrived, and there's so much to see. You should visit Main Street or go ice skating."

"I suppose I should explore. I haven't been in Vermont in years." Emma nibbled the shortbread. "My best friend Bronwyn made the reservation."

"Of course—Bronwyn is the woman who called today!" Betty said excitedly. "You must be Emma. I can't tell you how glad I am that you're here. The woman I hired to run the kids' club has the flu, and I panicked. One of the key selling points is a kids' club. Guests want to know they can relax without having to build snow-men or follow their kids down the bunny slope." She paused. "Then right after I called Bronwyn back, the funniest thing happened."

"Something happened?" Emma asked uneasily.

"A family with three children canceled at the last minute, and another guest called and said her son is spending the week with his father instead. So only one child is signed up for the kids' club. It's a shame; the father was counting on his daughter playing with other children," Betty said, and her tone brightened. "I'm sure you'll keep her entertained; there's so much to do in Snowberry."

"That's what Bronwyn said." Emma nodded. "I forgot how gorgeous Vermont is in the winter. I was supposed to spend the week in Hawaii with my boyfriend, but it didn't work out."

"That sounds like a story in itself." Betty poured two cups of tea. "I'd love to hear it."

"I can't seem to make a relationship last more than three hundred and sixty-five days," Emma said. "My friend Bronwyn thought Scott was the one to break the curse, but it didn't work out."

"That's the thing about love. In the beginning it's as sparkly and fresh as new snow, but there's no way of knowing if it's going to stick," Betty mused. "True love is magical. It casts a spell that nothing can break."

"That sounds like a line from one of Bronwyn's daughters' books," Emma laughed.

"There's a lot of wisdom in children's books." Betty nodded. "Why did Bronwyn think you should come here?"

In her exhaustion from driving, she'd forgotten about Fletcher! What if he walked in while her hair was a mess and there were shortbread crumbs on her jeans?

"A change of scenery," Emma said quickly. "So I don't sit around feeling sorry for myself that I'm not sipping mai tais and kayaking at sunset."

She couldn't confide in a stranger that she'd come to possibly reconnect with her first love. Anyway, it wasn't exactly true. Bronwyn thought she and Fletcher could restart their relationship, but Emma was afraid it was impossible.

"You'll love Snowberry. There's a museum with some of Robert Frost's poems, and we offer snowshoeing and guided tours to see moose in the forests. And most nights I hold a talent contest for the guests."

"A talent contest?" Emma raised her eyebrows.

"It's more fun than chess or those stodgy board games other bed and breakfasts offer." Betty's eyes twinkled. "Don't worry, I offer a selection of wines at dinner, so everyone is relaxed."

Emma squeezed her suitcase into the closet, and couldn't help feeling gloomy. The room was pretty, with a floral bedspread, but it wasn't an oceanfront suite with fresh fruits delivered daily and a card announcing the day's activities: surfing lessons, followed by zip-lining in the jungle.

What if she couldn't find anyone to talk to? And looking for moose sounded exciting, but probably meant shivering in rubber boots while longing for a hot chocolate.

The thought of running into Fletcher was the real reason she was nervous. He was a well-known director and had lived on two continents, while Emma had only changed apartments once since she'd arrived in New York. And while she loved her job, conjuring up ways to sell concealer was hardly as glamorous as attending cast parties with famous actors and actresses.

The FaceTime icon on her laptop blinked, and she pressed ACCEPT.

"You made it!" Bronwyn appeared on the screen. She was sitting in the living room, wearing a dress and knee-high boots. "I saw the weather report and was afraid you might get stuck on the road."

"You're fibbing." Emma sank onto the bed. It was nice to see a familiar face, even if only on a computer. "The skies are completely clear. You're FaceTiming me because you thought I might be hiding out in my apartment."

"The thought had occurred to me," Bronwyn admitted. "Driving four hours to Vermont to meet your old college flame is pretty brave."

"I must have been on a sugar and caffeine rush when I agreed," Emma sighed. "It was eleven years ago; this is all a terrible mistake."

"It's destiny, and destiny doesn't make mistakes," Bronwyn chided her. "Tell me about the inn. Is it as charming as in the brochure?"

Emma told her about Betty and the talent show, and how Main Street had been so festive when she arrived.

"The only thing is, a couple of families canceled, and there's only one child signed up for kids' club. I'm going to have to entertain her by myself."

"That will be even easier—you can do whatever you like. It all sounds heavenly," Bronwyn said. "I'm green with envy. This is only the second day of our staycation, and already I'm calling Carlton just to hear a voice that isn't high pitched and begging me to change channels."

"Why are you dressed up?" Emma asked. "You vowed to stay in sweats all week."

"Carlton saw Trixie's new bangs on Skype and suggested I take the girls out for afternoon tea," Bronwyn admitted. "He made reservations at the Plaza, and asked his cousin to meet us so I could get a pedicure at the hotel afterward. He's a good husband; sometimes I wonder how I got so lucky."

"You're both lucky," Emma said. "But it's not going to happen for me. I'll spend seven days getting fat from eating maple syrup, and then I'll go back to New York. I'll meet a cute Latin musician who seems like a good catch because he'll have a healthy glow in January. We'll get three hundred and sixty-four days of spicy dinners and great sex until next Christmas, when I realize I can't spend the holidays in Brazil with a dozen nieces and nephews I've never met. I'm thirty-three years old and I'll always be alone."

"You keep forgetting Fletcher's watch," Bronwyn persisted. "All those failed romances were keeping the way clear so you would be available when you and Fletcher reconnected."

"You make my life sound like a driveway that needs shoveling," Emma said, laughing, but she did feel better.

Maybe Bronwyn was right about Fletcher; Snowberry was so pretty. Outside the window the sky was turning a milky pink, and she heard the sounds of boots crunching in the snow. It wouldn't hurt to put on a warm coat and explore the village.

"I have to go. Carlton called a taxi, and it's waiting downstairs." Bronwyn sighed happily. "For the next three hours I will not wipe a single smudge mark or worry about slipping on Cinderella's plastic slipper. Trust me, you're in the right place. Just let synchronicity do its work."

The first place Emma entered was The Cider Mill, where there was an actual cider vat in the back. Emma was tempted to settle down in one of the comfy beanbags, but the guy behind the counter kept insisting she try a donut fresh from the oven, and Emma knew donuts and apple cider hardly constituted a healthy snack.

She reluctantly pulled herself away and explored the Snowberry General Store, where kitchen utensils were on display next to a case of pocketknives. She couldn't believe it was open on Christmas Eve, but the owner said it was one of the busiest days of the year. Upstairs there were Icelandic wool sweaters and rabbit-fur hats. Emma made her excuses to the guy behind the counter and hurried out the door. How could anyone wear a dead rabbit on her head?

Now she ambled down the snowy sidewalk and the empty feeling returned. It was all right for Bronwyn to talk about synchronicity. Bronwyn was gliding through her thirties with a successful dermatology practice and preschool Christmas concerts and Friday date nights with the guy she loved. Meanwhile Emma's life was like the donuts at The Cider Mill. It was missing a center. Without that special person to share things with, the ups and downs were becoming hollow.

There was an ice skating rink, and Emma was tempted to rent some skates. She used to love skating. But three years ago she'd dated a professional ice hockey player named Dane, and since then she'd felt uncoordinated on ice. Tonight the rink was filled with people having fun, and none of them seemed to worry about their form.

She exchanged her boots for a pair of skates and cautiously edged onto the ice. Music blared from a loudspeaker, and she smelled warm pretzels from a kiosk next to the rink.

A girl of about ten was skating by herself. For some reason, Emma couldn't take her eyes off her. It wasn't that she was that good; there were other little girls showing off with twirls and jumps. It was more that she was enjoying herself. Her hair was a halo of reddish ringlets, and she wore a fantastic coat: as if the wild pattern had been designed by a child, but it was made of the finest wool.

A man and a woman joined her, and Emma looked away. She wasn't going to become one of those single women who glanced longingly at every couple and wondered if she would ever be part of a family.

But there was something familiar about the little scene, and she dragged her eyes back to the group. The man was wearing a leather jacket, and the woman was young, with the kind of white-blond hair seen on women exiting expensive hair salons in Manhattan.

The man looked up and Emma gasped. He seemed even taller than she remembered, and his dark hair was cut short, but it was Fletcher! How could Fletcher have a daughter? And who was the stunning blonde? If that was his ex-wife, it seemed like a very friendly divorce.

Emma wished she had never let Bronwyn talk her into coming to Vermont. What if Fletcher had seen her? A man in his late thirties was tying his skates, and she skated up to him.

"Would you skate with me?" she asked.

"You want me to skate with you?" He straightened up.

"Yes, please." She nodded. "I haven't been on skates in years, and I'm afraid to skate alone."

"I suppose so." He shrugged and put out his hand. "I'm Luke; it's a pleasure to meet you. I just drove up from Boston. Where are you from?"

"I'm Emma," she said, but she was too nervous to answer his question. She ducked behind him until Fletcher was blocked from view. She was dying to take another look: did Fletcher still have that dimple, and was there a wedding ring on his finger? But she was afraid if she poked her head out, he might see her.

"Are you here for the whole Christmas week?" the man was asking. "There's a bar on Main Street that serves delicious hot toddies."

The little group skated toward her, and Emma panicked. No matter which direction she took, Fletcher could run into her. The entrance to the rink lay ahead of her, and there was only one thing she could do. She turned to Luke and gave him her warmest smile.

"Perhaps another time," she said, nodding. "I really have to go."

"I don't have your phone number!" he called after her.

Emma didn't even turn and wave. She felt incredibly rude;

perhaps she'd see Luke again and could explain. Right now the only thing that mattered was untying the skates and getting as far away as possible.

Emma opened the door of her room and stripped off her coat. Of all the ways to almost run into Fletcher, she'd done it when he was with one of the most beautiful women she'd ever seen and a girl in a fabulous wool coat, while Emma was floundering on the ice.

How could Bronwyn not have discovered Fletcher had a daughter? Emma couldn't help but wonder what she was like. Had she inherited Fletcher's kindness and love of the theater?

And could the blond woman be her mother? She seemed too young, and her stomach was flat in her skintight pants.

It was almost dinnertime, but Emma was too embarrassed to go downstairs for Christmas Eve dinner. She was going to drink the tea Betty had left on a tray and do some work.

She could always get up early and drive back to New York. Staying at the same Vermont inn as Fletcher didn't seem like a wonderful stroke of fate that would change her life forever. It seemed like the most terrible mistake.

Four

Seven Days Before New Year's Eve
Snowberry, Vermont

FLETCHER SAT IN THE LIBRARY of The Smuggler's Inn and flipped through the guestbook. His excuse for leaving the guest-room was that he had to put through a business call to New York, but that had been a little white lie. He couldn't tell his fiancée, Megan, the real reason; he could hardly admit it to himself. He could have sworn he'd seen Emma on the skating rink.

His therapist would have a field day with this piece of information, but that's why Fletcher hated the idea of a therapist, let alone the fact that now he visited the offices of Doctor Margaret Neal every other Tuesday.

But apparently having a therapist was part of the fallout of di-vorce, along with the other new developments he could hardly stomach: that he only saw his daughter Lola every other Friday through Sunday, and Wednesdays when he drove from Manhat-tan to Connecticut to take her out to dinner for the one hour his ex-wife, Cassandra, thought Lola could spare on a school night.

He could almost hear Margaret's nasal voice: "You're having the dream holiday: eight nights in a romantic Vermont inn with your fiancée and your daughter. Why are you spoiling it with imaginary sightings of a woman you haven't seen in more than a decade?" She'd lean over her huge teak desk. "At some point you have to allow yourself to be happy, Fletcher. No one scores points for being miserable."

Of course he was happy: he was finally in love. Christ, in six months he'd be married! And Margaret was right: the whole vacation was planned so that Megan and Lola could get to know each other. He'd made a list of things the three of them would do: take sleigh rides, go cross-country skiing, make pottery in one of the artists' studios that lined Route 100 on the way into town.

There was only one person he could talk to. It was 7 P.M. in Vermont, which meant it was midnight in London. Thank god Graham was a night owl. If Fletcher was lucky, Graham would have had a scotch or two with dinner and wouldn't mind listening to him.

"Fletcher, Merry Christmas!" Graham's clipped British accent came over the line. "You're lucky you caught me. I was about to get a quick bite at the Savoy."

"Merry Christmas! Dinner at almost midnight?" Fletcher asked. "Isn't that a little late, even for you?"

"Tomorrow is opening night of the new play," Graham reminded him. "I had to stay at the theater and keep telling the lead actor he was going to be the hit of the Christmas season. It never changes; famous actors turn into scared schoolchildren when they're about to be reviewed in *The Sunday Times*."

Fletcher had met Graham when he'd started working at the Old Vic. Graham had been twenty-five and already a well-known producer, with his name on a few critical successes.

"I'm sure it will be a success; they always are," Fletcher returned.

"Is anything wrong? Is Lola all right?" Graham asked.

"Your goddaughter is fine," Fletcher acknowledged. "You didn't have to buy out Fortnum & Mason's for Christmas. They do sell Christmas cookies in America."

"Not shortbread biscuits with orange curd marmalade," Graham corrected him. "I wanted to show her how much I miss her."

"She misses you too; she's made you a CD of her singing Christmas songs," Fletcher replied. "Lola isn't the reason I called. Megan and Lola and I were skating and I saw Emma. This time I was positive it was her: same light brown hair, and those high cheekbones. When I looked again she was gone."

"Just like it was Emma on the subway and Emma on the escalator at Bloomingdale's?" Graham asked.

Fletcher flinched, remembering taking Lola to Bloomingdale's the week before Christmas. He'd been sure it was Emma, and had made Lola ride the escalator to the top floor. But it wasn't Emma, and Lola had wondered why they'd ended up in home furnishings when they were meant to be shopping for party shoes.

"Look, Fletcher," Graham counseled. "The divorce was hard, and you're afraid you ruined Lola's life. But it wasn't your fault and it's behind you. You're engaged to a beautiful woman and your daughter is fine, and you're about to open a play on Broadway." He paused. "Even repeating it, I'm green with envy."

"You could have been engaged to a dozen girls," Fletcher chuckled.

"None of them understood why I had to stay at the theater until midnight and on weekends," he sighed. "I know how important Emma was to you. I was there when you arrived in London, remember? I could feel your pain. But it doesn't help to keep conjuring her up. Stop looking for ghosts of the past, it will only make you unhappy."

"Now you sound like my therapist," Fletcher grumbled.

"You haven't heard from Emma in a decade, and you're engaged," Graham continued. "Give my love to Lola and enjoy that fiancée. You're a lucky man, Fletcher. Try to remember that."

Fletcher hung up and ate a handful of cashew nuts. Graham was probably right; what would Emma be doing in Vermont?

It was just odd that he was positive he kept seeing her. And it hadn't started when he'd returned to America; it had been happening in London for years—in the food hall at Harrods, or hopping off a double-decker bus.

The funny thing was, the first time he'd thought he saw Emma, when he had only been in London for two weeks, was the reason he'd met his ex-wife Cassandra in the first place.

July, 2008
London, England

Fletcher stood in the living room of the London townhouse and tried to look like he'd been holding champagne flutes for years. Everyone else at the party—the actresses draped over couches, the producers smoking cigars—all seemed like they'd been raised on a diet of champagne and fancy hors d'oeuvres.

This was his first theater party, and he didn't belong in the smart townhouse in Belgravia. His title at the Old Vic was assistant director, but he was more of a glorified gofer. He spent his days running out for sandwiches, and his nights making sure the lead actor and actress weren't drinking large amounts of whiskey or making out in their dressing rooms before the five-minute warning.

His new friend, Graham, the only person who had really talked to him at the theater outside of his boss, had scored an invitation with a plus-one and insisted Fletcher join him.

"Don't look like we're about to face the Spanish Inquisition," Graham hissed. "This is a party; you're supposed to have fun."

"What if someone notices my suit is borrowed?" Fletcher whispered. "I should have worn my sports coat; at least it fit at the sleeves."

"It fits fine," Graham said, surveying Fletcher's dark suit. "Anyway, no one will be looking at your suit. The women will be enthralled by your American accent, and the men are only here for the champagne and pretty women."

Graham sauntered away and Fletcher approached the buffet table. British food was so odd: mini hot dogs sticking out of pastries, and some kind of dessert that looked like an exploded cake. He grabbed a plate and wondered what tasted good.

That's when he saw Emma, wearing the yellow dress she'd worn at graduation. He remembered her looking so pretty standing on the Colby Green, he had wanted to break the promises he made to himself and tell her this was crazy, they had to be together.

Could Emma have followed him to London? The woman walked toward the entryway and he had to follow her. He stumbled over the rug and spilled champagne over a woman with wavy red hair and a multicolored blouse.

"Look what you've done." The woman in the blouse glowered. "You got champagne all over raw silk."

"I'm sorry," he stammered. "Here, you can have my napkin."

"Americans are supposed to be coordinated." The woman accepted the napkin. "You're all pro athletes or race car drivers."

"Not all of us," Fletcher said gruffly. He was still thinking about the woman in the yellow dress and realizing it probably wasn't Emma after all.

"No, I can see that." She studied his gangly body. "Please be more careful next time; this is one of my best designs. How am I going to show it off if there's a huge stain?"

Fletcher turned, and the woman claimed his full attention. Her hair was gorgeous, like a red flame shooting over her shoulders. And her outfit was unique: the blouse was hand-painted, and she wore a flared skirt that showed off her shapely waist.

"Did you make that blouse?" he asked.

"I made all of it," she said, waving her hand over her body. "I'm a costume designer. Well, I will be a costume designer once I get my lucky break. Do you know how hard it was to get an invitation to this party? I had to go on four dates with a guy who smelled like liver and seemed to have more than two hands. It was worth it; everyone in theater is here."

"Where is the offending date now?" Fletcher asked curiously.

"He left me as soon as I told him that if his hands ever wandered near my blouse again, I'd break his wrists." She smiled impishly. "He's chatting up some brunette in the den."

"Fletcher Conway." Fletcher held out his hand. The champagne had made him bold, and he liked the woman's smile.

"Cassandra Davies." Her handshake was firm. "Why are you at the party? No offense, but that's a cheap suit, so you can't be an investor. And you're not quite handsome enough to be an actor."

"That stings my ego just a little," Fletcher said, smiling. "I came with a friend. I'm an assistant director at the Old Vic." He looked at Cassandra. "Why do you want to be a costume designer if you don't like anyone in the profession?"

"For the same reason you're willing to stand around a drafty theater for less than minimum wage," she said, and her smile was as intoxicating as the champagne. "Because the theater is the only place I feel properly alive."

Seven Days Before New Year's Eve
Snowberry, Vermont

Fletcher blinked, and the memory of his first meeting with Cassandra dissolved like ice in a glass of scotch. Graham said the divorce wasn't Fletcher's fault, but Graham had never been married. But Graham was right about one thing: Megan was smart and beautiful. Fletcher wasn't going to let an imaginary sighting of Emma get in the way of the first Christmas he and Megan and Lola spent together.

"Dad! There you are." Lola appeared in the doorway. Cassandra still designed many of Lola's clothes, and she had the most amazing wardrobe: dresses with matching leggings, wildly patterned coats, and bright scarfs and hats. Lola had her mother's red wavy hair, and the smile that had bowled him over.

"Megan and I are waiting in the lobby." Lola entered the library, wearing a smock with ribbed tights and pink boots. "She said you disappeared and she hasn't seen you in ages."

"I was doing some work," Fletcher said hastily, putting away his phone. "Let's go, I'm suddenly hungry as a bear."

"You'll still be hungry after dinner." Lola grimaced. "Megan said the restaurant serves soups and organic vegetables. On Christmas Eve! I'd rather eat at the inn. I walked by the dining room and they're serving turkey and stuffing with gravy."

"Megan chose the restaurant tonight, but you can decide where we eat tomorrow night." He took Lola's hand. "How about we pick up a pint of ice cream after dinner? You pick the flavor. What should we get?"

Lola looked up at Fletcher and the love in her eyes made him melt. "Ben and Jerry's Red Velvet Cake, of course," she said with that blazing smile. "Why do you have to ask?"

Fletcher and Lola entered the lobby, and Megan turned toward them. She really was stunning: blond hair tied in a neat ponytail and long legs fitted into leather boots. It wasn't just her looks that had attracted him. Megan had graduated from Yale's drama department four years ago, and she still had that wonderful enthusiasm and drive. Fletcher was a little tired of the whole game: producers who pulled their money at the last minute, actors whose demands were longer than a child's Christmas list. Megan made him recall why he'd fallen in love with theater.

"There you are." Megan kissed him. "You were gone for a while, and I missed you. I was afraid you got lost and Lola and I would have to eat by ourselves."

Fletcher wound his scarf around his neck and opened the door. Snow blanketed the sidewalk and the sky was full of stars. He was with the two people he cared about most at Christmas. What more could he ask for?

Five

IT WAS THE MORNING AFTER Emma arrived. She peeked out the window of her room. The sky was a swirl of clouds and fat snowflakes falling on the pavement. The church spire was almost invisible, and the village looked like it had been dipped in a bowl of warm milk.

She flopped back on the bed and thought of Fletcher and the blond woman and the little girl in that fantastic wool coat. There was no chance of staying at The Smuggler's Inn and interrupting Fletcher's family vacation. She had to go back to New York.

But she couldn't just leave; she'd promised to run the kids' club. Betty said only one child was signed up, but perhaps Betty could take care of it herself. And what about the roads? If she waited, they might not be passable.

She threw on a pair of jeans and a sweater and raced to the door. Then she turned back and glanced in the mirror. Even if Fletcher was with another woman, she didn't want his one memory of her to be without any makeup. She rubbed on lipstick and combed her hair. There was a cashmere scarf in her luggage, and she draped it around her neck. She was a successful advertising woman, after all; she didn't want to look the same as she had in college.

"Emma, you look lovely this morning," Betty said when Emma descended the staircase. The parlor was empty, and Emma felt silly. She had been worried about how she was dressed, but Fletcher wasn't even here.

"Thank you." Emma fiddled with the scarf. "I was wondering what the road conditions were like."

"The road conditions?" Betty repeated, running a duster over the fireplace mantel.

Emma was too embarrassed to say she was thinking about leaving.

"I was thinking of taking a drive," Emma volunteered. "The countryside is so pretty."

"The Green Mountains are breathtaking, but I'm afraid you won't see them today," Betty chuckled. "We're supposed to get six inches of snow by nightfall. You're not going anywhere unless you're a tow truck."

"Are you sure?" Emma winced.

"Don't worry, tomorrow is supposed to be clear," Betty offered. "You can always take a walk. A few of the guests already snapped on snowshoes and are trudging around the village. And the little girl signed up for the kids' club is going on an outing with her parents. I don't expect them back until dinnertime, so you have the afternoon to yourself."

"I don't feel like a walk," Emma said, deflated. She was completely stuck, and there was nothing she could do about it.

"Then you'll have to enjoy my breakfast," Betty said, beaming, and led her into the dining room. "You're the last one down, but there's plenty of biscuits and sausages."

Emma ate a bite of scrambled eggs and put down her fork. The eggs and warm biscuits with fresh-churned butter had looked delicious, but she wasn't the slightest bit hungry. She'd explore the inn, and then go upstairs and take a bath. One day of relaxing at The Smuggler's Inn wasn't so bad; tomorrow she'd go back to New York.

There was a honey jar shaped like a bear on the dining table, and she remembered her first date with Fletcher. Not their first kiss, because driving to Kennebunkport had been part of the trade for playing piano. The first time was when he'd picked her up wearing a blazer borrowed from his roommate, holding lilies that were wilted because they'd spent the afternoon in his dorm room.

October, 2007
Waterville, Maine

Emma sat across from Fletcher at the all-night diner and poured honey into a cup of tea. It was three weeks after their kiss at the seashore, and Emma had been certain Fletcher had forgotten about her. The kiss had meant nothing; it was the thrill of the sea spray combined with the exhilaration of being far from campus. They had been two puppies that momentarily escaped the litter.

When Fletcher did call and ask her to see a play at the Waterville Opera House, she'd thought it was a bad idea. Her senior thesis was taking up all her time, and there were only six months until graduation. But she'd blurted out yes, and spent the afternoon frantically searching for something to wear. Then she put the lilies Fletcher gave her in water and squeezed into his borrowed Corolla.

The play was entertaining, but the Corolla got a flat tire on the way home and they had to cancel Fletcher's dinner reservation at a French bistro. By the time he changed the tire, it was almost midnight, and they settled on burgers and fries at the diner near campus.

"A theater major who can change a tire," Emma said mischievously, pouring ketchup on lettuce. "I thought actors didn't do mundane things like work on cars or cook or do laundry."

She should have been disappointed that they'd missed out on soufflé and caramel flan, but she was strangely elated. Being with Fletcher was like putting her hand close enough to a fireplace to feel the warmth but not get burned.

"I've done my own laundry since I was in high school, and I make a decent tuna salad." Fletcher ate a handful of fries. "Anyway, I don't want to be an actor."

"You don't?" she asked in surprise. "You made me play the piano for your one-man show."

"You need a huge ego to face an audience across floodlights without wanting to run away," he explained. "I'm happier behind the scenes. I've wanted to be a director since I was a kid."

"Are you going to move to Hollywood and make blockbusters and drive around in a convertible?" She was joking, but underneath her light tone was the question of whether they would end up on different coasts.

"Movies are important, but there's no connection with the audience. I want to direct plays," he explained. "The greatest thrill of being a director is standing in the back of the theater and sensing the excitement ripple through the crowd. When they leave their seats at the end of the night, they all experienced the same adventure."

The possibility of them both living and working in New York made the weak tea taste delicious. But she didn't know how Fletcher felt about her. Maybe he simply had two tickets to the Waterville Opera House and didn't want to go by himself.

"What do you want to do after graduation?" Fletcher's words cut into her thoughts.

"Move to New York," she said simply. "I want to visit the museums and ride the subway and buy a carton of milk at midnight."

"Isn't that a little vague?" he said, grinning. "Will you be a dog walker, or go to law school and become a judge?"

"I'll do something with my English degree." She flushed. "Publishing, or work at a magazine. I've seen *Breakfast at Tiffany's* a dozen times, and every episode of *Sex and the City*." She stirred her tea. "You might think that's shallow, but we can't all have a burning passion."

"Wanting to live in New York isn't shallow. Passion doesn't have to be about your career; it can be for anything that makes you happy." He touched her hand, his eyes serious. "Maybe I'll be an assistant director at an off-off-Broadway play and convince you to be in the audience."

Emma gulped and looked straight into Fletcher's eyes. "You won't have to convince me. Whatever you direct will be wonderful."

Except that Fletcher had gotten an offer from the Old Vic in London, so they ended up living five thousand miles apart. And when one of her friends had a connection at Ogilvy & Mather, Emma gratefully accepted a job. She told herself she might be writing three-word ad copy instead of editing literary fiction, but Madison Avenue had its own glamour, and it was still New York.

So why was she sitting in the dining room of a Vermont inn chasing an eleven-year-old dream? She finished breakfast and walked down the hallway. There were framed landscapes of Vermont: barns with red roofs, hillsides alive with color. It all looked so beautiful that for a moment she was sad to leave.

She peered into a room with a bay window and a piano. There was an ancient rug and a crystal chandelier that could use a good dusting.

Emma sat on the piano stool and ran her hands along the keys. It was perfectly in tune, and tentatively she began to play. First she tried simple chords, and then she played a Christmas medley: "We Wish You a Merry Christmas," "Silent Night," and her favorite: "So This Is Christmas" by John Lennon.

"That was good—will you play it again?" a small voice asked.

Emma looked up and saw the little girl in the striking wool coat. Except now she was wearing something completely different: a striped sweater with flared jeans and a pair of green clogs.

"I didn't know anyone was listening," Emma stammered, recognizing Fletcher's daughter.

"There's nothing else to do." The girl perched dejectedly on a chair. "My father was supposed to rehearse with me for the talent show, and then we were going to see the covered bridges. But he went out hours ago and he's not back."

"I'm sure he'll be back soon." Emma's eyes traveled to the door, half-expecting Fletcher to appear.

"He's gotten so unpredictable lately," the girl sighed. "My best friend Cammi said the same thing happened when her parents got divorced. My father is different—we're like this." She twisted her fingers together. "At least we were, until the good witch entered the picture. Now I have to remind him I'm alive."

"The good witch?" Emma asked.

"That's our code word for his new girlfriend." She rolled her eyes. "Well—fiancée, technically. You should see that ring. I was hoping it was a prop for the new play. But Cammi confirmed it's real. She should know; her mother practically lives at Tiffany's."

"Your father is engaged?" Emma tried to sound calm.

"Honestly, I would have expected better from him," the girl said knowingly. "But Cammi said if you present a divorced man with a long pair of legs attached to a twenty-something body, they can't help themselves. She showed me all these articles about how men can't be alone." She looked at Emma. "Did you know that most single men don't know how to do laundry? And don't even get Cammi started on cooking. After her parents got divorced, she learned to make macaroni and cheese and lasagna."

"Your friend sounds very accomplished," Emma laughed. "How old are you?"

"I'm almost ten, but age is only a number when you're in the theater. I plan on being a big star by the time I'm fourteen." She looked at Emma nervously. "Eighteen at the latest."

"That's inspiring, and I'm sure you'll achieve it." Emma stood up. "I have to go, but it was nice talking to you."

"Please don't go, there's no else to talk to," the girl said, and suddenly was excited. "You can help me rehearse for the talent show."

"Me?" Emma repeated.

"I was going to sing a Christmas song." She moved over to the piano. "Please—my father won't come back for ages, and I won't have practiced at all."

"No, I can't." Emma shook her head. What would happen if Fletcher and his fiancée appeared and she was sitting at the piano with his daughter?

"It's snowing too hard to do anything else," the girl argued. "If my father sees how good I am, maybe he'll pay me some attention."

"I'm sure he pays you attention," Emma said.

"Not when the good witch is around," the girl said. "I didn't mind at first. I want my father to be happy, and he hadn't smiled much since he moved to New York. But then he gave her a part in the play and now she's practically moved into his apartment and soon they'll be married." The little face crumpled. "If I don't do something drastic, he'll forget I exist."

"I suppose I could practice a few songs," Emma said, her resolve wavering. "I don't even know your name. I'm Emma."

"I'm Lola." The girl held out her hand. "My father taught me that an actress has to have a good handshake. It shows the director you have confidence in yourself. Can we start with 'Have Yourself a Merry Little Christmas'? Some people say it's a cliché. But if it's good enough for Mariah Carey, it's good enough for me."

Lola started to sing and her voice took up the whole room. For a moment, Emma forgot about Fletcher and was swept up by the clear notes.

"Bravo," a female voice called.

Emma looked up. Betty was standing at the door, carrying a laundry basket.

"I'm sorry." Emma stopped. "I should have asked before I played your piano."

"Nonsense, that's what it's for." Betty beamed. "You're both so talented. And I'm so glad you found each other."

"Found each other?" Emma repeated.

"Lola is the little girl signed up for kids' club," Betty said and turned to Lola. "I didn't know you were here. Your father told me you would be out all day."

"We were supposed to be." Lola shrugged. "But Megan wanted to go snowshoeing with my father first, and they haven't come back." She looked at Emma brightly. "I'm glad because I got to rehearse with Emma. She's going to accompany me in the talent show."

"No, I'm not," Emma said, startled. "I was just helping you rehearse."

"Why not?" Lola asked. "If you're going to watch the show, you may as well perform. And we can practice again later this afternoon. If it's still snowing then, it'll be more fun than playing Scrabble."

"Lola is right." Betty set her basket on the floor. "And I'm preparing a special dinner, since we're practically snowed in: venison and baked potatoes and plum pudding for dessert."

Emma looked from Lola to Betty and couldn't think of a reason to say no.

"All right." She nodded. "I'm going to go up and take a bath. I'll see you in a couple of hours."

"One more thing," Lola said as Emma walked to the door.

Emma turned around and thought, she really was a beautiful child, with that flaming hair.

"Do you have something special to wear?" Lola asked. "Clothes are very important. You have to wear something the audience wants to watch."

Emma sat on the bed in her room and turned on her computer.

"Emma!" Bronwyn appeared on the screen. There was some kind of mud mask on her face and she was holding a cocktail glass.

"What's on your face, and are you drinking?" Emma momentarily forgot her own problems. "It's two o'clock in the afternoon."

"We had a little incident at lunch. Sarah decided to cook. She set the table with Barbie plates and served noodles and meatballs." Bronwyn sipped her drink. "I swear I was only gone from the kitchen for a minute. I don't know how she mixed Trixie's dry dog food into the Bolognese sauce." She winced. "I only found out because I almost broke a tooth. I'm hoping the scotch will neutralize the kibble in my stomach."

"Why are you wearing a face mask?" Emma tried not to laugh.

"That's so Sarah can't see my expression." Bronwyn grimaced. "She did it by accident, but I have the extremely un-motherly desire to strangle her.

"Enough about me—I want to hear about you and Fletcher. Let me guess: You ran into each other last night at dinner, and he asked you to join him. You roasted chestnuts until midnight and talked about everything you missed. Then you stumbled up to his room and made love all night. Now you're going to join him in the outdoor Jacuzzi, where you'll sip schnapps and make heart-shaped rings with your breath."

"That's definitely the movie version," Emma said, nodding. "The real-life version is, I went ice skating yesterday and saw

Fletcher with some leggy blonde and a beautiful little girl. I was too embarrassed to go downstairs to dinner and was determined to leave this morning. Only it's snowing, so I decided to play the piano." She took a breath. "Then Fletcher's daughter heard me playing and convinced me to accompany her in tonight's talent show."

"Could you repeat that, please?" Bronwyn said. "Liv is crying for her pacifier and I didn't hear what you said."

"Liv doesn't use a pacifier, and you heard me perfectly!" Emma's voice cracked. "You missed a few things in your investigating. Fletcher *is* divorced, but he's also engaged. And he has a nine-year-old daughter named Lola who acts like she's twenty and is determined to be the next big thing."

"Is his fiancée nice?" Bronwyn asked.

"I don't know! Fletcher hasn't seen me, and I don't know what to do when he does," Emma moaned. "Lola calls her the good witch. Apparently since she came into the picture, Lola feels ignored."

"What did you say?" Bronwyn was suddenly alert.

"Lola is afraid the new fiancée is stealing her father away," Emma explained. "That's why I couldn't say no. She's desperate to perform in the talent show so Fletcher will notice her."

"Don't you see? It's synchronicity all over again." Bronwyn peeled the mud off her cheek. "You were planning on coming back to New York, but then you got snowed in. Of all the people who heard you playing the piano, it was Fletcher's daughter. You're going to perform in the talent show together, and it will all work out perfectly."

"You forgot about the blond fiancée with a diamond ring that's as big as a bird's egg," Emma reminded her.

"It's probably a rebound relationship. I see it all the time at the practice. Newly divorced men come in for Botox, and a few months later they're making dual appointments for themselves and their new girlfriends." She leaned toward the screen. "You and Fletcher have a history together. That's why you're both in Vermont."

"I'm in Vermont because you made it sound like Fletcher was single and broken-hearted," Emma said.

"If it was a healthy relationship, his daughter wouldn't call her the good witch," Bronwyn insisted. "Let synchronicity do its work. All you have to do is sit at the piano and play 'Jingle Bells.'"

"I didn't really have a choice. Lola is worried that since the fiancée entered the picture, Fletcher has forgotten all about her." Emma sighed. "Not to mention the fact that she's the only child signed up for kids' club."

"Lola is the little girl who's doing kids' club!" Bronwyn couldn't have been more excited. "You saved the best news for last. If that isn't destiny at work, I don't know what is. You're going to spend the whole week with Lola; you'll get to know her intimately. You see? You're going to rekindle your great love and save Lola from a mean stepmother."

"Life isn't a fairy tale, even if it is Christmas," Emma said, but she remembered Lola's trembling mouth and couldn't help feeling sorry for her.

"Life is whatever you believe it will be." Bronwyn pulled the mud mask off her other cheek. "I have to go and cleanse. Enjoy yourself, and wear something sexy tonight—you don't want to look like Lola's piano teacher."

Emma hung up and rifled through her suitcase. She wasn't going to wear the low-cut red sweater because Bronwyn had told her to look sexy, or because Lola wanted her to impress the audience. She was going to wear it because she'd bought it with last year's Christmas bonus, and it hadn't done anything all year except sit in the back of the closet.

It did look good with the black slit skirt she had packed at the last minute. She held them both up to the mirror and groaned. What was she thinking? She could sit at the piano in a lace negligee and she wouldn't be any match for a twenty-something blonde with impossibly long legs.

Six

FLETCHER LATHERED SHAVING CREAM ON his cheeks and thought it had been a surprisingly good day. It had started off shakily. Megan had been disappointed that The Smuggler's Inn didn't have a fitness center and insisted that they get some exercise. Fletcher had stared out at the rooftops shrouded in snow, longing to spend the day reading scripts by the fireplace.

But at his last physical, the doctor hadn't liked his blood pressure and prescribed a daily workout routine. So Fletcher had gamely accepted the snowshoes Betty offered, and followed Megan outside. The village that yesterday had been full of the sights and sounds of Christmas was one of those abstract paintings that, no matter how you looked at it, was just different shades of white.

Now it was five o'clock in the afternoon and he was glad he'd joined her. Trekking through the snow had been so peaceful. The pine trees were hung with icicles and there were squirrel tracks in the fresh powder. The pressures of New York and the play fell away.

He and Megan had only planned on snowshoeing in the morning, but then Megan discovered a farm-to-table restaurant that offered a five-course tasting menu. The chef happened to be standing at the door and informed them that everything served in the dining room—the graham-cracker-crusted duck frites and lamb sliders made with fig jam—was prepared from local ingredients. Fletcher had read about Vermont cheese, but he hadn't imagined it was different than the selections at his local gourmet food store. But the blue cheese was nutty and sweet, and the sheep cheese melted in his mouth, and the tangy cheddar served with warm bread was better than anything he'd ever tasted. The waiter served them pale ale flecked with gold, and he grudgingly agreed Graham was right; he was a lucky man.

He tried to call Betty and ask if Lola could do kids' club this afternoon, but there was no cell reception. But it was only lunch; they wouldn't be gone very long. There had been a moment of panic when they finally got up from the table and Fletcher realized it was already mid-afternoon. He'd promised Lola he would help her rehearse before tonight's talent show, and now it was going to be too late. But Lola was in a particularly good mood when they returned to the inn. He offered to listen to her song, but she smiled that mysterious smile that made her look older than nine and told him he'd hear it at the talent show.

"You smell good." Megan appeared in the bathroom. "I just woke up, but seeing you makes me want to go back to bed."

Even in a flannel robe and with her hair pinned back, Megan was beautiful.

"So do you." Fletcher was tempted to wipe off the shaving cream and kiss her. "But shouldn't you be dressed? Dinner and the talent show start in half an hour."

"I was taking a nap and thinking about the first time you saw me act in a play." Megan stood beside him in front of the mirror. "Do you remember? I think I fell in love with you the moment I spotted you in the theater. You were so calm, and I was a nervous wreck."

"Of course I remember." Fletcher nodded, wondering as he often did how much his life had changed in six months. "It was at that little theater in SoHo. The acting was worse than anything I'd seen in college, and the writing was so leaden, I had to pinch myself to stay awake." He smiled. "But you came onstage for three minutes at the end, and it was like arriving at the top of Mount Olympus."

"Afterward we had a beer at the bar next door," Megan said, taking up the story. "I was so anxious, and you said I was too talented for the production. The director would be lucky to be the guy handing out programs in the plays I was going to perform in. You had so much faith in me, and it made me feel like I could do anything."

"I was right," Fletcher said, beaming. "You're going to be fantastic as the older sister in *Father of the Bride*."

"I've been rereading the script." She wiped shaving cream from Fletcher's cheek. "I think I should play Kay."

Fletcher stiffened, and the feeling of warm benevolence evaporated like fresh snow on the windowpane. "That's the starring role—and we've already got an actress attached. Haley Thomas was nominated for a Tony for her last performance."

"Think about the publicity," Megan urged. "Megan Chance plays the lead role in the Broadway remake of *Father of the Bride* directed by her fiancé, London-based Fletcher Conway. The fashion designers will go crazy wanting to design my real wedding dress, and we can do all sorts of tie-ins. I can shop for my going-away outfit at the same department stores we feature onstage; we can even mention some real New York wedding planners."

"You're too old to play Kay," he said without thinking.

Megan flinched, and he reminded himself of the cardinal rule of theater: never mention age to an actress if you want to stay in her good graces.

"I'm in my mid-twenties," Megan reminded him. "That's hardly too old to play a bride."

"Of course not. But Elizabeth Taylor was twenty in the original movie," Fletcher said hastily. "The whole point of the story is that Kay's father can't bear to give his little girl away. You're so womanly and self-assured."

"She did seem quite immature," Megan said thoughtfully and Fletcher breathed a sigh of relief. He couldn't wait to tell Graham how he'd avoided disaster with a few carefully chosen words.

"But that was one interpretation, and I'll make the character my own," Megan debated. "I've dreamed of working with Alec Baldwin. He's going to be an amazing father of the bride. Anyway, Alec is sixty; he could easily have a daughter who's twenty-four."

This wasn't the time to point out that Megan was twenty-six, and the theater lights would make her look even older.

"That's the angle for the remake. Kay is Alec's second chance at fatherhood, and he's even more reluctant to see her go than he was on the first go-around," Fletcher said gently. "And Broadway is different than Hollywood. It doesn't need outside promotion; people buy a ticket to see the play."

"Everything needs promotion. They teach you that at Yale," Megan answered. "The play will open in September, and we'll have our wedding at the Plaza in June. Just think about it! The wedding will make all the papers, and it will be wonderful for the show. I love you so much; I want your first play on Broadway to be a success."

This was the first that Fletcher had heard of the wedding being at the Plaza. Megan was the bride, and he wanted her to be happy. He didn't care where they got married, as long as they spent their lives together.

He really was in love. Megan made him feel confident and alive. Even here, standing in the slightly chilly bathroom of an inn in Vermont, he felt more vital than he had in months.

"Why don't we talk about it at dinner?" Fletcher proposed. "Lola is so excited about the talent show, and I don't want to keep her waiting."

"We had such a big lunch that I'm not really hungry." Megan reached up and kissed him. "I thought we could stay in our room. Why don't you finish shaving, and we can go back to bed?"

It took all Fletcher's willpower not to follow Megan to the bedroom. But he'd promised himself when he started dating Megan that he wouldn't become the kind of single father that put his girlfriend first. Lola meant the world to him, and he would never want to disappoint her.

There was a knock at the door, and he went to answer it. Lola stood in the hallway, wearing a long purple skirt. Her hair was tied with a pink ribbon, and she wore high-top sneakers.

"We were just talking about you." Fletcher ushered her inside. "You're so grown-up. I keep forgetting you have your own room."

"I have my own room at home; why shouldn't I have one here?" Lola pointed out. "Anyway, it was the only arrangement that worked. Megan would much rather have you as her roommate."

"As long as you're right next door." Fletcher's cheeks turned red.

"Betty promised me it's perfectly safe. I'm dying to hear this mystery song. I'll just finish shaving."

"We should hurry. I don't want Betty to give away my spot in the talent show." Lola's small face was pensive. "Megan isn't dressed."

"Would you mind if I skipped it?" Megan turned to Lola. "Snowshoeing tired me out, and your father and I ate a late lunch."

Fletcher was about to protest, but Lola put on her sweetest smile.

"I don't mind at all; you should rest up. Snowshoeing must have been grueling." She nodded thoughtfully. "My friend Cammi showed me an article that said it's difficult to take up a new sport after a certain age."

Fletcher laughed out loud and tousled Lola's hair. "Let's go. I'll show Cammi that she's wrong. I had a great time snowshoeing, and I've got the appetite of a boy to prove it."

Fletcher sat across from Lola in the dining room and dipped a baguette into his pumpkin soup. Betty had decorated the room with mistletoe, as well as a tall Christmas tree strung with colored lights. The piano had been pushed into the corner, and the fireplace was hung with stockings.

"Are you sure you don't mind that Megan isn't here?" Fletcher asked Lola. "Why don't I go up to the room after dinner and get her?"

"Megan won't come," Lola said matter-of-factly. Her small body was perched on a chair, and a napkin was placed neatly in her lap. "She doesn't want to watch me sing."

"Of course she wants to support you," Fletcher insisted. "She always says how talented you are."

"It's natural for her to feel threatened by the father–daughter bond," Lola continued. "Cammi said all her father's girlfriends are the same. First they try to win Cammi over, and if that doesn't work, they tell her father how great Cammi is. Then if there's a disagreement, Cammi's father will take the girlfriend's side." Lola ate a bite of glazed chicken. "It took her father going through three girlfriends for Cammi to figure it out."

"There's not going to be three girlfriends, and there's nothing to figure out!" Fletcher put down his fork. "Megan and I are getting married this summer, and we're going to be a family."

"We *are* a family," Lola said stoically.

"Of course we're a family." Fletcher was suddenly flustered. It was time to take a different approach. "Megan wants to have the wedding at the Plaza. Do you remember reading the Eloise books? You always wanted to have afternoon tea at the Plaza, and now there will be a wedding! We'll buy a beautiful flower girl dress, and you can help choose the cake."

"I'm too old to be a flower girl, and Megan doesn't eat regular cake. It will probably be gluten-free and low in sugar." Lola shuddered. "Maybe I could be in charge of the bubbles. My mom took me to a wedding and they blew bubbles at the bride and groom because throwing rice is bad for the environment."

Discussing Megan with Lola was like trying to keep a bumper car on track at an amusement park. It was better to change the subject.

"Tell me about this song. Who's going to accompany you?"

Lola looked around the room, and her mouth pursed.

"She isn't here," she said uncertainly. "I hope she didn't forget."

"I could play," Fletcher suggested. "My sight-reading is a little rusty, but I can get through 'Silent Night' or 'We Wish You a Merry Christmas.'"

Lola's eyes sparkled and she jumped up. "There she is! I have to go talk to her."

Fletcher turned, but Lola had disappeared into the lobby. Megan and Lola had so much in common; Lola just needed some time. Maybe getting married at the Plaza was a good idea. How could Lola not get excited about having a wedding in the setting of her favorite children's book?

The lights dimmed, and Betty stood in front of the microphone. "Welcome to The Smuggler's Inn. I'm glad everyone could join us." She gestured to the icicles on the windowpane. "I promise I didn't order the snow to keep you inside, but it is nice to see a full house.

"Without further ado, I would like to introduce our first contestant. She's the youngest performer we've ever had, but I think you'll agree she has big things ahead of her. Please welcome Lola Conway!"

Lola appeared next to Betty and curtsied awkwardly at the audience. Fletcher glanced at the piano and almost dropped his wine glass.

God, he was in trouble if he was imagining Emma was sitting right in front of him! The woman's hair was shorter than Emma's, and her cheeks seemed more sharply defined, but she sat up completely straight the way Emma always did at the piano. Even in the low light he could make out large brown eyes like Emma's under thick lashes.

This wasn't like the time he'd seen the woman on the subway who turned out to be six months pregnant and not Emma at all.

Or the girl standing outside the Four Seasons last summer who he'd been certain was Emma. It had been mortifying when he'd followed her into the restaurant and she was with another man.

The woman glanced in his direction, and Fletcher gulped. If it *was* Emma—if he hadn't drunk too much wine, and wasn't seeing things because he'd spent too much time in the cold—what was Emma doing at The Smuggler's Inn? And how had she ended up accompanying Lola on the piano?

Fletcher didn't really believe in coincidences, and even Graham would have scoffed that the scenario was impossible. And yet looking at her, seeing the way she concentrated as if each note had to be extracted from the keys, he knew without a doubt it was Emma.

When had he last seen her? Not at graduation, though that had been the last time he'd considered breaking the barriers they'd put up by talking to her. No, it was the next day, when he was loading his parents' car. He'd thought Emma had already left; to see her standing outside her dorm, her arms full of boxes, was a gift he had no business receiving.

There hadn't been any point in approaching her; his parents would appear at any minute. He remembered wishing he hadn't seen her, that it would have been better if his last minutes on campus were full of mundane goodbyes. Instead, she would be engraved in his memory like the wording on his Colby diploma.

The song ended and the room flooded with applause. Fletcher pulled his eyes away from Emma and gave Lola his full attention. His daughter, who always seemed more mature than the actresses he worked with, was a bright-eyed little girl soaking in the love of everyone around her.

Lola floated off across the room toward Fletcher.

"How was I?" she asked. Her cheeks were flushed and her ponytail swung behind her.

"You were fantastic," Fletcher said enthusiastically. "Mariah Carey never sung it better."

"First prize is a gift voucher at the Sugar Shack." Lola sank down in her chair. "I can buy presents for Cammi and Emma."

"For Emma?" Fletcher repeated.

"The woman who played the piano." Lola pointed across the room. "It's important to thank your accompanist."

"Emma," Fletcher intoned, reaching for his wine glass.

"I said she has to come and meet you." Lola jumped up. "I'll go get her."

Fletcher wondered if he could make an excuse and leave, but before he could flesh out a plan, Lola was dragging Emma to the table.

"Dad, this is Emma," Lola announced. "Emma, this is my father. He's a big director and one day our names are going to be together under a marquee on Broadway."

Should he tell Lola that Emma was an old college friend? If he did, what questions would Lola ask? And what would Megan think when she discovered his first love was staying in the same inn in Vermont?

Before he could say anything, Emma was holding out her hand. Her face lit up in a smile and there was laughter in her eyes.

"It's nice to see you," she said. "You have a talented daughter."

"Thank you." Fletcher nodded. "It was kind of you to accompany her on the piano."

"I'm glad it went well," Emma said and turned to Lola. "I really have to go. Enjoy the rest of your dinner."

"It's snowing, and there *is* nowhere to go," Lola reminded her. "Stay for dessert. Betty made a mini chocolate cake for our table, and my father doesn't like chocolate."

"I like chocolate," Fletcher cut in. "If I eat it at night, I get a headache."

"It would be rude to send some back," Lola said to Emma. "You have to stay and have a slice."

"Another time," Emma assured her. "I left a pile of work upstairs, and I have to finish it."

"It's Christmas," Lola persisted. "No one works during Christmas."

"I'm afraid one of my clients doesn't believe in holidays, even at Christmas." She smiled. "It was nice to play for you. I hope you win."

"She's pretty," Lola said when Emma left.

Lola forked chocolate cake into her mouth. Fletcher was staring into space and wishing he had a double martini. Perhaps he needed something even stronger, like a whole bottle of gin.

"Who's pretty?" Fletcher asked.

"The woman on the piano," Lola said. "She reminds me of an actress on television, but I can't remember which one."

Fletcher looked at Lola. He was the father and Lola was the child, and he wasn't going to sit around and critique the woman he had been in love with eleven years ago.

"That narrows it down to about a million actresses." He handed Lola a napkin. "Wipe your mouth and let's go upstairs. Nine-year-old actresses still have bedtimes."

"We can't go yet," Lola implored. "Betty hasn't announced the winner."

"I suppose you're right." Fletcher slouched in his chair.

The lights lowered and Betty returned to the microphone.

"Shh, she's going to say the winner now!" Lola put her hands to her ears. "I'm so scared. I'm going to block out the sound; you tell me what she says."

"Hello again. I hope you enjoyed the performances as much as I did." Betty beamed. "Who knew there could be so much talent under the roof of The Smuggler's Inn?" She smiled expectantly. "Without further ado, tonight's winner of a gift certificate to the Sugar Shack is Miss Lola Conway!"

Lola took her hands out of her ears and jumped up and down. She ran up to the podium and Betty handed her the envelope.

"I won! I won!" Lola practically flew back to the table. Her eyes were bright and her cheeks were full of color.

"I never doubted you would," Fletcher responded. "You're the most talented performer here."

"I'm so glad we came to Snowberry," Lola said and hugged him. "This is the best Christmas ever."

The Christmas tree twinkled in the corner and the room bubbled with laughter. It was Christmas week, and he was celebrating with his daughter and fiancée. He should have been the happiest man in the world. Then why did he have an ominous feeling, like when he staged a new play and knew before the final act that it was going to be a flop? Only this wasn't a play; it was his life, and he couldn't mess it up.

Seven

BETTY WAS RIGHT. THE NEXT morning the sky was blue and the sun gleamed down on the fresh snow. Emma stood at the window and had never seen so much white. The mountains were white, and the church steeples were wrapped in snow like fluffy marshmallows. Even the cars parked below were white rectangles waiting to be dug out.

Last night had been so embarrassing: worse than when she gave a presentation to a client and realized too late that the slides for the PowerPoint were photos of Bronwyn's dog and not her mock-ups for cosmetic ads. Emma couldn't even remember how they'd been mixed up in her briefcase. It took her twenty minutes to assure the account executives she wasn't going to use a cocker spaniel to sell mascara.

Even if Betty agreed to take over the kids' club, it was too late to go back to New York. Fletcher knew she was here. And he hadn't even acknowledged her to Lola. Emma hadn't admitted they knew each other either. It had been too overwhelming to look up from the piano and see Fletcher sitting at the table. There were lines around his mouth and his hair was shorter, but he looked exactly the same.

Her laptop chimed and she flipped it open.

"I checked the weather report in Vermont, and it's going to be a beautiful day." Bronwyn appeared on the screen. She was sitting in the room off of the laundry nook that she used as her home office. The walls held her diplomas, and the desk was cluttered with picture frames. "I made a list of things you should do. Start with a breakfast of blueberry waffles and Canadian bacon at The Maple Company on Main Street. Then you and Lola can watch the sled dog races on the frozen lake. There are six teams, and each sled is pulled by sixteen dogs. The brochure promises it will be one of the most exciting events of your holiday. After that, I recommend a visit to the Vermont Teddy Bear factory on Route 100. Lola would love it." Bronwyn looked up from her notes.

"I suppose I could ask Betty. I don't know if excursions are in the kids' club budget," Emma commented.

"If you do go, you can do me a favor. Trixie chewed the ear off Liv's teddy bear, and I was wondering if you could buy a new one. Since every meal in Vermont seems to include either hard cheeses or maple syrup, you'll need some exercise. You could start a snowball fight or try ice fishing. It's a wonderful way to explore Vermont's covered bridges in the wintertime."

"You don't have to convince me to stay—I promised to run the kids' club, and I won't let Betty down," Emma stopped her. "It's too late anyway. Fletcher knows I'm here."

"What happened?" Bronwyn picked up a nail file. "I want a play-by-play commentary."

"I accompanied Lola on the piano at the talent show, and Fletcher was in the audience," Emma said. "Lola dragged me to the table afterward and introduced me."

"She introduced you?" Bronwyn repeated.

"It was more awkward than that time five years ago when my boyfriend Matt insisted on singing karaoke at your Christmas party. Do you remember? His previous girlfriend told him he had a wonderful voice, and he couldn't sing a note."

"His family owned a jewelry store, and she wanted a diamond ring on her finger," Bronwyn recalled. "Maybe you shouldn't have broken up with him. He was handsome, and he kept asking me if you liked emeralds or rubies."

"I was too young to get engaged, and we didn't have that much in common." Emma sighed.

"Speaking of being engaged," Bronwyn cut in. "I want to know everything about Fletcher's fiancée. Is she a bottle blonde, or is it natural?"

"I wouldn't know," Emma said. "Megan wasn't at dinner."

"What do you mean, she wasn't there?"

"She must have been in the room. Fletcher and Lola were eating alone."

"Fletcher's hot fiancée was alone in their room during their romantic holiday?" Bronwyn said archly. "It sounds like trouble in paradise."

"Or they spent the afternoon in bed and she didn't want to get dressed," Emma retorted. "It's none of my business. Fletcher pretended not to know me."

Bronwyn brandished the nail file at the camera. "That's the best news I've heard. Don't you see? If he thought of you as an old college friend, he would have told Lola all about you. Your presence stirred up old feelings, and he doesn't want his daughter to know."

"Or it means I'm the last person Fletcher expected to see at The Smuggler's Inn," Emma retorted.

"Just keep making yourself available," Bronwyn said encouragingly. "Synchronicity will do the rest. Look how well it's working! Not only are you practically forced to spend time alone with Lola, but Megan wasn't at dinner last night. What are the chances that Fletcher's fiancée would miss dinner on the first night Fletcher saw you? It has destiny written all over it."

"I told you, I have no idea why Megan wasn't there," Emma said reflectively. It was odd that Megan hadn't been at dinner, and it had been nice seeing Fletcher alone with Lola. But she was imagining things. There was probably a simple reason why Megan hadn't been at the talent show, other than fate trying to bring Emma and Fletcher together.

"You're right, I need to keep busy. I don't want to run into him again," Emma said reflectively. "I'll go sledding or take a walk through the forest this morning. Tonight I'll eat dinner in the village, and tomorrow I'll take a morning excursion to a glassblowing factory."

"You haven't told me anything about Fletcher. Does he have that extra roll some men get in their mid-thirties, and is he losing his hair?" Bronwyn asked.

"He looks exactly the same." Emma remembered how his eyes were the palest shade of blue. "His hair is a little shorter, but it suits him."

"You see! You get all swoony when you talk about him. Look around this room." Bronwyn turned the computer so the camera scanned her office. "Do you know why my diplomas are on the wall, even though no one comes in here? And why I have photos of Liv and Sarah on my desk, when both girls are usually a few steps away in the playroom? The diplomas represent how hard I've worked to achieve my career. And the family photos remind me of the two small people I love most in the world." She paused. "You have a great career; it's okay to want a family too. Being a wife and mother is the greatest thing I've ever done."

"That's why you're my best friend," Emma said softly. "You can be a little opinionated, and I don't agree with your taste in rap music, but you know me better than anyone."

"Mothers need to be opinionated, so they can be heard over a three-year-old banging on her Sesame Street piano. And I only listen to rap music because Carlton likes it." Bronwyn leaned into the camera. "Go enjoy Vermont. And wear that white angora sweater, it makes your hair look extra glossy."

"How did you know I packed the angora sweater?"

"You knew Fletcher would be there," Bronwyn gloated. "You would have been crazy not to pack the angora sweater."

Emma descended the staircase and inhaled the scent of cinnamon buns. It would be lovely to have one of Betty's delicious breakfasts, but there was the chance of running into Fletcher in the dining room. She'd grab a muffin and a piece of fruit from the kitchen before she went outside.

As the kitchen doors swung open, she saw Betty hunched over the oak table. There was a notebook in front of her, and she looked like she'd been crying.

"I'm sorry, I didn't mean to intrude," Emma said, stumbling over her words.

"Please come in," Betty said, closing the notebook. Emma thought again how beautiful she was. Her sweater was camel-colored cashmere, and she was wearing tan slacks. "Would you like a cup of coffee? I just brewed a fresh pot."

A fresh cup of coffee was too good to pass up. Emma spied the plate of Danishes on the counter and was suddenly starving.

"I'd love one. And those apple turnovers smell heavenly," Emma said, nodding.

"There's an apple tree in the garden." Betty handed Emma a turnover. "The garden is one of my favorite things about living in Vermont. In Boston I had one tomato plant on the balcony that could never survive the summer humidity. Here, I grow apples, and rhubarb for my homemade raspberry-rhubarb pie. I would miss the garden so much if I had to move."

"Why would you move?" Emma inquired. "You love running the inn."

Betty waved at the notebooks. "Money, I'm afraid. It's silly to fret over a house when I lost the most important thing in the world. John and I were married for thirty-three years. I was twenty when we met, and he was the first boy I properly dated.

"I was trying to make it as an actress, working in the mens-wear department at Saks during the holidays. John said it was fate. He was a big believer in everything happening for a reason. Every year he gave his father a box of chocolates for Christmas, but that year he decided to buy a tie."

"That's a wonderful story, but why are you worried about money?" Emma asked. "The inn is fully booked, and your clothes . . ." She had been about to say that Betty dressed so elegantly, but realized it was none of her business.

"Are all cashmere and the finest wool?" Betty said, finishing her sentence. "John was a successful surgeon, and we lived quite well. It's my fault; I tried to keep him alive too long."

"What do you mean?" Emma wondered.

"John said one of the first things you learn in medical school is that you can't save every patient, and sometimes you have to let go. But that's impossible when it's someone you love. We spent a month at a clinic in the Swiss Alps, and a winter in Mexico where it rained so much I had to go to the market in a rowboat. Then there were the doctors pushing medicines that weren't covered by insurance." Betty pointed to the notebook. "If only the medical bills had stopped when John died . . . but new ones arrive every day."

"There must be someone who could help," Emma suggested.

"My son is married and starting his own family, and my daughter is getting a PhD and will be paying off student loans for years." Betty shook her head. "I did the budget when I opened the inn: how many rooms needed to be occupied, and how much it would cost to heat all the guests' rooms. I miscalculated the hotel tax. If I fall behind, they can close the inn."

"Where would you go?" Emma inquired.

"I wouldn't want to live in Boston without John; there's nothing for me there. The Smuggler's Inn is my home now." Betty finished her coffee. "When I'm here, I feel John watching over me. But you're on vacation, you don't want to hear any more of my problems." She looked at Emma expectantly. "Let's talk about you. You're young and pretty and obviously successful," she said, waving at Emma's cashmere scarf. "There must be someone you want to spend Christmas week with."

"Not everyone can find love." Emma ate a bite of turnover. "I have a nice apartment, and I love my job; I'm a copywriter at an advertising agency. I have drawers of cosmetic samples and an expense account that pays for cab fare when I work late."

"I loved being an actress, but I couldn't have lived without love. John and I fought our feelings in the beginning: he was accepted to medical school in Boston, and I was trying to make it on the stage in New York," Betty recalled fondly. "I remember the second Christmas we were apart; I missed John so much. I cashed the check my parents sent me and bought a train ticket to Boston." She smiled. "Only when I arrived, John wasn't home. His roommate said John had left that morning and didn't say where he was going.

"He was at my apartment, of course, banging on the door and waking the neighbors." She laughed. "Isn't it funny? We often wondered what would have happened if we'd missed each other, but my next-door neighbor told John where I was. He took the first train back to Boston, and we celebrated Christmas with Kentucky Fried Chicken because that was the only place that was open. After that, I moved to Boston and we got married and had children. We bought this house, and I performed in the summers at the local playhouse." She looked at Emma. "I said last night that being onstage is the best place to dream, but I didn't just dream of being an actress. I also wanted to fall in love and have a family. Since John died, I miss having someone to share things with." Betty put her coffee cup in the sink. "You're young. Keep chasing your dreams; it's the only way to make them come true."

Emma walked past the conservatory and heard the sound of crying. Lola was sitting on the piano stool, her knees tucked under her.

"Lola?" Emma entered the room. "Are you all right?"

Lola straightened up. "I was practicing for tonight's talent show."

"I've heard 'White Christmas' a dozen times, but it never made me cry," Emma said, glancing at the songbook.

"Who said I was crying?" A few tears escaped Lola's small fists and fell on her collar.

"I sell cosmetics for a living, and unless you've started wearing mascara at the age of nine, I can't explain the smudges on your cheeks." Emma pointed to the wet blotches. "You're the second person I've found crying this morning."

"The second person?" Lola said curiously.

Emma sat on the stool beside her. "Sometimes it helps to talk to someone. Do you want to tell me what's wrong?"

Lola fiddled with her hair as if she was trying to decide between flavors of ice cream.

"I won first place in the talent show, and the prize was a tour of the Sugar Shack," Lola began. "Betty told me all about it: they show you the taps on the trees and tell you how they extract the sap in the spring. You get to see the vats where they make the maple syrup and there's a gift shop that sells maple candy and jams."

"That doesn't sound like a reason to cry," Emma said.

"My father said we could go this morning. But he and Megan went on a sleigh ride, and I don't know when they're coming back."

"It's not even lunchtime; they'll return soon," Emma assured her.

"I heard my father and Megan arguing," Lola sighed. "When he came out of the room he had that dejected expression, like I get when I study for a spelling test and still get words wrong. He's probably trying to make up with Megan, and they won't be back for hours."

"You heard them arguing?" Emma said before she could stop herself. Fletcher and Megan were none of her business.

"I wasn't eavesdropping. I was about to knock on their door," Lola insisted. "Cammi's mother is always listening outside her bedroom. She says it's her responsibility to make sure Cammi is happy."

"That might apply to mothers, but it doesn't to nine-year-old girls," Emma said gently. "And you probably misheard them. I'm sure your father and Megan were just having a conversation."

"Megan was saying something about her part in the new play, and my father said they already talked about it and it wasn't a good idea," Lola reflected. "Then it got muffled and before I could knock, Megan opened the door."

"It couldn't have been a serious argument if they were already coming downstairs," Emma suggested.

"Megan had on her jacket and the boots my father gave her for Christmas. My father was wearing a shirt and loafers. Megan wouldn't have been bundled up if she was going to eat in the dining room, and my father would have worn his coat if he was going outside," Lola finished triumphantly. "They didn't match, so something was wrong."

"You would have made a great Nancy Drew, but I'm sure it was nothing." Emma smiled. "They'll probably be back soon."

"The sleigh only had two seats, so my father suggested I go with Megan. She said that sounded like a great idea, but she's not that good an actress. I could tell she was lying." Lola looked at Emma and her eyes brightened. "*You* can go with me to the Sugar Shack this afternoon during kids' club!"

"I suppose we could do that." Emma nodded. "If Betty doesn't mind that we leave the property."

"Why should she mind? It's my gift certificate, and the sun is finally out. I love it when you step on the snow and it crunches. We don't want to stay cooped up here all day."

Lola was right; spending the afternoon at the Sugar Shack was a good idea. Lola was like a flower blooming in front of her eyes. Her wavy red hair was tied with a yellow ribbon, and she wore a velvet dress and clogs.

"All right." Emma nodded. "I'll tell Betty our plans."

"I'll get my coat." Lola jumped off the stool. "You should put on something warmer. It might be sunny, but the thermometer on the porch says it's twenty degrees."

A sleigh picked them up and drove along Route 100 to the Sugar Shack. The scenery was completely different than yesterday, when the landscape had resembled a buttery cake mix. Red barns dotted the fields, icicles shimmered on pine trees, and Emma saw herds of cows and sheep.

The Sugar Shack was a brick building nestled at the end of a dirt road. The tour guide introduced them to a goat that liked to nuzzle visitors and a horse that ate Cheerios for breakfast. Lola didn't believe him until the guide took Lola into the horse's stall and showed her the box of breakfast cereal.

The tour of the vats was fascinating. Emma learned that Vermont had fifteen hundred sugar houses and produced half a million pounds of maple syrup a year. They sampled amber maple syrup that was the color of spun gold, and dark maple syrup that reminded her of a rich claret.

Then they sat at a table in the cafe and shared the Sugar Shack's signature dessert of boiled maple syrup on fresh snow.

"I've never eaten snow before." Lola dipped her spoon into the syrupy concoction. "It's better than ice cream."

"Vermont is terrible for a diet," Emma sighed. "Betty makes the best bacon I've ever tasted, and her turnovers are delicious."

"My favorite thing about America is hamburgers and hot dogs. In England we have sausage rolls, but no one eats them with ketchup, and that's the best part. Megan fills the fridge with green smoothies and vegetables that smell bad after two days." Lola wrinkled her nose. "I don't know how my father puts up with it. Cammi says it's because Megan is a blonde. Something about the chemicals in a blonde's hair attracts men and makes them do things they wouldn't normally do."

"I doubt that," Emma laughed. "Maybe your father is trying to eat healthy."

"We used to fight over who ate the last bite of macaroni and cheese, and now he says it's bad for his cholesterol." Lola rolled her eyes. "I'm never going to be a blonde. I have the same hair color as my mother, and she has the best hair in the world."

Emma was dying to ask about Fletcher's ex-wife. Why did she move to Connecticut? Had she remarried? But it was none of her business, and it didn't matter anyway. Fletcher was engaged.

"You have nice hair, too," Lola said. "I told my father you were pretty."

"You did what?" Emma's eyes widened.

"At the talent show last night." Lola ate a spoonful of gold-colored snow. "My father and I used to talk about things like that: who were the prettiest actresses, and which ones I wanted to be like when I grow up. Now he's always with Megan, and we don't talk about anything at all."

"Megan can't be around all the time," Emma insisted.

"She's like our neighbor's cat that spends all day preening in front of the window," Lola sighed. "Sometimes I think I should just pack my overnight bag and run away."

"You can't do that," Emma said. "Your father would be heart-broken."

"He doesn't notice me anymore," Lola said dramatically. "Every other Sunday we used to go out for pancakes. Now he and Megan spend all day talking about the wedding." Lola looked at Emma curiously. "Why aren't you married?"

"Me?" Emma repeated and her cheeks flushed.

"You don't want to get left on the shelf," Lola instructed her. "When I grow up, I'm going to marry a famous actor and we're going to have a penthouse apartment with an indoor swimming pool."

"You don't have to get married to live in a penthouse," Emma said. "If you're a successful actress, you can afford it by yourself."

"It's much better to be married." Lola licked her spoon. "Swimming is no fun alone."

Emma sat at the piano in the conservatory and ran her hands over the keys. After they'd left the Sugar Shack, the sleigh brought them back to The Smuggler's Inn and Lola went up to her room.

The lights on the Christmas tree twinkled, and the afternoon sun made patterns on the rug. The whole inn was quiet. Betty was out and the other guests were trekking through the forest or drinking hot chocolate on Main Street and watching the ice skaters.

Today two people had told her that love was the most important thing in the world. How could Lola know that at the age of nine, and how could Betty still believe in love when her heart was broken? Emma wondered if she was capable of having a lasting love, or if all her romances would end at Christmas, when other couples were exchanging presents and going on romantic vacations.

She remembered the first time Fletcher had told her he loved her. It was just before Christmas break of their senior year. She had thought she'd never hear him say those three words.

December, 2007
Waterville, Maine

It was the week before Christmas vacation at Colby, and Emma was strangely out of sorts. Other students were spending the last days on campus having snowball fights and singing Christmas carols. Emma stared out her dorm window at the quad and couldn't shake the empty feeling.

At first she'd thought it was exam nerves, but she received an A on her thesis draft and passed all her tests. It was Fletcher. They had been dating for two months and neither of them had expressed their feelings. Should Emma tell Fletcher that she was in love with him? How did he feel about her? They were both going home for Christmas, and she wondered what would happen when they returned.

She hadn't even known what to get him for Christmas. It would be too embarrassing if she gave him something romantic and he bought her a pair of mittens. She finally settled on a wool scarf embroidered with his initials.

There was a knock on her door and she answered it. Fletcher stood in the hallway, holding a small bunch of tulips.

"You look beautiful," Fletcher said approvingly. "These are for you. The guy at the florist tried to convince me to buy a Christmas poinsettia, but I told him it would die by the time we got back from winter break."

"They're lovely." She set the flowers on her desk. "You haven't told me where we're going for dinner. I didn't know what to wear."

"That's because it's a surprise," he said happily. "C'mon. I borrowed Jake's car and I had to leave it running. It's almost out of gas and if I turn it off, it might not start."

"How can we drive without gas?" she asked, grabbing the box with the scarf.

"I told him I'd fill it up." Fletcher took her hand. "I can't be choosy. I'm lucky I found a car."

Emma sat across from Fletcher at the Village Inn and thought she should be enjoying herself. The tavern was incredibly festive, with a roaring fire and a giant Christmas tree that made the restaurant smell like pine needles.

But the anxious feeling wouldn't go away. She had to tell Fletcher her feelings, but she should wait until after dinner and they were alone. She finally put down her fork and pushed the wrapped box across the table.

"I hope you like it. Merry Christmas."

Fletcher opened the box and took out the scarf.

"It's perfect." He looked at Emma and his smile seemed slightly awkward. "I don't have a present for you here."

"You didn't have to get me anything," Emma said quickly. "Dinner and flowers is enough."

"The tavern is famous for its twelve-hour duck. They stuff it with herbs and spices and roast it for twelve hours." He pointed at her plate. "But you've hardly eaten anything."

"It's all delicious," she assured him. "I guess I studied too hard. I haven't slept in days," she said lamely. "Maybe we can take some home."

"I'll ask them to box it up." He nodded. "But I wasn't planning on going straight back to campus. I wanted to show you something first."

Fletcher took her hand and led her through the lobby of the inn. They climbed a staircase and he took a room key out of his pocket.

Emma peered inside and caught her breath. The room was all white, with a queen bed and white wool rug and white robes hanging on old-fashioned pegs. There was a white Christmas tree and a stand that held a television.

"I wanted to take you to New York for Christmas, but I couldn't afford the train fare." He took her hand. "So I rented Christmas movies set in New York: *Miracle on 34th Street,* and *You've Got Mail.* And I put together a Christmas CD. Did you know that John Lennon and Yoko wrote 'So This Is Christmas' when they spent eight days at the St. Regis in New York?"

"It's the most wonderful thing anyone has ever done!" Emma noticed the little touches: chocolate Santas on the bedside tables, and a bottle of Bailey's Irish Cream. "It must have cost a fortune! Don't tell me you're going to be washing dishes over break, I'll feel terribly guilty."

"I offered, but they didn't need a busboy." He grinned.

"Then how did you pay for it?" Emma asked.

"I sold my signed autograph of Robert De Niro," he admitted.

"You did what?" She turned around. Robert De Niro was one

of Fletcher's idols. The autograph was his most treasured possession, along with a program of *The Producers* signed by Matthew Broderick.

"I'll get his autograph again when he stars in one of my plays." Fletcher put his arm around her. "Right now nothing is more important than spending one night before Christmas with the girl I love."

She reached up and kissed him and he kissed her back.

"I'm falling in love with you. I know we're young and we have so much ahead of us, but all I want is to be together," he whispered.

"That's all I want too," she breathed, and kissed him again.

Five Days Before New Year's Eve
Snowberry, Vermont

Emma watched the lights twinkle on the Christmas tree in the conservatory of The Smuggler's Inn. How could she have let Bronwyn convince her that some magic twist of fate had brought her to the jewelry store in the East Village? And how could she have believed that a man's watch would change her life?

She was here now, and The Smuggler's Inn was so charming. It had been fun going to the Sugar Shack with Lola, and the village itself was one of the prettiest places she had ever seen.

It was Christmas, and she was determined to enjoy herself. She'd only been on one sleigh ride, and she wanted to check out the scented candles at the Snowberry General Store. All she had to do was avoid Fletcher. Emma closed the piano and hoped that it would be easier than it seemed.

Eight

FLETCHER SAT IN THE LIBRARY of The Smuggler's Inn and wondered how he could be happy and miserable at the same time. It had been his idea to spend Christmas in Snowberry. Megan had wanted to lie on a beach in the Bahamas, and Lola had made a list of shows she wanted to see on Broadway. Fletcher had piled them into the car and promised seven days of roasting chestnuts by the fire and trekking through the snow to see live Christmas trees.

But this morning Megan had asked again why she couldn't play the lead in *Father of the Bride*. He stood in front of the closet in his boxers and wished they could forget about it and go back to bed. Megan wasn't like that; she would never use sex to get what she wanted. He tried to tell her that the producers had the final say, but she insisted that he was the director, and if he really believed in her, he could make them see she was right for the role.

She'd kissed him on the cheek and said she was going out for breakfast. He got dressed faster than he thought possible and ran out the door after her. Lola was standing in the hallway and he had to pretend everything was all right.

And everything was all right. It had taken all afternoon and a romantic sleigh ride through the forest for Megan to relax. When they argued, she became like a cat caught in the rain. Her skin was prickly and those almond-shaped green eyes shut him out completely.

He knew Megan loved him; she told him all the time that he was one of the most brilliant people she'd ever met. So how could he blame her for caring about her career? When he was at the Old Vic, he'd had to fight to direct his first play. The executive producer had taken one look at Fletcher in his Colby sweatshirt and said that if that longhaired American kid was going to direct Shakespeare, he would withdraw his money faster than anyone could say Violet Crumble.

Fletcher finally agreed to consider Megan for the part, and the rest of the afternoon was magical. The sleigh drove through a forest carpeted in fresh powder, hung with icicles as bright as diamonds. They held hands under the blanket and listened to the clopping of horse hoofs and Fletcher had that elusive feeling of being exactly where he wanted to be.

Then why now, sipping a brandy before dinner, was there an anxious feeling in his stomach? It was because of Lola. Originally he had signed her up for kids' club so she could be with other children, but apparently she was the only child staying at the inn. And to make things even more complicated, Emma was in charge of the program! When Betty explained how the woman in charge of kids' club had come down with the flu and Emma stepped in at the last minute, Fletcher's skin got clammy. What were the chances of Emma and Lola being thrown together all week?

When they returned to the inn, Lola couldn't wait to tell him about her afternoon with Emma. She showed him the postcards she was writing to Cammi and her mother and promised to give him a preview of the song she was going to sing at that night's talent show. Fletcher could hardly tell Lola that she shouldn't do kids' club when she was having such a good time.

His phone buzzed and he pressed ACCEPT.

"Fletcher, it's Graham." His British accent came over the line. "How is the holiday? Are you and Megan drinking schnapps by the fire, and is Lola making friends with goats?"

"I'm glad you called." Fletcher put the brandy on the table. "I need to talk to you."

"Any more imaginary sightings of Emma?" Graham asked cheerfully. "Emma eating hot biscuits at the inn, or Emma snowshoeing outside your window?"

"Emma accompanied Lola at the talent show last night," Fletcher replied. "Lola sang 'Have Yourself a Merry Little Christmas' and Emma played the piano."

"That's almost as good as the dream I had about Meghan Markle," Graham chuckled. "She and Prince Harry invited me to Buckingham Palace for afternoon tea."

"This isn't a joke," Fletcher said sharply. "Emma is staying at The Smuggler's Inn."

"Your college sweetheart turned up in some tiny town in Vermont that isn't even on a map?" Graham asked. "I'd say go easy on the brandy, you were never a good drinker."

"I didn't want to believe it either," Fletcher said. "Lola brought her over to the table. Her hair is different, but she looks exactly the same."

"You're serious! You don't think she followed you there?" Graham gasped in surprise. "You haven't talked to her in a decade."

"I doubt that. Emma seemed as shocked as I was," Fletcher said slowly. "It's more like . . ."

"Like what?" Graham cut in.

"Some crazy trick of fate, I suppose. I still can't believe that she's here. It's made me think about things. I thought Megan and Lola would get along wonderfully, but they can't agree on anything," Fletcher began. "And Megan and I got into an argument about the new play. She wants to play Kay, and I don't think she's right for the part."

"What does that have to do with Emma?" Graham wondered.

"Maybe Emma being here is fate saying I should slow down," Fletcher said, pondering. "Megan and I have only been together for six months; maybe it's moving too fast."

"That doesn't sound like you; you've never been a big believer in fate. Emma being in Vermont is most likely a sign that The Smuggler's Inn ran a Christmas special in *New York Magazine,*" Graham countered. "It's like dining at the Savoy. I know half the people at the American Bar on a Friday night."

"Odd things keep happening," Fletcher persisted. "The woman who runs kids' club got the flu, and Emma took her place at the last minute. Emma and Lola spend every afternoon together," he said pensively. "It's like some magic Christmas spell hangs over the whole inn."

"I thought New Englanders don't believe in spells—they burned all the witches," Graham chuckled. "I'm sorry, I don't mean to make light of your situation. I know what strong feelings you had for Emma, but that was a decade ago. You have to remember your life before you met Megan. Cassandra left you for an architect in Connecticut, and you had to follow her to America or you'd only see Lola summers and Christmas holidays. And don't you recall the first month after you arrived in New York? You kept calling me because you were so miserable."

"I herniated my back moving boxes into my new apartment, and my ninety-two-year-old neighbor brought over chicken soup," Fletcher said. "Then I was about to get fired because the producer was worried I wasn't up for the task. I tried to get a taxi to the theater to save my job, but it was pouring rain and the taxis were all taken." Fletcher remembered the first time he'd seen Megan. "A beautiful blonde carrying a copy of Tennessee Williams's plays offered to share her cab, and we talked about *A Streetcar Named Desire* on the drive."

"If anything was a twist of fate, it was meeting a woman with movie-star looks and a Yale education when you were at the lowest point of your life," Graham said, finishing Fletcher's story. "You're my best friend, and I just want you to be happy. I saw you and Megan together at Thanksgiving and it's the real thing. Don't throw it away because a figure from your past magically appeared in Vermont at Christmas."

"I love Megan, but it's complicated," Fletcher worried. "When I'm with Megan, I feel like I'm disappointing Lola."

"I have an idea. Take them both out for ice cream. No one can be miserable when they're licking a vanilla ice cream cone."

"I supposed you're right," Fletcher grunted.

"Megan is a gift from the heavens. Please, Fletcher, try to forget about Emma and not complicate your life," Graham counseled him. "If you slip and hurt your back again, the ninety-two-year-old neighbor with the chicken soup might be dead."

Fletcher hung up and picked up his brandy. Graham was right; Fletcher had to stop thinking about Emma. He was addressing the problems between Megan and Lola all wrong. He was expecting

Megan and Lola to find common ground, but he had to do it for them.

First he had to show Lola how much he loved her. He finished the brandy, and was suddenly in a much better mood. Sometimes it was difficult to see your own life clearly; you needed a kick in the right direction.

Lola was sitting cross-legged on her bed when he knocked on the door. She was wearing one of Cassandra's creations, a blue dress with a floral hem, and white tights.

"I thought you'd be practicing for the talent show," he said, poking his head in.

"Betty canceled the talent show." Lola looked up from her postcard. "She had some kind of emergency."

"That's too bad, but it opens the night to possibilities." Fletcher perched on the bed. "How about we eat somewhere special? The Goose Duck Inn has a Christmas tree that's ten feet tall."

"Every restaurant Megan chooses serves spinach salad or some weird liver." Lola wrinkled her nose. "I'd rather stay here and make peanut butter sandwiches."

"Megan didn't choose it, I did," Fletcher offered. "I read in the guidebook they have the best maple walnut cake and their stuffing comes with extra gravy. But we can go anywhere you like."

"Megan thinks gravy is a waste of calories," Lola said suspiciously.

"Then she can ask for hers on the side," Fletcher suggested.

"I know what you're doing. You're trying to make me feel better because there wasn't room in the sleigh," Lola replied. "I don't mind about Megan. Cammi says if her father doesn't remarry he'll get old and only have their dog for company. We don't even have a dog, so you'd be all alone."

"I'm only thirty-four; that's a long way off," Fletcher laughed. "You're my favorite dining companion, and I want to go somewhere you enjoy."

"It is Christmas, and maple walnut cake sounds yummy." Lola brightened. "Can we visit the village square afterward? They hold a concert every night, and maybe they'll let me sing."

"Most little girls would be more interested in watching Christmas movies," Fletcher said, and kissed her on the forehead.

"Most girls haven't decided on a career on Broadway." Lola put away the postcards. "I have to perform all the time if I want to be a star by the time I'm fourteen."

The Goose Duck Inn was a white clapboard house with a gray-shingled roof and a plaque that said it was established in 1890. The interior was quintessential Vermont: a lobby with a roaring fire, Norman Rockwell prints on the walls, and the scent of pine trees and candle wax.

The maître d' led them to a table that was set with porcelain plates and gleaming silverware. The Christmas tree took up a whole corner, and every branch was decorated with ornaments. Waiters carried silver bread baskets, and the brick fireplace was hung with stockings.

Megan looked gorgeous in an emerald-green dress and gold earrings. Her face was artfully made up, with the sheer arrogance of youth: a touch of blush to accentuate her cheekbones, and red lipstick. Lola wore a plaid coat over a matching dress and green stockings.

"I'm the luckiest guy, to have such beautiful dinner dates." Fletcher was in a good mood: the wine selection was excellent, and everyone liked something on the menu. Megan ordered the mushroom Wellington, Lola was excited about the burger with Belgian fries, and Fletcher was having pork chops in an apple bourbon sauce.

"We should make reservations here for New Year's Eve," he suggested. "They're serving duckling and a choice of maple crème brûlée or salted caramel ice cream for dessert."

"I'm having a wonderful time, but I thought we could go back to New York a day early," Megan said, looking up from her salad. "We received an invitation to Jordan Roth's New Year's Eve party. It's the party of the season, and it would be the perfect place to announce I'm going to play Kay. Everyone will be there."

Jordan Roth was the wunderkind producer responsible for *The Book of Mormon* and half the hit shows on Broadway. But Fletcher had promised Lola they would celebrate New Year's Eve in Vermont.

Fletcher was about to answer when something familiar caught his eye. The blood drained from his cheeks and he picked up his wine glass.

Emma was sitting at a table on the other side of the restaurant. Her face was half-hidden by the menu, but it was definitely her. She was wearing a white sweater and talking to the waiter.

"Dad." Lola turned and followed his gaze. "It's Emma! She's all alone, I should ask her to join us."

"That isn't a good idea." Fletcher stopped her. "She's probably meeting someone."

"She doesn't have anyone to meet," Lola said authoritatively. "She doesn't have a boyfriend and she's never been married. I told her she should find someone soon, or it would be too late."

"It's never too late to fall in love," Fletcher said to Lola.

"That's the wonderful thing about love; it happens when you least expect it."

"Your father is right. I was waiting at a taxi stand in the pouring rain when I saw your father. I had no idea I was going to meet the man of my dreams." Megan touched Fletcher's hand and turned to Lola. "But who's Emma?"

"Emma is in charge of the kids' club. Yesterday she accompanied me on the piano in the talent show, and today we went to the Sugar Shack," Lola said. "She's really cool. She let me eat fresh snow. I'm going to ask her to join us."

Lola darted across the dining room before Fletcher could stop her. Lola tugged Emma's arm and the sinking feeling in Fletcher's stomach became a crater.

"I guess Betty recommends the Goose Duck Inn to everyone," Emma laughed when they returned to the table. "It's nice to see you again."

Fletcher studied Emma in the candlelight and suddenly felt like the gawky college student coming across a pretty girl playing the piano. But that was ridiculous; he was a grown man eating dinner with his fiancée and daughter.

"Megan, this is Emma," he volunteered. "Emma and I were friends in college. She's staying at The Smuggler's Inn."

"Really!" Lola's eyes widened. "You didn't say you knew each other."

"It was a complete surprise," Emma said hastily, and Fletcher felt grateful to her. "I haven't seen your father in eleven years."

"Wouldn't it be great if Emma joined us?" Lola prodded. "You two must have so much to catch up on."

"I don't want to intrude," Emma said, shaking her head. "Besides I already ordered."

"Tell the waiter to bring your food here," Lola encouraged. "Food tastes better when you have company."

"Lola's right, there's no reason to dine alone." Fletcher smiled wanly. Lola wasn't going to stop until Emma agreed. "I'll ask the waiter to set an extra place."

"Lola tells me that you're a famous director," Emma said after they had finished the main courses and the waiter brought a plate of artisanal cheeses. "I'm not surprised." She turned to Lola. "Your father was the most talented student in the drama department."

"Success in the theater all depends on your next play," Fletcher said modestly, eating a bite of blue cheese laced with walnuts.

Dinner had gone better than he'd expected. Lola and Emma kept up a lively discussion about the best Christmas songs, and even Megan chimed in with suggestions. He described life in the theater, and Emma told a funny story about being a copywriter.

"Are you in theater too?" Emma said, turning to Megan.

"I'm an actress," Megan said, nodding. "I graduated from Yale's drama department, and I'm going to be performing on Broadway."

"Megan has only been in one proper play. Now that she and my father are getting married she's going to get lots of roles." Lola concentrated on her ice cream. "Megan wants to play the lead in the new play."

"It's a remake of *Father of the Bride*. Alec Baldwin is going to play my father, and I'll be the bride." Megan scooped up parfait and looked at Fletcher. "Fletcher and I have an uncanny connection. As soon as I suggested it, Fletcher saw I was perfect for the part."

After they finished dinner, Emma said she was going to stop at the General Store and Fletcher and Lola and Megan returned to the inn.

Fletcher sent Lola downstairs to find a board game and stood in front of the closet, unbuttoning his shirt.

"Dinner was delicious, but wasn't that the oddest coincidence?" he began. "Running into Emma after all these years."

"Most of the guests seem to be from New York." Megan unzipped her boots.

"We were at college together," Fletcher pressed on. "But I haven't thought about Emma in more than a decade."

"That's what Emma said." Megan looked at Fletcher quizzically. "You don't think I'm jealous, do you? We love each other, and I trust you completely."

"I love you too, and there's nothing to be jealous of," Fletcher agreed hurriedly. "I just thought it might seem like a strange coincidence."

"Things like that happen all the time." Megan shrugged off her jacket. "When I was studying abroad, I was sitting in a café in Florence and across the street was a guy from my French literature class at Yale. He joined me for an espresso and we caught up for hours."

"That must have been a surprise." Fletcher pictured Megan and some Yale jock with a blond crew cut sharing biscotti.

"I suppose Emma is pretty, in a faded way. But she's not the kind of woman one would be jealous of." Megan blotted her lipstick. "I'm glad Lola has Emma to hang out with. That gives us more time."

"More time?" Fletcher asked hopefully, wondering if Megan would suggest making love. Caressing Megan's milky skin was just what he needed to ease the nervous tension in his shoulders.

"Just more time to spend together. I'd love to take a long walk in the forest, or just curl up with you by the fire." Megan stroked his chest. "And we can rehearse my new role in the play."

"About that." Fletcher's skin felt clammy. "I can't make the decision alone. I have to consult with the producer, and . . ."

Megan dropped her hand and knotted a robe around her waist. "We discussed it this morning. You're the director; you can cast whomever you like. I'm going to take a hot bath. Oh, and think about going home early for Jordan's party. Vermont is gorgeous, but we don't want to miss the biggest New Year's Eve party in Manhattan."

"It's not that easy," Fletcher responded. "A play is like a giant jigsaw puzzle. If you start rearranging the pieces, the whole thing can fall apart."

"I trust you to figure it out," she said, and kissed him. "You're one of the most brilliant people I know."

Fletcher nursed a scotch and paced around the downstairs parlor. It was almost midnight, and the inn was quiet. Lola had finally gone to bed after beating Fletcher at four games of backgammon, and when he returned to his room, Megan was asleep. He tried to call Graham, but his phone went straight to voicemail. He debated calling his therapist, Margaret. But it was Christmas week and his old college flame showing up at The Smuggler's Inn hardly constituted an emergency.

Megan had shrugged the whole episode off as easily as her cashmere sweater. But sometimes Megan was impossible to read; that was part of the attraction. She had seemed more upset about the possibility of not playing Kay. What would the producers say when he suggested replacing a Tony-winning actress with his fiancée in the lead role?

He sipped his scotch, and his thoughts kept returning to Emma. It had been the strangest thing to sit across from her at dinner. And yet at the same time it had felt completely normal; she had that wonderful way of asking a question and being so interested in his answer. He found himself reeling off the names of the plays he had directed and telling her about London.

Even Lola seemed happier at dinner. She finished everything on her plate and thanked him for taking them to the Goose Duck Inn. On the way back to the inn, she held his hand and talked animatedly about seeing moose in the forest tomorrow.

Then why did he have this precarious feeling? Like when he was on the airplane at Heathrow Airport and the pilot said they were delayed by ice on the runway. Fletcher knew the plane wouldn't depart until it was safe, but he couldn't help clutching the seat and picturing crashing into the Atlantic.

Graham would say it was pre-wedding jitters, and he should drink another scotch and relax. Fletcher filled his glass again and remembered his wedding to Cassandra, and how thoughts of Emma had almost derailed the ceremony at the last minute.

December, 2008
London, England

It was the week before Christmas in London and Fletcher was sitting at the desk in his flat. He paused in the middle of writing his rehearsal dinner speech and marveled again at the four words that kept wafting through his brain like the smell of greasepaint at the Old Vic: he was getting married.

It seemed as unbelievable as the fact that Cassandra had agreed to go out on a date with him in the first place. After all, their first encounter at the party involved him spilling his drink on her. But they ran into each other at a performance a week later. He'd bought her a glass of champagne and asked whether she wanted to join him for a post-theater supper.

Fletcher had learned so much about Cassandra in the last five months: she was from a wealthy family, and her desire to be a costume designer was fueled partly by her love of theater and partly to escape from a future of garden parties and christenings. She never ran out of energy. While Fletcher could spend the whole day eating fish and chips and reading scripts, she insisted they go boating and take long walks in Kensington Gardens.

Would there have been a wedding tomorrow at Cassandra's parents' club in Belgravia if she hadn't announced she was pregnant? They probably would have waited until he was an established director and could afford more than a ground-floor flat, where the crib would be lodged next to their bed.

It was Fletcher who insisted they get married. Cassandra would have been quite happy to keep their relationship as it was. Her parents had agreed to support her, and she could bring up the baby with the help of her old nanny. But he loved Cassandra; she made his life as vivid as the clothes she designed, and he couldn't imagine life without her.

There was a knock at the door and he answered it.

"There you are." Cassandra entered the flat. She looked almost subdued in a pleated navy skirt and stockings. Her only allowance to her usual style was a pair of dangling glass earrings. "The rehearsal starts in an hour, and you're not dressed."

"I was trying to write my speech." He kissed her. "I have even more admiration for playwrights. I've been sitting here all afternoon, and only have one paragraph."

"The groom always says the same thing." Cassandra dusted biscuit crumbs onto a napkin. "He's grateful to the bride's mother and father for raising the woman of his dreams, and promises to take good care of her."

"I wish you had showed up hours ago." He smiled, scribbling on the piece of paper. "A few more sentences like that and I'll be done."

"I've been dealing with wedding cake emergencies. I love that we're having the wedding close to Christmas, but the bakery is so busy making Christmas puddings they messed up our cake." Cassandra moved toward the bedroom. "I'll get your suit while you finish your speech."

"The suit jacket is hanging in the closet," he called after her.

"What about cuff links?" Cassandra said from the bedroom.

"There's a box of cuff links in the third drawer." He tried to remember if his one pair of cuff links had actually made it to London.

Cassandra returned to the living room carrying a flat box.

"There aren't any cuff links, but I found this," she said, holding up a watch with a leather band. "What a beautiful watch. You should wear it to the wedding."

Fletcher looked up and his cheeks paled. He hadn't thought about the gift from Emma since he moved into the flat. What were the chances that Cassandra would discover the watch a day before the wedding?

"It's engraved." She turned it over and read out loud, "*To Fletcher, you have my heart. Emma.*"

Fletcher flushed and looked down at the floor. "Old college girl-friend."

"Where is Emma now?" Cassandra asked curiously.

"I have no idea, it ended before we graduated," Fletcher assured her. "You know what college students are like. Lots of grand gestures fueled by reading the Romantic poets. It doesn't translate into real life."

"We read Shelley and Keats in school and I thought they were boring," Cassandra said thoughtfully. "Doesn't it seem odd that you kept a present from an old girlfriend when you're about to get married?"

"I just told you," Fletcher said, but he could feel the color rising to his cheeks. "It doesn't mean anything."

"You might think that, but I studied Freud at university." Cassandra held the watch pensively. "Freud would say you deliberately held onto the watch to avoid making future commitments."

"Freud would be wrong." Fletcher's voice rose. "As you can see, I'm writing the rehearsal dinner speech for my wedding."

"I've said you don't have to marry me, I'm perfectly capable of raising the baby alone." Cassandra's mouth wobbled. "If you'd rather be with this Emma, I'd like to know that now."

Christmas music drifted up from the downstairs flat and for a moment Fletcher remembered the Christmas he and Emma had spent together at the bed and breakfast in Maine. They'd stayed up watching Christmas movies. It had been one of the best nights of his life.

Then he shook himself and counted his blessings: a loving fiancée, a baby on the way, and his position at the Old Vic. Emma was in the past, and he and Cassandra were going to have a wonderful life.

He took Cassandra in his arms and stroked her hair. "Do you really think I'm going to let you get out of marrying me that easily?" he said, and kissed her. "I love you. You've made me the happiest man in London, and I can't wait to meet you at the altar."

"I love you too." Cassandra kissed him back. "I really have to go." Her smile—the brilliant smile that lit up his day—returned. "I have to stop by the bakery and check on the lemon filling." She handed him the watch. "It's a pity you don't have Emma's address; you could send it back."

Cassandra left and Fletcher turned the watch over in his hand. Cassandra was right; he should get rid of the watch. If he couldn't return it to Emma, he'd sell it. He walked into the bedroom and put it back in the drawer. His wingtip shoes sat next to the bed, near a yellow tie and matching handkerchief.

Tomorrow he was getting married and he couldn't be happier. They were going to honeymoon in Ibiza and move into Cassandra's sunny flat and soon he'd be a father.

Life was good and he was a lucky guy. Now all he had to do was finish the speech for the rehearsal dinner.

Five Days Before New Year's Eve
Snowberry, Vermont

Fletcher paced around the parlor of The Smuggler's Inn and remembered his wedding day to Cassandra; it had rained all day, and everyone had laughed and said it was England, what did he expect?

But he was happy, and he would have kept on being happy if Cassandra hadn't fallen in love with someone else. His therapist would tell him that thinking about his marriage was as pointless as rereading last year's New Year's resolutions in December. The only thing he could do was be the best husband to Megan and father to Lola.

He still had an uneasy feeling, as if there was some Christmas spell at work that he had no control over. Ten years ago at Christmas, Emma's watch had almost stopped his wedding to Cassandra. Was it fate that had brought Emma to Snowberry now, and what did it mean for his engagement to Megan?

The clock struck midnight and he put the scotch glass on the side table. Graham would have laughed and reminded Fletcher that he didn't believe in destiny. Tomorrow he'd take Lola ice skating and then visit the antique stores with Megan. It would be nice to buy something together for the apartment.

The lights twinkled on the Christmas tree and he bounded up the stairs. Christmas really was the most magical time of year. He had a beautiful nine-year-old daughter, and he was engaged to be married. Everything was going to be perfect.

Nine

EMMA SAT AT THE DESK in the guestroom at The Smuggler's Inn and tapped at her computer keyboard. She had gone down-stairs to the dining room before anyone was up and fixed a cup of coffee and a plate of muffins. Then she'd crept back to her room and decided to catch up on her emails.

It would have been nicer to eat breakfast in the dining room surrounded by other guests, and the scent of Betty's hot cereal with maple syrup. But then she might run into Fletcher and Megan and Lola having breakfast, and that was too upsetting to think about.

A photo of Scott standing next to a surfboard appeared on her Instagram feed and she studied it carefully. No matter how em-barrassing last night had been, she still was glad she hadn't gone to Hawaii. You couldn't stay with someone you didn't love; it was as impossible as having a snowball fight in the sarong Bronwyn had bought her for Christmas.

The FaceTime light blinked and Bronwyn's face appeared on the screen. She was dressed in a lime-green sundress, and was wearing large sunglasses.

"Why are you wearing a sundress when a snowstorm is headed to New York?" Emma asked.

"Do you like it? I bought it from Saks's cruise collection," Bronwyn answered. "It's perfect for our little getaway to Palm Beach. Five nights at The Breakers; we leave the day after tomorrow."

"I thought you were on call at the clinic and can't go on vacation?" Emma reminded her.

"I promised Etta Parsons four weeks of free babysitting if she trades with me. I can't take it anymore. Carlton sprained his ankle and can't join us until Saturday, and Sarah and Liv decided to start a punk rock band. Sarah did Liv's makeup; my three-year-old is wearing a face full of Dior powder and blush. We leave tomorrow morning. Until then, I turned the heat on high. I'm chilling piña coladas in the freezer and I've got 'Kokomo' by the Beach Boys playing on repeat on Spotify."

"You're not making me want to get married and have children," Emma laughed.

"Fifty-one weeks a year, I'm perfectly happy," Bronwyn said, fanning herself with a magazine. "But if I ever say I'm going to have a staycation the week after Christmas while my husband is skiing and my nanny is visiting her mother, you have my permission to gag me."

"I saw a photo of Scott on Instagram. He's two shades darker than when he arrived in Maui," Emma sighed.

"Don't think about Scott. I want to hear about Fletcher." Bronwyn took off her sunglasses. "Have you seen him again?"

"I don't want to talk about it," Emma groaned. "It was the most embarrassing night of my life."

"You want to know embarrassing?" Bronwyn rejoined. "When you send a sexy text telling your husband what you're going to do when his sprained ankle is better and realize you sent it to the car service instead. I'm going to have to wear a disguise when the town car picks us up tomorrow."

"I had dinner at the Goose Duck Inn so I wouldn't run into Fletcher in the dining room," Emma began. "But Fletcher and Megan and Lola were sitting on the other side of the restaurant."

"Did you spend the whole night spying on them from behind your menu?" Bronwyn asked. "I did that once when my date stood me up at the Olive Garden. Two nights later I was having dinner there and he appeared with another girl. He wanted to use his coupon."

"It was worse than that," Emma replied. "Lola came over to my table and insisted I join them."

"You ate dinner with Fletcher and his fiancée?" Bronwyn gasped. "I might need to drink one of those piña coladas. Is she the Marilyn Monroe bombshell type of blonde, or one of those Scandinavian blondes who looks like she inhales her food through a straw?"

"She was stunning." Emma recalled Megan's perfect features. "She has this elegant nose and almond-shaped green eyes."

"The nose is probably bought, and even the eye color could be contacts," Bronwyn said knowingly. "Nothing is real these days. Mrs. Peterson's lip implants are paying for three nights at The Breakers in Palm Beach. What was she like? Did she hang all over Fletcher and gush at everything he said?"

"She graduated from Yale, and she's going to be starring on Broadway," Emma corrected her. "She's hardly a theater groupie."

"There must be something wrong with her," Bronwyn offered. "An eye twitch or an allergic reaction to dairy products."

"I did notice some kind of friction between them," Emma mused.

"You see!" Bronwyn beamed. "The watch brought you to Vermont to stop Fletcher from making a terrible mistake. He's going to fall back in love with you and you'll live happily ever after," she predicted. "But make sure he buys you a new diamond ring. If Megan gives the engagement ring back, you don't want to wear the same one."

"I'm not even going to think about Fletcher. I have some copy to write for a new lipstick," Emma laughed. "Don't post too many photos of Palm Beach on Instagram. If I see any more pictures of white-sand beaches, I might be tempted to get a spray tan."

"They never work evenly," Bronwyn said. "And you look beautiful with pale skin, like Snow White before the prince kisses her."

Emma descended the staircase and slipped down the hallway. The parlor was empty, but she didn't want to take a chance of running into Fletcher and Megan. She was about to open the door when she heard someone calling her name.

"Emma!" Lola's small face appeared. "Where are you going?"

"It's not time for kids' club yet. I didn't know you were back," Emma said, turning around. "I thought you and your father went ice skating."

"We had a wonderful morning!" Lola nodded. "Dad took me to the Crêpe Café and I had a stack of pancakes this high." She waved her hands. "Then we skated circles around the skating rink before anyone was there. The best part was that Megan stayed at the inn because she wanted her beauty sleep," Lola said thoughtfully. "The last thing Megan needs is to get more beautiful."

"I don't think anyone can be too beautiful," Emma reflected.

"Some people have a sparkly beauty. My mother is beautiful because when she smiles you feel happy," Lola mused. "Megan's beauty is scratchy, like a wool sweater that looks pretty in the store but itches when you put it on."

"Your mother sounds lovely," Emma offered.

"She's my best friend," Lola agreed. "Besides my father and Cammi, of course. My mother would do anything for me."

"So would your father. He loves being with you."

"I always thought so, but Megan wants all his attention," Lola said doubtfully. "We had so much fun at breakfast because she wasn't there. We played tic tac toe while we ate our pancakes, and when we ice skated we sang our favorite Christmas songs." Lola giggled. "My father has a terrible voice. He's lucky he never tried to be an actor."

"The first night we met in college, he acted in a one-man show," Emma recalled. "He only told me later that it was because he couldn't get any other students to perform."

"Were you really good friends?" Lola inquired.

"It was a small college; everyone knew each other," Emma said, and stopped herself. She shouldn't be talking to Lola about Fletcher. "I have to go. I'll see you this afternoon for kids' club. I thought we could go sledding and build a snowman."

"Can I come to breakfast with you?" Lola asked.

"But you already ate," Emma said, puzzled.

"I'd rather be with you. Megan just got up and my dad wants to visit boring antique stores," Lola said, rolling her eyes. "Anyway, I'm a growing girl, I'm always hungry."

Main Street was bustling with tourists in knitted ski sweaters and après-ski boots. Christmas songs blared over the loudspeakers, and the shop windows were filled with New Year's Eve streamers and colored tinsel.

Lola kept up a constant chatter about moving to America: her mother said she would love bagels with cream cheese, but they weren't as good as warm crumpets with orange marmalade. Then she ticked off the things she missed about Christmas in London: the food hall at Harrods, with its cases of English toffees; seeing the Christmas lights from the top of the London Eye; ice skating at Trafalgar Square.

"You have all that in New York," Emma said as they entered a diner with a linoleum floor and red booths. There was a jukebox and a blender with a sign that offered Ovaltine milkshakes. "You can ice skate at Rockefeller Center, and Zabar's sells every kind of Christmas treat. You can even take a cruise and see the Christmas lights on the Statue of Liberty."

"My mother was too busy to come into New York during the holidays, and my father spent the week before Christmas with Megan's parents in New Jersey." Lola shrugged. "Even Cammi wasn't available. Her parents are trying to outdo each other with vacations. Her father dragged her to Aspen for Christmas, and now she's stuck in the Bahamas."

"That doesn't sound too terrible," Emma said, laughing.

"Everyone knows hotel Santa Clauses aren't real," Lola said. "And Cammi hates the beach. She has sensitive skin."

"I can't think of anywhere I'd rather be than Snowberry, Vermont." Emma picked up the menu. "There's nothing better than making new friends."

"Especially when I get to eat more pancakes!" Lola said happily. "I'll have the hot apple crumble special. It's a crêpe filled with cooked apples and cinnamon."

The waiter brought two hot chocolates topped with whipped cream. Emma ordered a crêpe filled with sliced strawberries and bananas and a side of blueberry compote.

"I know who was crying yesterday," Lola said, biting into her crêpe. "It was Betty."

"Who told you that?" Emma asked in surprise.

"No one, I figured it out. She canceled the talent show because of an emergency, and this morning I heard her talking on the phone," Lola replied. "She sounded upset."

"Lola, you can't eavesdrop on people," Emma counseled her. "You're going to get into trouble."

"I didn't listen on purpose. I was in the mudroom putting on my boots. They have long laces, and it takes forever to tie them," she insisted.

"Betty is having money problems, and might have to shut down the inn," Emma acknowledged.

"She can't do that!" Lola exclaimed. "I want to ask my dad if we can come back in the summer. We could go fishing and ride bicycles."

"I wish there was a way to help her," Emma sighed. "Her husband died, and the inn is all she has."

Lola dipped her spoon into her hot chocolate. "We can hold a fundraiser; it's done all the time in the theater. Last Christmas when my dad directed *The Nutcracker,* the lead actress's house burned down in a fire. There was a special performance, and the ticket sales went to buy her family a Christmas tree and turkey with all the trimmings."

"That's a lovely idea, but I'm leaving in four days and so are you. We can hardly put on a play before New Year's."

"We could hold a talent show on New Year's Eve and invite everyone in Snowberry to enter," Lola said eagerly. "We'll put up posters around the village. The entry fee will be fifty dollars, and all the proceeds will go to Betty."

"I doubt that would be enough money to make a difference," Emma said, her resolve wavering.

"There's lots of wealthy tourists, " Lola pondered. "If they know it's for a good cause, maybe they'll donate more. Once the theater held a fundraiser for a stagehand who broke his leg in a motorcycle accident, and somebody donated a car." She ate a spoonful of whipped cream. "We found out later that his mother put up the money because she wanted him to stop riding a motorcycle. You never know, we could raise enough to save the inn."

"How would we publicize it?" Emma wondered. It really was a good idea. Betty had spent every summer and Christmas in Snowberry for years; people would want to help her.

"Let's go back to the inn and make posters," Lola suggested. "I'm pretty good at drawing, and you can think up what to say. Then we can put them all around the village. Everyone will know about it by night time."

"We should ask Betty first." Emma was suddenly excited. "She might not want to accept charity."

"Christmas is about doing things for others," Lola reminded her. "Betty will be doing a good deed by allowing people to help her. And maybe it was fate that made me hear her on the phone."

"What do you mean?" Emma's ears pricked up.

"My mom believes in destiny—you know, that there's some big mystical plan that guides you through life," she said earnestly. "Maybe it was fate that made me take so long to tie my shoelaces and overhear Betty's conversation. Now we're going to have a fundraiser and help her save the inn."

Emma thought about Bronwyn's belief that destiny had caused Emma to find Fletcher's watch and go to Snowberry.

"We haven't saved Betty's inn yet." She ruffled Lola's hair. "But that's pretty clever. Sometimes I forget you're nine years old."

Lola looked up from her hot chocolate, and there was a spot of whipped cream on her nose. "I told you. In the theater, age is just a number."

"A New Year's Eve talent show!" Betty said when Emma told her their plan. Emma and Lola sat at the kitchen table while Betty arranged a tray of shortbread. "That's a wonderful gesture, but I don't know if we could raise enough to make a difference."

"Lola said some people would donate more, and she's right," Emma replied, and Lola nodded eagerly. "The Smuggler's Inn is part of Snowberry. Everyone would want to help."

"We do get a lot of wealthy visitors from New York and Boston," Betty said thoughtfully. "We could ask some of the shopkeepers to be the judges: Molly at the flower shop, and Gunther who owns the ski store. But we couldn't hold it here. The fire code limits the number of people allowed in the dining room."

"I hadn't thought about that," Emma said, feeling deflated. The talent show wouldn't work if there wasn't a big enough venue.

"We could hold it at the playhouse," Betty said, brightening. "It's usually only used for the summer festival, but there's a stage and a piano and plenty of seats."

"It sounds perfect." Emma beamed. "Lola and I will make the

posters, and you can call the shopkeepers and arrange the play-house."

"I'll get my pens." Lola jumped off her chair. "And when my dad comes back, he can help us."

"Your dad?" Emma gulped. For a moment she had forgotten about Fletcher and Megan. How was she going to avoid Fletcher if they were working together on the talent show?

"I'm only nine years old," Lola said, and there was something mischievous in her eyes. "I can't do everything myself."

"Those are good drawings." Emma picked up a sheet of poster board.

Emma and Lola were sitting on the floor in Lola's room. There was a box of colored markers and a selection of posters with Lola's pictures. One had a snowman standing in front of The Smuggler's Inn with Emma's caption: "Help Frosty keep his home."

"My dad says I get my drawing talent from my mom—she's a costume designer." Lola sat back on her heels. "Well, she was one in London. Then she married Chuck and moved to Connecticut. Now she drives me to school like the other mothers, and spends the day baking and rearranging the furniture."

"I'm sure she does more than that," Emma suggested.

"One time I came home and the sofa from the living room was in the family room. She says it's because she's never had a big house. And she doesn't want a job. When she was a costume designer, I hardly ever had playdates." Lola paused. "I didn't mind. I loved going to the theater on school nights. I hung out backstage and someone always offered to help with my homework."

"Your parents were lucky they could take you to work," Emma agreed. "My best friend Bronwyn is a dermatologist, and her girls have a nanny. Bronwyn doesn't get home until dinnertime, and she misses them so much."

Lola jumped up and walked to the bedside table. She opened a drawer and took out a photo.

"This is my mom and dad and me on the set of *Oliver Twist*." Lola handed it to Emma. "Dad was the director and Mom designed the costumes and I played an orphan."

In the photo Lola was wearing a pinafore and her cheeks were smudged with makeup. Fletcher's head was close to hers, and on the other side was a woman with Lola's flaming hair. Her eyes were green and she was wearing a satin blouse and dangling earrings.

"What a lovely photo," Emma commented.

"Since her parents' divorce, Cammi has two of everything. She has two American Girl dolls and two of the same pair of UGGs. She even has two guinea pigs; Harry Potter lives at her mom's, and Hermione stays at her dad's. I think that's the worst part. My bedroom used to be my favorite place because it had everything: my doll collection and my songbooks and my clothes. Now everything is spread out between two houses, and neither of them feel like home."

"You haven't been in America long," Emma said, and touched her arm. "Soon both places will be familiar."

"There's no place like Broadway if you want to be an actress, so I should love New York." Lola's mouth wobbled. "But I miss London. My dad and my mom and I were a team, and it will never be the same."

Emma stood at her window and looked out on the snow-covered landscape. They had finished the posters and Emma had returned to her room. It was early afternoon and the scene outside was like a postcard. Children dragged sleds down the sidewalk, and the white fields were dotted with wooden barns and clapboard houses.

She remembered the photo that Lola had showed her, and felt a sense of longing. What would it be like to be part of a family? To know that someone cared about you more than anything in the world. And to love someone so much that you would do anything to make him happy.

Emma leaned against the windowsill and remembered when she and Fletcher had been so in love. They'd been a team; there was nothing they wouldn't do for each other.

April, 2008
Waterville, Maine

Emma opened the window of her dorm room and inhaled the scent of fresh-cut grass. It was the first day of classes after spring break, and the whole campus was alive with color. The gardens had bloomed while she was away, and the trees were finally green.

After almost four years at Colby, Emma knew that there could be another snowstorm; the real warm weather—when you could bicycle around campus without bringing a sweater—was weeks away. But it was lovely to allow the breeze into her room and think about the outing she and Fletcher had planned for tomorrow: seeing a play at the Waterville Opera House, and then having a picnic in the park. They hadn't seen each other in a week, and she couldn't wait to be together.

There was a meowing sound, and Emma glanced at the box on the floor. She had gotten herself into a bind, and if she didn't fix it, there might not be an outing tomorrow. Worse, she might get in trouble with her resident assistant and get kicked out of her dorm.

When she arrived at her dorm this morning, a kitten had been crouched next to the entrance. She waited for someone to claim it, but no one came. Finally she found a box in the storeroom and took the kitten up to her room.

There was a knock at the door, and she stuffed the box in the closet.

"Oh, it's you," she said when Fletcher appeared in the doorway.

"That's not a very effusive greeting when we've been apart for a week." Fletcher entered the room. "I missed you. You were flying around the country, while I was stuck serving ice cream cones to tourists in Kennebunkport who wondered why there were snow showers during their spring vacation."

"I was hardly jetting around; I flew to Wisconsin to see my family." She perched on the bed. "And there couldn't have been snow showers." She waved at the trees outside the window. "The whole campus is in bloom."

"The snow melted after the first day. Spring is wonderful." He sat beside her. "It makes it almost real: graduation and summer and starting our lives."

The months since Fletcher told her he loved her at Christmas were the best she'd ever had. They did everything together: ate their meals in the dining commons and studied at the library and took long walks around the quad. Emma brought her textbooks to rehearsals, and Fletcher said the only thing that kept him from collapsing after ten hours onstage with no break for lunch was knowing that Emma was in the back of the theater.

Neither of them talked about what would happen after graduation. Their relationship was like the kites students flew on the Colby Green: bright and beautiful, but if you tugged at the string too hard they could come crashing back to earth.

There was a scratching sound in the closet, and Fletcher frowned.

"What's that noise? Don't tell me you have another guy in here!" he said. "Is that why I got the cold welcome?"

"It's a male, but not the kind you're thinking," Emma laughed and opened the closet. The kitten brushed against her ankles and she picked him up. "I found him outside. I waited for an hour but no one came."

"He's a beauty." Fletcher stroked his fur. "Pets are forbidden. The guy on the next floor hid a ferret in his room. The ferret chewed his roommate's speaker wire and he almost got kicked out of school."

"I'll take him to the shelter in Waterville tomorrow," Emma agreed. "But I have a study session for an Econ exam in the library in an hour. If I leave him in my room, someone might hear him."

"I'll take him," Fletcher offered.

"You have a performance, and cats aren't allowed in the theater," Emma reminded him.

"I'll think of something." Fletcher picked up the box. "Othello and I will be fine."

"Othello?" Emma repeated.

"If I call his name, people will think I'm talking about the play." Fletcher kissed her. "Don't worry, we'll see you tonight."

Emma stood in front of the library and inhaled the night air. It was at moments like this, when the sky was black velvet and every star was a diamond, that she wanted to stay in college forever.

What would happen after May? Even if they both ended up in New York, it might not work out. Fletcher would be swept up in the theater world, while Emma was grinding away at an office job. They would be too broke to go out on proper dates, and with different schedules, they might lose touch altogether.

She tried to imagine life without Fletcher, and there was a hard feeling, like Othello's bony frame pressing against her chest. It didn't matter that they were young and inexperienced; they were in love, and she didn't want it to end.

"There you are." Fletcher appeared in the dark. A scarf was wrapped around his neck and he was carrying a cardboard box.

"Is Othello all right?" She scooped up the cat.

"He's a trouper." Fletcher grinned. "He never made a sound."

"What did you do with him during the performance?" Emma stroked his fur.

"One of the actors carried him in a wicker basket during the market scene."

"Othello was onstage?" Emma gasped. "What if he meowed or tried to jump out?"

"The basket was supposed to hold a loaf of bread, but a cat was more authentic." Fletcher grinned. "There were lots of stray cats at the markets in the sixteenth century. I might use Othello again."

Emma reached up and kissed Fletcher. "Thank you; I was so worried."

"One of the stagehands lives off-campus and offered to keep

him," Fletcher said. "I wanted to check with you first—you're his adoptive parent."

"That's a wonderful idea." Emma beamed. "You have to thank him for me."

"The theater is a family; everyone helps each other," Fletcher said, and was suddenly serious. "I want you to be part of that family, too."

"What do you mean?" Emma wondered.

"We don't talk about graduation. It's like discussing the final episode of a favorite show that's going to be canceled." He touched her cheek. "I don't know where we'll be or what we're going to do, but I love you and I want to stay together."

"I want that too," she whispered.

Fletcher pulled her close, and there was a meowing sound.

"I think we're squishing Othello," Emma laughed, handing him the cat.

"At least we know he's a male." Fletcher grinned. "He can't stand me kissing you."

Four Days Before New Year's Eve
Snowberry, Vermont

Emma looked out her guestroom window at the church steeples wrapped in snow and took a deep breath. They had been so in love; she'd thought nothing could tear them apart.

That had been eleven years ago, so there was no point in thinking about it now. Fletcher had a child, and he was engaged. He probably didn't even remember the promises they'd made to each other. Emma was just an old college girlfriend.

She grabbed her coat and opened the door. She and Lola were going to blanket every store in Snowberry with flyers about the talent show. Maybe Bronwyn had been wrong. Perhaps Emma was in Vermont to do a good deed for someone at Christmas. If she could help Betty save The Smuggler's Inn, she could believe that the pain of seeing Fletcher again was worth it.

Ten

FLETCHER FELT LIKE A NEW man. Breakfast at the Crêpe Café with Lola this morning had been so much fun. Fletcher had eaten a savory crêpe with cheddar cheese and ham and been reminded of the meals he and Lola had shared at Tutton's in Covent Garden before a performance at the Old Vic.

People thought he was crazy to take a little girl to an elegant restaurant when they could have eaten fish and chips backstage. But Fletcher loved watching the pre-theater crowd sipping Pimm's, and Lola couldn't take her eyes off the women in their cocktail dresses and fur stoles. Lola would eat Cumberland sausage with mushy peas, and Fletcher would order steak and kidney pie, which he swore brought him good luck; then they'd share a dessert from the glass case, like sticky toffee pudding or white-and-black chocolate brownie with Dorset clotted cream.

Cassandra would already be at the theater putting the finishing touches on costumes, and he cherished those meals with Lola alone. Lola loved hearing stories about being a director: the actress who wouldn't go onstage unless her poodle was waiting in her dressing room, the actor who demanded Fletcher fix him bourbon with honey before every performance. And Fletcher loved listening to Lola's dreams of playing Maria in *The Sound of Music* or Mary in *Mary Poppins*.

This morning after breakfast, Fletcher took Lola ice skating, and they practically had the rink to themselves. Lola slipped her small hand into his and they glided around the ice to "Jingle Bells" and "Silent Night."

Then they'd returned to The Smuggler's Inn, and Fletcher and Megan went to the Antique Mall. It reminded Fletcher of the markets at Covent Garden, where you could find everything from heirloom jewelry to jars of preserves. Each dealer had a selection of antiques: potbelly stoves and pewter tea sets and kerosene lanterns. Megan fell in love with a pair of silver candlesticks, and Fletcher found a pair of bookends and bought Lola an antique doll. A vendor tried to sell them an old-fashioned rocking horse, and Fletcher felt a surge of excitement. Perhaps one day he and Megan would have a baby, and they could return to Vermont and buy a nineteenth-century jelly cupboard to hold the baby's blankets and bibs.

Now Megan was in the village getting her hair done. Fletcher bounded up the stairs of The Smuggler's Inn to Lola's room.

"Here you are." Fletcher opened Lola's door. "I brought you a present."

Lola unwrapped the tissue paper and discovered a doll wearing lace pantaloons.

"The vendor swore it's from the nineteenth century, but the shoes are plastic," he said, pointing to the doll's red slippers. "But her hair reminded me of yours, and I thought you'd like it."

"It's lovely, thank you." Lola placed it on the desk.

"What are you doing?" Fletcher surveyed the posters spread out on the floor.

"I'm making posters for a fundraiser," Lola said. "We're going to hold a talent show on New Year's Eve."

"New Year's Eve?" Fletcher repeated. "I don't know if we'll still be here."

"We have to stay." Lola's eyes widened. "Betty is in danger of losing The Smuggler's Inn, so we're going to charge a fifty-dollar entrance fee. The talent show is going to be held in the playhouse, and we're going to put posters up all around Snowberry."

"There's an important theater party in New York, and Megan doesn't want to miss it."

"But The Smuggler's Inn is Betty's home. If she loses it, she won't have anywhere to go," Lola said. "You're the one who said the best part of being in the theater is helping others. Is it more important that Megan shows off at a fancy party, or that we help Betty keep her home?"

"Megan isn't showing off," Fletcher said loyally. "She has my best interests at heart. She's trying to create interest in the new play."

"You've directed more plays than she's seen in her whole life, and you never go to theater parties. They are a waste of time, and you'd rather stay home and read scripts."

Once Fletcher became an established director, he'd told Graham he didn't want to attend any more parties. The smoked salmon gave him stomach acid, the champagne gave him a headache, and he'd rather stay home with Cassandra and Lola.

"Megan says networking is important, and she's right," Fletcher offered. "No one knows me in New York."

"There will be other parties. Please, can we stay?" Lola begged. "Betty is counting on us and I don't want to let her down."

"Us?" Fletcher repeated.

"I sort of told her that you would put up posters and help with the sets," Lola admitted. "Betty's husband died and her children live far away. The Smuggler's Inn is all she has."

"I'm glad I was consulted," Fletcher chuckled, admiring Lola's tenacity.

"I'm asking now," Lola said hopefully. "All you have to do is say yes."

"Our reservation at The Smuggler's Inn is through New Year's," Fletcher wavered. "And we've been invited to another theater party at the end of January. It's at the home of some big critic, and Dustin Hoffman is going to be there."

"I don't know who that is, but I'm sure Megan will find someone there to show off to." Lola jumped up. "You carry the posters and I'll tell Emma."

"Emma?" Fletcher stopped.

"Emma helped make the posters." Lola gestured to the poster board. "We're going to hang them around town together."

"Emma helped you with this?" Fletcher glanced at a drawing of a sled stacked with wrapped boxes. The caption read: THE BEST CHRISTMAS PRESENT IS BEING WITH FRIENDS. CELEBRATE NEW YEAR'S EVE AT SNOWBERRY'S FIRST ANNUAL NEW YEAR'S EVE TALENT SHOW.

"First annual talent show?" Fletcher raised his eyebrow.

"Emma said it's an old advertising trick. You make people think they're missing out on a tradition." Lola looked at Fletcher. "She's really good at this stuff. You should hire her to write your playbills."

"We have that covered," Fletcher said uncomfortably.

"Well, let's go." Lola grabbed her coat. "I have to tell Betty first, and Emma is waiting in the mudroom."

Emma was zipping up her boots when Fletcher reached the mudroom. Seeing her perched on the bench with her mouth set in a firm line reminded him of the long winters at Colby: Emma hurrying to put on her boots and not be late for class, Fletcher offering to carry her backpack, and Emma smiling and saying she'd be fine.

"Oh, hello." Emma looked up. "I never seem to find a pair of boots with a working zipper. I should give up and move to a warmer climate."

"It's remarkable to see you," Fletcher said without thinking. It had been one thing to discover Emma playing the piano in the dining room of The Smuggler's Inn. Even dinner at the Goose Duck Inn was manageable, because they'd been surrounded by Megan and Lola. But now, finding Emma in the mudroom while Lola was in the kitchen with Betty, there was nothing to separate them from the past.

"Remarkable?" Emma repeated, curious.

"It's such a crazy coincidence," Fletcher said quickly. "I've only been in New York since last spring. What are the chances of us staying at the same inn in Vermont at Christmas?"

"I know what you mean," Emma replied. "I was going to say the same thing."

"Well, it's very . . ." Fletcher stopped as Lola hurtled into the mudroom.

"I'm sorry I took so long." Lola turned from Fletcher to Emma. "I know you're old friends, but you're not going to talk about how when you were in college no one looked at their phones, or how much better life was before Facebook." She rolled her eyes. "I promised Betty we'd get the posters up before dinnertime."

"We wouldn't dream of it." Fletcher took Lola's hand and

opened the door for Emma. "It seems we're on a mission. We'd better get started."

The Christmas tree in the village square was lit with gold and silver lights, and the lampposts were adorned with green bows. Children were making snowballs, and there was the sound of laughter and the scent of pine needles and cinnamon rolls.

Lola darted into a store and Fletcher found himself standing next to Emma. Fletcher was used to awkward situations: coaxing an actress to go onstage after she read a devastating review in the London *Times,* or having to tell a producer the last play had lost money while asking him to back the next venture. For the first time since he'd spilled champagne on Cassandra at the theater party years ago, Fletcher didn't know what to say.

"Your daughter is very special." Emma watched through the window as Lola talked animatedly to the shopkeeper. The man hesitated and then took the poster and placed it in front of the cash register.

"I've learned often the best thing to do is to stay out of Lola's way," Fletcher said, chuckling. "She once convinced her teacher to take the whole class to a matinee showing of *Paddington.* Lola claimed it would be educational to see the most loved figure in children's literature on the screen. She even got the manager to give each child a box of mints if their parents promised to write a review."

"I can't believe she's only nine," Emma said. "She's more mature than I was in high school. And she has a wonderful sense of style."

"She gets that from her mother. Cassandra could turn a Hanes

T-shirt into something to wear to a cocktail party," Fletcher agreed. "I do worry about Lola. There's a whole world outside the theater. And it's a hard life; you can be talented and still never get a break."

"You've done well," Emma said. "Lola told me about the time that Prince William and the Duchess of Cambridge came to a performance."

"It was last Christmas for *The Nutcracker*," Fletcher recalled. "Lola wrote a letter to Santa Claus, saying the only thing she wanted for Christmas was to see the Duchess of Cambridge in person. Graham gave the letter to the Duchess before the first act. At intermission, the Duchess stopped by Graham's private box to say hello. Lola almost fainted."

"Who's Graham?" Emma asked.

"My producer," Fletcher said and smiled. "Also my best friend, and the only guy who tells me when I'm about to ruin my life. I'm lucky to have him."

"I have a best friend like that. Bronwyn is a dermatologist with a stockbroker husband and two gorgeous little girls. She's the kind of friend who will say that my shirt is unbuttoned or I have something between my teeth when my date is waiting impatiently downstairs." Emma blushed.

There was a strained silence. What was he doing chatting with Emma when Megan wasn't even there? He should make an excuse; he needed to send an urgent email and go back to the inn. He opened his mouth to say something, but Lola ran out of the General Store.

"The owner promised to put posters in every section of the store," Lola announced. "The store is really cool. There's a shelf of comic books and a selection of Christmas cookies. He even sells doors—not just doorknobs, the whole door."

"Maybe I should go back to the inn and let you two do this by yourselves," Fletcher said brusquely. "Megan is getting her hair done, and I should be there when she returns."

"You can't stop now." Lola tugged at his arm. "And Megan will be ages. Mom says she'd never go blond because you have to spend all day at the beauty salon. It's too time-consuming."

"You two can hang the posters," Emma suggested. "I really should buy presents for my goddaughters."

"I didn't mean . . ." Fletcher began, and Lola cut in.

"We all have to work together. I approach the shopkeepers and Dad carries the posters and Emma is in charge of making sure we don't run out of tape."

Fletcher looked at Lola and his shoulders relaxed. He wasn't doing anything wrong; he was helping Betty save the inn.

"I suppose we have our marching orders," he said to Emma, and turned to Lola. "What unsuspecting shopkeeper do we ask next?"

They left posters at the ski shop and the travel bookstore, which oddly didn't sell travel books, only guides to Vermont. Everyone knew Betty and wanted to help. The woman who ran the haberdashery store offered to whip up costumes, and the girl at the party store said they should fill the playhouse with balloons for New Year's Eve. The owner of Snowberry Sweet Shop gave them samples of "Vermonsters"—dark chocolate with caramel and nuts— and suggested wrapping them in red ribbon and giving them to all the contestants.

"Look, it's the playhouse." Lola pointed to a brick building with white columns. The roof was strung with Christmas lights and there was a sign with black lettering.

"You must be Lola," a man in his early sixties said, greeting them. "Betty called and said I should be expecting you. I'm Stephen Green."

"This is my father." Lola pointed to Fletcher. "His name is Fletcher Conway and he's a big Broadway director. And this is Emma—she helped with the posters."

"With that kind of introduction, you don't need a publicist." Stephen grinned, shaking hands with Fletcher and Emma. "Please come inside. I turned the heat on and rustled up some hot cocoa and cookies."

The playhouse lobby was simple: wood floors, a concession stand, and a few benches with striped cushions. But then Stephen led them into the theater, and Fletcher was mesmerized. There was thick red carpet and velvet seats and a stage outfitted with a gold curtain. Spotlights hung from the ceiling, and the walls were papered in silver wallpaper.

"This is fantastic," Fletcher said, admiring the art deco lighting fixtures.

"I'm glad you like it." Stephen beamed. He was tall, dressed in a flannel shirt and corduroys. "When I bought this place, the wood floor was so rotted, the actors could have fallen through it. And the insulation was terrible; I couldn't pay workers enough in winter to make the renovations.

"But I could have sunk my savings into the stock market and spent my retirement fretting whenever the Dow went down. Or I could put the money into something I love and be happy every day." He looked at Fletcher. "It's an honor to meet you. I saw your production of *King Lear* in London."

"Jude Law was an amazing King Lear," Fletcher agreed. "But how did you recognize me? No one notices the director."

"I'm a bit of a Shakespeare groupie," Stephen admitted. "I've seen *Hamlet* performed in Sydney, and a production of *Romeo and Juliet* in Thailand." He chuckled. "I didn't understand a word, but the costumes were breathtaking."

"When I was seven I was a fairy in *A Midsummer Night's Dream*," Lola piped up. "I got to wear a fairy costume with silver wings and sparkly tights."

"Then you have to come back to Snowberry next summer. I'm planning on doing *A Midsummer Night's Dream*." He turned to Fletcher. "In fact, you could be the guest director. With Fletcher Conway in charge, ticket sales would go through the roof."

"That's very flattering," Fletcher said modestly. "But I'm new to Broadway; no one knows who I am."

"You're not giving yourself enough credit. And you might enjoy it," Stephen insisted. "Actors come from Boston and New York, and the audience is very enthusiastic. Your daughter would love Snowberry in the summer: there's fishing, and a stable where you can ride horses."

"Please, can we?" Lola jumped up and down. "Betty said that on the fourth of July there's a parade. Everyone gets their face painted and eats red-white-and-blue popsicles."

"It's a wonderful invitation, but I'm getting married this summer," Fletcher explained.

Stephen turned to Emma and smiled. "My apologies; I should have consulted the bride. You could get married in Snowberry. There's a lovely church, and my friend Ernie is the minister."

"Emma isn't the bride, she's a friend," Lola announced before Emma could answer. "The bride's name is Megan. She wants to have the wedding at the Plaza Hotel in New York."

"Why don't we talk about summer later?" Fletcher interjected. "We have a talent show to plan, and apparently Lola has volunteered me to help with the sets."

"I apologize if Lola embarrassed you," Fletcher said to Emma after they left the playhouse. Lola had run ahead to the Main Street Confectionary, and Fletcher and Emma strolled along the sidewalk.

"You mean with Stephen trying to marry us off?" Emma laughed.

"Why aren't you married?" Fletcher asked, and immediately regretted it. "I'm sorry, I shouldn't have asked that. It's none of my business."

"My friend Bronwyn asks the same thing every year." Emma stopped in front of the shop window. "I have a habit of breaking up with guys just when they're about to propose. I'm supposed to be on a beach in Maui with my boyfriend, but I canceled and he went by himself."

"You have a boyfriend in Hawaii?" Fletcher wondered.

"An ex-boyfriend," Emma corrected. "My relationships run like clockwork: the first eleven months are perfect, and then in the twelfth month I suddenly can't imagine spending our lives together. I've spent the last eleven Christmases alone."

"So that's why you're in Snowberry at Christmas," Fletcher mused.

"Bronwyn thought it would be good for me to get out of New York." Emma nodded. "I resisted at first, but I'm glad I came."

"You are?" Fletcher asked.

"Betty is wonderful and Snowberry is charming and I met Lola." She nodded.

"Lola," Fletcher repeated, and wondered why he felt deflated.

"Dad!" Lola dashed out of the confectioner's holding a gold box. "Look what the owner gave me: handmade chocolate fudge dipped in maple syrup."

"But the Sweet Shop already donated Vermonsters—what will we do with more chocolate?" Fletcher asked.

"These aren't for the talent show." Lola popped one in her mouth and smiled her impish smile. "She gave them to me because I'm hungry."

Fletcher opened the door of his room and took off his jacket. Emma and Lola were in the kitchen telling Betty the good news, but Fletcher had wanted to go upstairs before Megan returned from the hair salon.

It had been an enjoyable afternoon; he hadn't seen Lola so animated since they'd arrived in Snowberry. And Emma was such a good sport, standing on the pavement in the frigid air while Lola charmed the shopkeepers.

He tried to analyze how it felt to spend time with Emma. At first it had been uncomfortable, but Emma was easy to talk to. And it had been perfectly innocent. He was madly in love with Megan, and even Megan thought it was good for Lola to have a friend.

The door opened and Megan entered the guestroom. Her blond hair fell down her back, and she was wearing a scoop-neck dress and knee-high boots.

"You're back." He kissed her. "You look gorgeous—and is that a new dress?"

"Thank you. I was worried about trusting my hair color to a salon in Vermont." Megan checked her reflection in the mirror.

"But there won't be time to get it done in New York before the party. I saw the dress in a boutique window; I hoped you'd like it."

"I love the hair and the dress," Fletcher agreed. "But I'm afraid we're not going to Jordan's New Year's Eve party."

"What do you mean, we're not going?" Megan asked. "I already RSVP'd."

"You'll have to RSVP again," Fletcher said. "Betty is in financial trouble, and Lola suggested we have a talent show on New Year's Eve to raise money. We spent the afternoon putting posters up around Snowberry."

"Lola decided to have a talent show," Megan repeated incredulously.

"Ever since Lola was a child, I taught her that helping each other is one of the most important aspects about being part of the theater."

"You do realize Lola is still a child. I love you, and I know it's difficult building our relationship and keeping Lola happy at the same time," Megan pleaded. "But don't you see what's happening? A nine-year-old is dictating our New Year's Eve plans."

"This has nothing to do with what Lola wants. It was my decision. I made a promise to Lola and Betty," Fletcher returned. "And what would we do with Lola if we went back to New York? It's too late to get a babysitter, and we couldn't leave her alone."

"I hadn't thought about that. I suppose you're right," Megan agreed. "I love you, and I'm only thinking about your career. Meeting the right people is important."

Fletcher was suddenly flustered. He had promised he would help with the talent show; he couldn't back out now. "I love you too, and I know you want what's best for us. We got an invitation to another party in January; the guest list includes Dustin Hoffman."

"Then we'll attend that instead," Megan said brightly. "Why don't we go somewhere special for dinner tonight? There's a dinner theater just outside town. They're performing *A Christmas Carol,* and the milk-fed lamb is supposed to be superb."

"I don't feel comfortable leaving Lola," Fletcher said, his resolve wavering.

"Lola should come with us, of course. She'd love the play. I'll see if they have a table for three." Megan unzipped her dress. "Let's take a Jacuzzi until dinnertime. I'll change out of this dress and we can go downstairs."

Fletcher grabbed a robe from the closet. He had been worrying about Megan's reaction for nothing. She understood how important Lola was to him.

A light snow was falling, and it looked so romantic. He was going to sit in a hot tub with his fiancée, and then he and Megan and Lola were going to have a festive dinner. He was doing exactly what Graham suggested, and he wasn't going to let anything get in the way of being happy.

Eleven

Four Days Before New Year's Eve
Snowberry, Vermont

EMMA SIPPED A CUP OF tea with honey and scrolled through her emails. It was early evening, and she had just returned from handing out flyers with Fletcher and Lola. So many thoughts ran through her head, it was like riding the carousel in Central Park.

At first when Fletcher had appeared in the mudroom, she'd wanted to run away. How could she act naturally with the only guy she'd ever loved? Could they even have a conversation without rehashing everything that had happened?

Then Lola had barreled into the mudroom, and it was too late to make up an excuse. Lola kept up a bright level of chatter, and Fletcher was so easy to talk to. By the time they reached Main Street, Emma's worries had receded and she was relaxed.

Now that she was alone in her guestroom, the mixed-up feelings returned. What was she doing, getting involved in Fletcher and Lola's lives? Lola had a mother, and Fletcher was getting married. There was no room for Emma, and she might get hurt.

The FaceTime icon on her computer blinked, and she pressed ACCEPT.

Bronwyn appeared on the screen wearing a yellow caftan, her face smothered in some kind of lotion.

"Why are you wearing a caftan? You aren't going to Palm Beach until tomorrow," Emma reminded her. "And what's on your face? You look like the Bride of Frankenstein."

"The girls asked me to model my new bathing suit, and I panicked," Bronwyn said. "This body hasn't seen a bikini in two years, and back then I had the excuse that it was still baby weight. I was going to cancel the vacation, but Liv and Sarah have been running around in matching pink bikinis. So I ordered this caftan and it just got delivered." Bronwyn peered into the camera. "As long as I never leave the lounge chair, no one can tell that my boobs reach my navel."

"Those anorexic Palm Beach socialites would kill for your boobs," Emma scoffed. "What's on your face?"

"It's a rejuvenating lotion from Paris. French women understand that if you have perfect skin, men never look below the neck. By the time Carlton arrives, I'm going to have cheeks as smooth as a newborn baby." Bronwyn paused. "You don't look as pale as you did this morning. Did you buy a spray tan? It might look good now, but when you go to bed your pillow will turn orange and tomorrow you'll have stripes like a tiger."

"It must be the hot tea." Emma held up her cup. "Tea always makes me flushed."

"You're not flushed, you're glowing," Bronwyn said suspiciously. "You spent the afternoon with Fletcher! You both realized how much you missed each other, and you can't wait to pick up where you left off."

"You forgot a couple of key factors: Fletcher has a daughter. And he's engaged to an actress who spent all afternoon at the hair salon just to make sure she's the most beautiful woman in Vermont," Emma said with a sigh.

"You *are* still in love with him," Bronwyn insisted. "I can tell by the dreamy look in your eyes, like I get when I'm imagining dinner at The Breakers Restaurant with Carlton. The girls will be in the hotel room with a babysitter, and the only thing that could distract us from eating seared halibut in melted butter will be the sound of the surf crashing against the sand." She shivered. "I get goose bumps thinking about it."

"Fletcher and Lola and I spent the afternoon handing out posters around Snowberry," Emma admitted. "But it was completely platonic. Fletcher and Megan are getting married at the Plaza in July."

"It's only December," Bronwyn said, waving her hand. "And you and Fletcher have a history. Megan is like a cup holder that kept Fletcher warm until you arrived."

"You haven't seen her—any man would fall in love with her," Emma said dismally. "I do feel bad for Lola. She had her father to herself, and now she has to share him with a live Barbie doll who graduated summa cum laude from Yale."

"Megan is no competition. Fletcher needs a stepmother for Lola, and children love you." Bronwyn inspected her fingernails. "Whenever you leave, Sarah and Liv ask why I don't read them stories for hours. In my next life, I want to be a godmother, and you can do the hard work: combing out Liv's hair after the bath, and cutting out pictures from magazines for Sarah's kindergarten collages."

"Lola is special," Emma said slowly. "But she has a mother, and Fletcher is engaged. I shouldn't get involved; I'm setting myself up for disaster."

"Let me tell you a story. I have a client who comes to the clinic for Botox in her neck," Bronwyn began. "In the sixties she ran away to San Francisco. She was seventeen, and fell in love with a hippie with long hair and a guitar. They were going to elope, but her father found out and flew her back to New Jersey. Fast-forward fifty years, and the client is divorced and living in Manhattan. She takes the love of her life, a Yorkie named Pickles, to the doggie beauty parlor every Saturday. Pickles becomes friends with a Cockapoo whose owner is the guy she fell in love with in San Francisco. His hair was short and he didn't have a guitar, but she recognized him right away. They moved in together, and now they get a two-dog family discount at the doggie beauty parlor. What are the odds that they'd both be living in Manhattan and taking their dogs to the same beauty salon fifty years later? You can't argue with fate; it works every time."

"That's a lovely story, but I don't have a dog and Fletcher isn't single," Emma reminded her.

"He has Lola, and Lola likes you more than Megan," Bronwyn replied. "Keep doing what you're doing and let synchronicity do the rest. Who knows, this time next year you might be honeymooning at The Breakers in Palm Beach."

There was a knock at the door, and Emma signed off. She opened the door and Lola stood in the hallway, wearing a striped sweater over a long skirt and pink clogs.

"Lola, come in." Emma ushered her inside. "You look lovely. Are you going downstairs to dinner? Betty is making shepherd's pie with mashed sweet corn from her garden."

"Dad and Megan and I were going to a dinner theater." Lola perched on the bed. "They're doing *A Christmas Carol,* and Santa Claus delivers presents to the tables."

"That sounds like fun," Emma said. "When are you leaving?"

"Dad and Megan already left." Lola shrugged. "I decided to stay here."

"Why would you miss it?" Emma asked. "*A Christmas Carol* is one of my favorite Christmas stories."

"My dad was really upset that I wouldn't go. Megan reserved a table for three right next to the stage," Lola replied. "I told him I had the worst stomachache and finally he let me stay here. He was going to cancel altogether, but Megan really wanted to see it."

"But why wouldn't you want to go? Especially if Megan went to all that trouble."

"It wasn't about Megan. She was being really nice. She said she wished her hair was thicker like mine. Whenever she tries to curl it, it turns into frizz." Lola hesitated. "But I found out something and I was afraid I'd start crying at dinner."

"I told you not to eavesdrop," Emma warned. "You'll hear something you shouldn't know."

"It wasn't my fault, I was Skyping my mother," Lola insisted. "She was standing in the kitchen, showing me the blender she got for Christmas. We've never had a blender before. There isn't time to mash up vegetables when you have to be at the theater. I heard Chuck's voice. He asked about her doctor's appointment."

"Doctor?" Emma repeated, wondering if Cassandra had a disease.

"Mom looked nervous and said it was fine." Lola's mouth curled down at the corners. "Then Chuck asked when they'd find out the sex, and whether it would be corny to buy blue or pink cigars for the guys at the office."

"Oh, I see," Emma breathed.

"My mom is going to have a baby, and no one told me!" Lola's eyes filled with tears.

"Maybe she just found out," Emma assured her. "You should be excited. There's nothing more fun than having a little brother or sister."

"At first I thought I wouldn't mind," Lola said, blinking. "I could dig out my old Beatrix Potter books and give the baby my Paddington Bear. I still have him, even though the toggles on his jacket are gone and he's missing an ear. But don't you see? Everyone has someone new, and no one needs me anymore."

"Of course your mother needs you. You're her daughter," Emma replied.

"Cammi warned me this would happen. The new baby will get all the attention, because it belongs to both of them," Lola said. "Cammi goes to her father's for a few days, and her mother doesn't even call because she's busy buying up the baby department at Macy's. When Cammi is home, all her mom and her new husband talk about is what color to paint the nursery."

"I didn't know Cammi's family had a baby."

"Her mom is pregnant." Lola wiped her eyes. "Cammi's afraid that her mom and her new husband will forget about her when the baby is born."

"You're worrying too much," Emma said to comfort her. "My brother is five years younger, and we were close as children."

"That's different—you shared the same parents. But my mom and Chuck will always love the new baby more than me." The tears started again. "I know, because my father loves me more than anything in the world."

"Yes, he does," Emma said soothingly. "And that's not going to change."

"But it will!" Lola hiccupped. "Megan is in her twenties; at some point she'll want a baby. I'll probably be a teenager, so she'll make me babysit while she goes to the gym." The tears came faster. "I won't have time to do theater, and my dreams of being a star by eighteen will drown in a plastic baby bath."

Lola collapsed on the bed and Emma stroked her hair. How could Lola be so mature and childlike at the same time?

"Even if Megan has a baby, nothing will change the way Fletcher feels about you. And your mother and Chuck have room in their hearts to love two children." Emma had an idea. "Why don't we go to the toy store and you can pick out a gift for the baby? Afterward, we'll get dinner in the village and watch the Christmas concert."

"Go to a toy store now?" Lola asked, drying her eyes.

"I have to get gifts for my goddaughters, and I haven't made it to the Vermont Teddy Bear factory," Emma said, nodding. "And I'm starving. This afternoon we passed a restaurant that serves fried fish fillets and apple pie with vanilla ice cream for dessert."

"That sounds even better than Betty's shepherd's pie." Lola rubbed her stomach. "We better hurry, I don't want them to run out of ice cream. Apple pie without ice cream is boring."

It felt so festive walking through the village with Lola. They passed the Snowberry Lodge, which sat on a hill and was much grander than The Smuggler's Inn. It had white columns and a plaque saying that the spot was the site of a battle in the Revolutionary War of 1776.

They stopped at the Old Cheese Shoppe and sampled Vermont cheddar that smelled so sharp, Lola held her nose and ate the wedge of cheese at the same time. There was a store called The Mountain Goat that sold snowshoes, and a dress shop named Miss Frances's Frocks that had lace dresses with real petticoats. Emma and Lola thought they were costumes until Miss Frances appeared in one of her own creations.

The Snowberry Toy Shop had a Christmas tree that could have used a good dusting and two floors of dolls and trains. There was a section for blocks and a back room crammed with books.

"What should I get Liv and Sarah?" Emma asked.

"It's after Christmas—didn't you already give them presents?" Lola inquired, picking up a wooden duck.

"I wasn't supposed to be in New York at Christmas," Emma replied. "I haven't bought them anything yet."

"Where were you supposed to be?" Lola wondered.

"In Hawaii with my boyfriend," Emma said. "But it wasn't working out, so I broke up with him."

"You gave up surfing for this?" Lola gestured to a couple of faded beanbags and a plate of sliced fruitcake.

"I was afraid he was going to propose, and it didn't seem right to go on vacation together," Emma explained.

"You're braver than I imagined." Lola scrunched her nose. "I thought you weren't married because you're kind of old, but you actually turned someone down."

"My friend Bronwyn doesn't think I'm brave," Emma sighed. "She thinks there's some kind of curse."

"Bronwyn is wrong," Lola said knowledgeably. "Waiting for true love is the bravest thing in the world. I'm not going to get married until I meet the man of my dreams. I don't want to mess it up."

"How will you know it's him?" Emma asked curiously.

"He'll kiss me and I'll wake up from a deep sleep like in *Sleeping Beauty*," Lola said, her eyes sparkling. "And once it happens, nothing will ever be the same again."

Emma bought two handmade cloth dolls with blond pigtails wrapped around their heads. Lola decided on a book of fairy tales and a squeaky pig for the bath.

Afterward they strolled down Main Street to a brick building with white shutters. Inside was a cozy dining room with a roaring fire and old photos on the walls. Lola ate fried fish and gravy-covered fries, and Emma ordered short ribs with a side of fingerling potatoes.

"Perhaps you should wait and let your mother tell Fletcher about the baby," Emma suggested after the waiter replaced their plates with apple pie for Lola and a slice of peanut-butter cheesecake for Emma.

"You mean he won't be happy about it?" Lola ate a bite of vanilla ice cream.

"It might be a bit of a shock," Emma said diplomatically. "It's better that Fletcher hear it from your mother."

"You and Dad were really good friends in college, weren't you?" Lola said.

"What makes you say that?" Emma responded.

"You're like me and Cammi. You can talk to each other forever and never run out of things to say. And Dad looks comfortable around you," Lola continued. "Sometimes when he's with Megan he gets this anxious look, like he's afraid of saying the wrong thing."

"Romantic relationships are more complicated than friendships," Emma said carefully. "But yes, your dad and I were good friends at Colby."

"Then why didn't you keep in touch?" Lola wondered.

"It's easy to drift apart when you move and go on to different things." Emma shrugged. "I'm sure you have friends in London that you won't see again."

"I was only eight when I left; that's still a child," Lola reminded her. "Cammi and I are going to be friends forever. I'm going to be an actress in New York and she's going to live in Beverly Hills, but we're going to meet once a year."

"Is Cammi going to be an actress too?" Emma asked, grateful to change the subject.

"Cammi doesn't like acting. She was choosing between being a marriage counselor and a divorce attorney." Lola licked her spoon. "She decided on divorce attorney—that's where the money is."

Emma and Lola emerged onto Main Street as the church bells chimed the hour. The shop windows were ablaze with lights, and there was a new dusting of snow on the pavement.

Lola slipped her small hand into Emma's and they strolled to the village square. There was a wooden stage strung with streamers, and the carolers were preparing to sing.

"Emma, Lola, I thought that was you." A man approached them. "It's Stephen Green. It's nice to see you."

"Of course—the owner of the playhouse." Emma smiled.

"I direct the carolers at Christmas." Stephen waved at the little group dressed in red sweaters. "'Jingle Bells' isn't Shakespeare, but tourists love it."

"It's very festive," Emma said, nodding.

"I'm glad I saw you," he continued. "I asked a buddy at the *Southern Vermont Gazette* to write an article about the talent show. It will be in tomorrow's newspaper."

"Betty will be pleased," Emma said, beaming.

"My wife and I were good friends with Betty and John. Anne

died five years ago, and they were so kind to me," he said. "Their Christmas parties are always a bright spot in my year. I'd like to help."

"Betty already got some calls this evening." Emma nodded. "The word is getting around."

"Tell her I'm here if she needs me." Stephen turned to the stage. "I better go, or my smallest caroler will need to use the bathroom again and we'll never get started."

The carolers sang "Come All Ye Faithful" and "O Holy Night." It was magical standing in the village square with snow softly falling and Lola's mittened fingers curled around her hand. Then the group sang "The Twelve Days of Christmas" and everyone joined in. Lola belted out the last verse and Emma's heart had never felt so full.

"What did you think?" Lola asked after they had stopped to buy maple fudge for Fletcher and Megan.

"The performance was wonderful," Emma said. "I'll have to tell Bronwyn to bring the girls. They would love Snowberry at Christmas."

"I'm not talking about the carolers." Lola looked up at Emma. Her cheeks were flushed from the cold, and the tip of her nose was red. "I mean about Stephen."

"Stephen!" Emma repeated, laughing. "I'm not looking for a relationship. Anyway, I may seem old, but I'm only thirty-three. Stephen is in his sixties."

"I've changed my mind about you being old. Being with you is fun," Lola reflected. "But I was talking about Stephen for Betty."

"Betty's husband just died. It might be too soon for her to think about men."

"Why would it be too soon? It's better to have someone to celebrate Christmas with," Lola said logically. "There's no greater joy at Christmas than giving gifts to someone you care about."

When they returned to The Smuggler's Inn, Lola ran upstairs and Emma entered the kitchen to find Betty.

"Emma!" Betty said, and gestured to the counter. "I saved you some pecan pie—let me cut you a slice."

"No, thank you." Emma shook her head. "Lola and I had dinner in the village."

"I was wondering where you were." Betty poured hot tea into a mug.

"We went to the toy store, and after dinner we listened to a Christmas concert."

"Your eyes are sparkling." Betty looked at Emma. "I haven't seen you so happy since you arrived."

"Lola is an exceptional little girl," Emma agreed. "She's smart and lively and so much fun to be around."

"All children are exceptional in their own way," Betty mused. "My daughter taught herself to do cartwheels at the age of six. I thought she was going to be an amazing gymnast, until she joined a class and there were a dozen girls who could do the same thing."

"What do you mean?" Emma asked.

"Maybe it's not Lola that's exceptional. Maybe it's you and Lola together," Betty said. "Perhaps that's why fate brought you and Lola together. To show you that you're a good mother. Not every woman is cut out to have children."

"You sound like Bronwyn; she believes destiny is in charge of everything." Emma laughed. "I hadn't thought of that, but it doesn't really matter. I don't even have a boyfriend."

"You're good at falling in love," Betty reminded her.

"I can't make it last," Emma said. "I'm destined to be the god-mother who gives too many birthday presents because I don't have anyone else to shop for."

"Or you can keep looking until you find the right man." Betty stirred her tea. "I can't think of anything that's worth fighting for more than a happy marriage."

"I'll think about it." Emma took off her jacket. "Before I forget, we ran into Stephen Green. There's going to be an article in the paper about the talent show. Lola said the funniest thing. She thought you and Stephen would be perfect for each other."

"Did she really? How interesting." Betty's cheeks colored slightly. She finished her tea and walked to the sink. "Well, you *did* say Lola was an exceptional child."

Emma entered her room and tossed the presents on the bed. Outside the window a soft snow was falling, and the streetlights bathed the sidewalks in a golden glow. It had been a wonderful evening. Emma had loved stopping in front of the shop windows while Lola pointed to the things she would buy when she was older: lipstick and leather boots and a faux-fur coat.

So why did she still feel so empty, as if there was a hole in her heart as big as one of Betty's Christmas ornaments? Everyone had someone to love: Fletcher had Megan and Lola, and Bronwyn had Carlton and the girls, and Betty had her children and Stephen and the other residents of Snowberry who wanted to help her.

How could it be so difficult to find someone she wanted to spend the rest of her life with? Someone to wake up with every morning, and decorate the tree with at Christmas. A guy who would do anything for her, and who made her want to do the same for him.

Maybe this time destiny had got it wrong, and she was looking in the wrong place. But where else could she look? No matter how hard she tried, her happy ending dissolved like slush on the sidewalk. Emma turned off the light and the darkness engulfed her. Lola was right; it was better to celebrate Christmas with someone. It was no fun being alone.

Twelve

Three Days Before New Year's Eve
Snowberry, Vermont

FLETCHER HURRIED THROUGH THE VILLAGE to the playhouse. It had snowed all night and the sidewalks were slippery. But he loved being out this early; it reminded him of when he jogged around campus before class. The sky was a winter blue, the snow was free of footprints, and everything looked clean and new.

He had been disappointed last night when Lola said she had a stomachache and wanted to stay at the inn. He'd suggested they cancel their reservation for *A Christmas Carol,* but Lola insisted Betty would take care of her. And he and Megan were only a short distance away; if Lola needed him, he could return.

It had been a lovely evening. The play was charming, and Megan looked beautiful in her new dress. They held hands across the table and talked about their favorite holiday traditions.

His phone rang as he was about to enter the playhouse, and he recognized Graham's number.

"Fletcher, it's Graham." Graham's voice came over the line. "I hadn't heard from you. I wanted to make sure you weren't eaten by a wild boar or any of those other strange animals you find in Vermont."

"So far I've only seen squirrels." Fletcher noticed a squirrel scurrying into a bush. "It snowed last night, and this morning the village is all white."

"You should be glad you're not in London," Graham grunted. "It's been raining for a week. They're predicting snow flurries for New Year's Day, and then more rain, so the whole city will be a sludgy mess."

"I'm quite enjoying Snowberry. Megan wanted to go back to New York early for a theater party, but we decided to stay until New Year's."

"What kind of theater party?" Graham asked.

"Jordan Roth is having a bash on New Year's Eve," Fletcher responded. "We're holding a fundraiser for the owner of The Smuggler's Inn, so I told Megan we couldn't go."

"Do you think that's a good idea?" Graham asked. "At this point in your career, should you be giving up a party thrown by the biggest producer on Broadway to raise a few dollars for a country inn?"

"It's important to Lola," Fletcher said. "She's grown fond of Betty."

"I'm all for charity, but it begins at home," Graham reminded him. "You're new in New York; meeting the right people is important to the success of the play."

Fletcher opened his mouth and then closed it. Megan had said exactly the same thing.

"So is teaching Lola to help others," Fletcher insisted. "Yesterday Lola and Emma and I passed posters around the village. Lola met all the shopkeepers, and it was very educational."

"You and Lola and Emma?" Graham repeated. "Where was Megan?"

"Megan was getting her hair done."

"I see you haven't taken my advice," Graham said. "About staying away from Emma and concentrating on your engagement."

"I didn't even know Emma was joining us," Fletcher replied. "Lola set the whole thing up. I couldn't back out when she'd gone to so much trouble."

"I'm beginning to believe there is some kind of magic spell at work," Graham mused. "Each time we talk, Emma is the subject of every other sentence."

"Now you're talking like one of those soothsayers in the booths at the Covent Garden market," Fletcher cut in. "Snowberry is a small village, and we're staying at the same inn. Of course we're going to do things together."

"I'm only trying to help you," Graham said gently. "When you get a chance, take a look in the mirror."

"What do you mean?" Fletcher asked.

"It's an old trick I use with actors when they're not getting their role."

"I look in the mirror every day when I button my shirt."

"Don't look at the buttons of your shirt, look into your eyes," he said. "That's the only way to see what's going on in your soul. I was raised on Christmas stories. I believe Christmas is the time when miracles can happen. But first you have to know what you really want."

Fletcher bounded up the steps of the playhouse, and Stephen met him at the door.

"Fletcher! I'm glad you called." Stephen beamed. He was wearing a wool jacket over a flannel shirt and heavy boots.

"Betty gave me your number." Fletcher followed him into the playhouse lobby. "I hope it isn't too early. I want to take some measurements of the stage; we only have three days until the talent show."

"I'm always up early. Bad habit from thirty years as a stockbroker." Stephen led him into the theater.

Fletcher took out a notepad and made a quick sketch of the stage.

"It won't be anything fancy, just a few props," he said when he finished drawing. "Lola is determined to raise enough money for Betty. The whole thing has captured her enthusiasm."

"You have a special daughter," Stephen agreed. "I ran into Lola and Emma at the Christmas concert last night."

"Lola and Emma?" Fletcher repeated. When he and Megan returned from the dinner theater, Lola had already been asleep. And he had left this morning before anyone was awake.

"Lola has an amazing voice. I could hear her over the carolers," Stephen said, smiling. "If you come back next Christmas, I'll give her a solo."

"I'll think about it." Fletcher was suddenly uncomfortable. Why was Lola having dinner with Emma, when she'd said she had a stomachache and was going to stay in bed?

"I'm glad you called," Stephen was saying. "I'd like you to take my offer seriously."

"Your offer?" Fletcher dragged himself back to the conversation.

"To direct *A Midsummer Night's Dream*. Snowberry in the summertime is the perfect place for a child. And you'd bring such wisdom to the production—it would be the best season we ever had."

"It's a tremendous opportunity, but I'm getting married," Fletcher said.

"Think about it," Stephen urged. "I spent enough summers in Manhattan to know that the humidity is unbearable, and all the good places to eat close for July and August. Up here we have working farms and outdoor markets selling fresh fruits and vegetables. Lola could learn to grow watermelons and milk a cow."

Fletcher strolled along Main Street, but he was too distracted to appreciate the smell of hot cinnamon buns coming from the bakery or the sight of the first skaters making circles on the ice.

What had Lola been doing with Emma? It was one thing for them to spend time together at kids' club, but Lola had said she had a stomachache and couldn't go to the dinner theater. Had Lola been telling the truth, or had she not wanted to go to dinner with Fletcher and Megan? Megan and Lola seemed to be getting along better. Megan had complimented Lola on her mane of red hair, and Lola had said how much she liked Megan's new dress.

It was Fletcher's fault; he was letting everyone tell him what to do. He and Megan and Lola were a family, and it was time he took control.

Lola was in the kitchen with Betty when he returned to the inn. Watching her scribbling furiously in a notebook, Fletcher was awed by the beauty and complexity of his daughter. She was so small; her legs barely touched the ground when she sat on the stool, but she had a drive combined with a clarity he couldn't have imagined at her age.

"You seem to have recovered from your stomachache," Fletcher said, waving at the plate of cinnamon rolls on the counter.

"Betty said I can't pass up cinnamon rolls at Christmas. Plus, they're delicious." Lola pushed the plate to Fletcher. "Try one."

"I think I will." Fletcher ate a bite of sticky bun and wondered what Megan would say about his cholesterol. Then he reminded himself he was in charge; one Danish wouldn't hurt him.

"Betty and I are making the program for the talent show." Lola showed Fletcher her notes. "It's going to be like *American Idol*. Stephen will be the emcee, and there will be three judges."

"I saw Stephen at the playhouse this morning," Fletcher replied. "I've got some ideas for decorating the stage."

"Yes, he called me." Betty poured two cups of coffee and handed one to Fletcher. "He's determined to make you take him up on his offer."

"What offer?" Lola asked, wiping icing from her chin.

"Stephen wants your father to direct the Shakespeare festival next summer," Betty said, turning to Lola. "The playhouse has never had a big-name director before; it would be good for all the businesses in Snowberry."

"I'm hardly a big director," Fletcher cut in. "This will be my first play on Broadway."

"Of course you're famous," Lola insisted. "Dad has been to a reception at Buckingham Palace. And he met Harry Styles; Mom was so impressed when I showed her Harry's autograph."

"My friend Graham takes me along every year to Elton John's Halloween party," Fletcher said modestly. "I never know who these people are, but he makes sure Lola gets the best autographs."

"You and Lola would love summer in Snowberry," Betty urged. "Lola can pick blueberries, and I'll teach her to make strawberry rhubarb pie."

"It is tempting. I love regional theater, and I'm anxious to direct more Shakespeare," Fletcher reflected. "But this summer won't work. Megan and I are getting married."

"You could get married at The Smuggler's Inn," Betty suggested. "My roses will be in bloom and the summer fruits will be in season. I can't think of a better place for a wedding."

"It's a perfect plan!" Lola piped up. "I can help Betty bake the wedding cake. And Emma can make the invitations—she's very good with words."

"Emma!" Fletcher exclaimed. Lola was like a runaway horse; he had to rein her in.

"You and Emma are old friends," Lola said logically. "I thought you would want to invite her."

"Megan and I haven't started a guest list." Fletcher put down his coffee cup. "I'll think about it, Betty, but right now I need to talk to Lola."

"We are talking," Lola replied. "We're planning a wedding."

"I need to talk to you upstairs," Fletcher said, and turned to Betty. "Thank you for the coffee and pastries."

"Is it something important?" Lola asked when they reached her room. "Because we need to get the program finalized by this evening."

"I want to help Betty save the inn, but that's not why we came to Vermont." Fletcher leaned against the desk.

"We're here so Megan and I can get to know each other better." Lola perched on the bed. "But babies don't get to know their parents before they're born. No matter what, they're stuck with them."

"Well, yes, but this is different."

"You mean, Megan doesn't have to like me?" Lola wondered.

"What gave you that idea?" Fletcher asked. "Megan thinks you're one of the smartest, most talented girls she's met."

"If she was my real mother, that wouldn't matter," Lola persisted. "If you had a new baby, you'd love it because it was yours."

"Megan and I aren't going to have a baby anytime soon," Fletcher assured her.

"But if you did, or if Mom and Chuck did, you'd love it even if it had a nose like Pinocchio."

"I haven't seen many babies with noses like Pinocchio," Fletcher chuckled. "These are odd questions—is something bothering you?"

Lola hopped off the bed and walked to the closet. "Cammi and I were just talking about babies. She's worried that when the new baby arrives, her mom won't have time for her."

Fletcher walked over to Lola and put his arms around her.

"I see what this is about." He hugged her tightly. "Parenting doesn't work that way. Parents can love all their children at the same time."

"That's what Emma said." Lola nodded. "But I didn't believe her."

"Why were you talking about babies with Emma?" Fletcher asked, startled.

"She was buying presents for her goddaughters, and we got on the subject of babies." Lola shrugged. "But let's talk about something else. Why did you want to come upstairs?"

"You said you had a stomachache last night. But Stephen saw you and Emma at the choir concert," he began.

"I know—crazy, right? I was feeling so bad I didn't want to get out of bed, and then poof"—Lola waved her hands—"I was all better."

"Miraculous." Fletcher was perplexed. Lola was obviously concerned about something, but she could close up like a turtle retreating into its shell. When he and Cassandra broke the news last year that they were divorcing and moving to America, Fletcher had expected an outburst of tears. Instead the only thing Lola said was she would miss Annabelle's birthday party, and there was going to be a magician.

It was only much later, when he recounted the scene to his therapist in New York, that he understood Lola had focused all the pain of the divorce on missing a birthday party with finger sandwiches and a magician in a black top hat.

"I'm glad you're better, because you and Megan and I are going to spend today experiencing Vermont," Fletcher said.

"Can we experience it tomorrow? I have kids' club this afternoon. And I can't ice skate today, I scraped up my hands on the ice," Lola said. "And I love pancakes with maple syrup. But Mom will get mad if I come home with cavities."

"I'll tell Emma you're not doing kids' club today. We're going to do something different." Fletcher tried to remember everything he'd read in the brochures. "We'll start with visiting a glassblowing factory."

"That sounds as thrilling as a school field trip," Lola groaned. "Are you sure this can't wait until we finish the programs? Betty hasn't watched *American Idol*. She won't pick the right judges."

"The programs can wait," Fletcher said sternly. "And you'll love the glassblowing factory. They even make glass candy canes."

Fletcher stood in the hundred-year-old mill that had been converted into a glassblowing studio and tried to concentrate. The excursion had started promisingly: he had hired a horse-driven sleigh outfitted with thick blankets. They drove along country roads, and Lola was so excited by the fields dotted with cows, she barely stayed in her seat.

And the mill itself was charming. It was a wooden building perched on the bank of a river. They crossed a snow-covered bridge and entered a two-story lobby with a glass Santa Claus.

But the tour guide had been explaining the glassblowing techniques for what seemed like hours, and even Fletcher couldn't hide his boredom. Megan inspected her fingernails, and Lola fidgeted with the buttons on her coat.

"So that's how a profession that started in 1813 at a glassblowing studio on the banks of Lake Dunmore is now one of Vermont's biggest industries," the guide was saying. "If you follow me to the gift shop, there is a selection of glass to choose from." He smiled broadly. "Children love the glass animals, and there are some vases that make perfect holiday gifts."

The guide led them into a separate building with huge windows and cases of glass objects. There were glass pumpkins and glass angels with gold wings. Lola fell in love with a glass hedgehog, and Fletcher thought the blue paperweight would look good on his desk.

"Look! Aren't these pretty. They would make exquisite wedding favors." Megan picked up a perfume bottle with a heart-shaped stopper and showed them to Fletcher. "For men, we could give the cologne bottles. You receive the same favor at every wedding in New York: a Tiffany's box housing some trinket for the women and a silk tie or pair of cuff links for the men. This would be completely different, and it would look dazzling in the ballroom of the Plaza!"

"But you might not get married at the Plaza." Lola inspected the perfume bottle. "You might have the wedding here in Snowberry."

"What did you say?" Megan looked at Lola.

"Dad wants to direct the Shakespeare festival next summer. So Betty suggested you have the wedding at The Smuggler's Inn," Lola said. "It was awfully nice of her. She even offered to make the cake."

"Have the wedding in Snowberry?" Megan turned to Fletcher. "That's news to me. You haven't said anything about this."

"That's because there's nothing to say," Fletcher returned quickly. "I saw Stephen this morning and he asked me to consider his offer. I told him it was out of the question because I was getting married. Betty suggested we hold the wedding at the inn."

Megan's expression was as frigid as the ice on the windowpane. She put the perfume bottle back on the counter and glowered at Fletcher.

"I don't think that's a good idea," she said, more loudly than Fletcher would have liked. "I've always dreamed of a big church wedding with a white poufy dress and a long train. And how will we squeeze three hundred guests into The Smuggler's Inn?"

"There's a church just outside of Snowberry," he stammered. "And the reception could be in the garden."

"But I already made an appointment to see St. Patrick's Cathedral on Fifth Avenue—all the top society weddings are held there," Megan said tightly. "That reminds me. We need to take engagement photos if we want our announcement to be in *The New York Times*. I ran into an old friend from Yale who's a photographer, and he offered to take some for free."

Fletcher wondered if the photographer was an old boyfriend.

Why else would he take free photos? But Megan had never given him reason to doubt her. She didn't even believe in flirting; she thought it belittled women.

"I didn't know you picked out a church," he said before he could stop himself.

"And I didn't know you moved the wedding to Vermont," Megan countered.

There was a crashing sound, and Fletcher turned around. The remains of a glass fish were scattered at Lola's feet.

"I'm sorry," Lola said when Fletcher hurried over to her. Lola had wandered away while they were arguing, and he hadn't even noticed. "I picked it up and it slipped out of my hands. Now you're going to have to pay for it, and it's my fault."

Fletcher remembered Cassandra always counting to ten when Lola did something wrong. If Cassandra was still angry by the time she reached nine, then Lola deserved a punishment. But this was Fletcher's fault. He'd practically told Megan they were getting married in Vermont. And he dragged Lola to a glassblowing demonstration when she wanted to work on the program.

"Accidents happen." He took Lola's hand and walked back to Megan. "I'm sorry. I shouldn't have considered getting married in Vermont without discussing it with you first."

"No, you shouldn't have," Megan replied, but her tone was softer. "And I was going to tell you about the appointment at St. Patrick's."

"Let's get out of here—the sleigh is waiting," he whispered to both of them. "I'm hungry, and I don't need to learn anything more about natural color striations in glass pumpkins."

Fletcher dipped sourdough bread into a bowl of corn chowder and felt much better. He'd picked the restaurant for lunch, and Megan and Lola agreed it was perfect; it had a slanted ceiling and round tables with checkered tablecloths. The flickering candles gave the room a warm glow, and the smell of butter and spices from the open kitchen was delicious.

The menu had all their favorite foods: a winter salad with cranberries and kale for Megan, lamb chops with creamed spinach for Lola, and saddle of venison in a walnut sauce for Fletcher. The first thing he did was order a bottle of red wine and a Shirley Temple for Lola. By the time he and Megan had each had a glass of wine and Lola finished the glazed cherry, everyone was in a good mood.

"I have a surprise for you," Fletcher said, pouring another glass of wine.

"I hope it's not a tour of a chocolate factory." Lola slurped her drink. "I'd rather just eat a peanut butter cup. I don't need to see how it's made."

"Betty did suggest a tour of the Ben and Jerry's Factory but that can wait until another day," Fletcher agreed. "This is more exciting. It's about the honeymoon."

"We already agreed on the honeymoon," Megan reminded him. "We're going to spend ten days in Greece."

Deciding on their honeymoon had been easy. They both loved the Greek islands, and Fletcher had planned a side trip to Athens to see the Parthenon.

"This is in addition to the honeymoon," Fletcher corrected her. "Since the wedding is in July and rehearsals for *Father of the Bride* don't start until September, we can take a bit more time." He paused, the wine and good food making him enjoy the suspense. "We can meet Lola in England. The English countryside is gorgeous in the summer, and we can catch a performance at the Old Globe Theater. We've never been to London together," he said to Megan. "It's the perfect opportunity to show you around."

"But Lola is only nine. Do you think it's safe for her to fly across the Atlantic by herself?" Megan said.

"She'll be ten by then, but I have it all figured out," Fletcher responded. "Graham is coming for the wedding, and he planned on staying an extra week. He and Lola can fly over together—he's her godfather."

"Yes, please!" Lola piped up. Her mouth was red from the cherry syrup, and her smile was almost as big as her face. "Graham is the best godfather. He takes me to lunch at the Savoy and introduces me to actors. Once we met an actress with really short hair and it turned out to be Emma Watson." Lola swooned. "I almost didn't recognize her because of the haircut, but she told me all about growing up at Hogwarts."

"That does sound tempting. I haven't been to London in years," Megan mused. "We could attend Wimbledon—the paparazzi love photographing the spectators, and it would be good to get international exposure. And we could set up some meetings—it would be fun to do a play in the West End."

The whole reason Fletcher had moved to America was to stay close to Lola; he couldn't direct a play in London. And the British press would be too busy snapping photos of celebrities like David Beckham to notice Fletcher and his new bride. But Megan and Lola were excited about the same thing, and he didn't want to ruin their enthusiasm.

"Let's order something to celebrate." He picked up the menu. "Warm gingerbread pudding or spice cake with eggnog ice cream?"

"Warm gingerbread pudding!" Lola and Megan said in unison.

Everyone laughed, and Fletcher signaled the waiter. Lola and Megan chatted excitedly about London, and Fletcher leaned back in his chair. He couldn't imagine a more perfect moment: Christmas lights twinkling in the window, logs crackling in the fireplace, Lola and Megan's heads pressed close together. They were going to create a wonderful family, and he didn't have a thing to worry about.

"Can we go tubing?" Lola asked when the sleigh stopped in front of The Smuggler's Inn. The hill behind them was filled with children on sleds. The sound of laughter mixed with the whooshing of rubber tubes scudding down the slope.

"I thought you wanted to help Betty with the programs," Fletcher reminded her.

"I do, but it looks like fun." Lola pointed to two teenagers spinning down the hill on tubes. "Please, let's do it together."

"You want all of us to go tubing now?" Fletcher asked doubtfully. The last thing Fletcher needed was to go back to New York with a cast on his leg.

"It's more fun to do it as a family," Lola urged. "Mom and Chuck took me inner tubing in Connecticut."

"You two should go—I'll watch," Megan suggested. "I don't want to ruin my leather jacket if I fall."

If Chuck with his bad tennis knee could ride an inner tube, so could Fletcher. And he wanted Lola to enjoy outdoor activities instead of only being interested in the theater.

"Why not? I was quite good in college," Fletcher said cheerfully and turned to Megan. "Don't worry about falling; it's easier than it looks."

Fletcher sailed down the slope and wished Graham could see him now. He was getting exercise and doing things with Megan and Lola together. And it was fun: the tube jumped easily over the bumps and he felt vigorous and alive.

"Let's go again," Lola said when Fletcher reached the bottom.

"That's enough for me." Fletcher climbed out of the tube. Other families glanced admiringly at Lola's flaming hair and Megan's long legs, and Fletcher thought they really were a beautiful family.

"Please, one more time," Lola begged. "When Mom and Chuck took me tubing, we were the last ones on the mountain."

The wind had picked up, and there was a small pain in Fletcher's side.

"Why don't we go back to The Smuggler's Inn?" he suggested. "You can finish the programs, and Megan and I will take a Jacuzzi."

"I'm not in a hurry," Megan interjected. She had been more effusive since he suggested extending their honeymoon. She leaned forward and kissed him. "You look so handsome coming down the hill. I'll stand at the bottom and referee."

"We're not going to race," Fletcher corrected her.

"Don't worry, I know you're getting kind of old," Lola said, examining Fletcher critically. "You can have a head start."

Fletcher perched on top of the hill and wondered if this was a good idea. But Lola was already waiting impatiently for him to start. As long as he went slowly, nothing bad would happen.

Megan waved from the bottom and he pushed off the slope. Lola's tube came up behind him and soon they were side by side. Lola was giggling and Fletcher felt a rush of joy.

But then Lola picked up speed and Fletcher tried to catch up.

Lola finished first, jumping out of the tube and waving her arms in the air. Suddenly Megan got knocked down into the snow. Megan screeched and his tube came to a halt.

"Are you all right?" He jumped out of the tube and ran to help her up.

"My jacket is soaking wet—it's ruined!" Her cheeks were pale, and her mouth was set in a firm line.

"I told you I was fast," Lola said and turned to Megan. "I'm sorry—I didn't mean for your jacket to get wet. Maybe Betty has something at the inn that can fix it."

"I'll have to take it somewhere when we get back to New York," Megan said and brushed away the snow in her hair. "If you'll excuse me, I'm going to change out of these wet clothes, and then I'm going to go to the beauty parlor and redo my hair."

Fletcher stood in the library of The Smuggler's Inn and nursed a large scotch. He hadn't even gone upstairs to change out of his damp clothes; he'd walked straight to the library and filled the tallest shot glass he could find.

If Megan's leather jacket hadn't gotten ruined, he and Megan would be sitting in the Jacuzzi by now. Instead she was at the beauty parlor getting her hair repaired, and Lola was upstairs taking a bath. What bad luck, almost crashing into Megan when they had been having fun.

The whole excursion had been somewhat stressful, like the opening night of a new play. There were moments of joy, and he was confident it would be a success, but until the last curtain fell and the audience broke into applause, his stomach was tying itself in knots.

He was in love with Megan, and he was certain marrying her was the right decision. But every day brought a new problem: Could he give Megan the lead in the new play? Why was Lola talking about babies? Should they consider holding the wedding at The Smuggler's Inn?

There was no reason not to get married in Vermont. Nothing was happening with *Father of the Bride* until the fall. Lola would blossom in Snowberry in the summer, and he would love to direct *A Midsummer Night's Dream*.

But Megan had her heart set on getting married at the Plaza. And he had gone about it all wrong. He should have asked Megan if she would consider getting married in Vermont before she heard it from someone else. It was like the time he'd brought home a puppy for Lola. He and Cassandra had talked vaguely about getting a dog, but he should have asked Cassandra first. Instead, he arrived home with a puppy that proceeded to chew their shoes and jump on the furniture.

The scotch warmed his throat, and his mind wandered to Emma. He remembered the first crack in their relationship. It had been his fault, but it had seemed so minor at the time. He'd been positive he could fix it.

April, 2008
Waterville, Maine

Fletcher stood behind the counter of Ye Olde Candy Shoppe in Waterville, Maine and wondered what hurt more: his eyes, from staying up all night studying; his legs, from bicycling the three miles from campus; or his back, from standing behind the counter.

There was nothing he could change about the situation. If he didn't study, he would fail his exams. He had to bicycle to work, because he still didn't own a car. And he had to earn enough money by graduation so he could move close to Emma.

Just thinking about Emma made filling paper bags with sticky taffy, and jelly beans that left orange dye on his hands, tolerable. The last few months had been the best of his life: cooking spaghetti for dinner on the hot plate in his dorm room, listening to the spring rain on the rooftops, taking long walks on Sunday mornings when the rest of the campus was asleep.

Emma was determined to move to New York, and he wanted to be near her. So, twenty hours a week, he wore a paper hat and dished out novelty candies: coconut Needhams made with chocolate and Maine potatoes, and gummy animals shaped like moose and lobsters.

The bell above the door tinkled, and a man wearing a navy blazer entered the store.

"I need a present for my wife," the man said as he approached the counter. "Some of that fudge and a few of the pralines." He deliberated. "And a separate bag of the Charleston Chews. My wife won't let me eat them because of my diabetes, but I'll finish them before I get off the plane."

The man handed Fletcher his credit card and waited while Fletcher filled two bags.

"I'm Harry Stone," he said, and held out his hand. "And you're Fletcher Conway."

"I'm sorry—have we met?" Fletcher asked.

"No, but my son goes to Colby," Harry said. "William Stone."

"That doesn't sound familiar." Fletcher shook his head.

"That's because William is studying to be a doctor, and doesn't approve of theater people, including his own father," Harry laughed. "But I saw your production of *Macbeth*. It was excellent; I've never seen so much energy in Shakespeare."

"Most students don't understand Shakespeare's English, so I direct the actors to use as much physical expression as possible," Fletcher explained. "Sort of like a football game with costumes."

"It worked brilliantly. I was impressed," Harry agreed. "The department head is an old friend and said I could find you here. I was wondering if you'd be interested in a job."

"You mean other than counting out milk balls?" Fletcher waved at the glass jars of candy.

"Being an assistant director at a theater company," Harry corrected him. "Not now, but when you graduate."

Fletcher felt like a bird was trapped in his chest, beating its wings.

"What kind of theater company?" he asked nonchalantly, as if he received offers all the time.

"Shakespeare, mostly—though we dabble in other great British playwrights." Harry ticked them off his fingers. "Harold Pinter and Somerset Maugham."

"Somerset Maugham!" Fletcher had devoured his writing, but he didn't know anyone who was familiar with his plays.

"The job will be tedious, with terrible working conditions," Harry said cheerfully. "Actors who refuse to go on if a cockroach scuttles across the stage; pay that is so low, you'll be living on biscuits and beef jerky. But you'll be working with some of the greatest names in theater, and I'll teach you everything I know."

"It sounds tremendous." Fletcher tried not to sound too eager. "Can I think about it and get back to you?"

"Here's my card." He handed it to Fletcher. "I'll be in town until Friday; then I return to England."

"England?" Fletcher repeated, noticing the card had a London address.

"Didn't I mention that?" Harry asked. "The job is in London. I'm the director of the Old Vic."

Fletcher walked out of the store at the end of his shift and noticed a girl leaning against the lamppost. Her head was hidden in a book, but he recognized Emma's sandals.

"Emma? What are you doing here?" he asked.

"I came to meet you." She put the book away. She was wearing a summer dress with a cotton sweater tied around her neck.

"I have something exciting to tell you." She kissed him. "If I waited until you got back to campus, I was afraid I'd burst."

"I have something to tell you, too." Fletcher unlocked his bicycle. "But you came all the way here—you go first."

"I told you that Julie's father works at Ogilvy & Mather in New York," Emma said. "He put in a good word for me, and I have a job interview."

"That's wonderful," Fletcher said, beaming.

"It's better than wonderful!" Emma exclaimed. "Ogilvy is one of the biggest ad agencies in the world. And the job isn't in the mailroom or secretary pool, it's as a junior copywriter. I'm taking the bus to Manhattan on Friday."

"You'll get the job," Fletcher said, and kissed her. "You're smart and talented, and they'd be lucky to have you."

"What did you want to tell me?" she said, turning to him.

Fletcher thought of Harry's card in his pocket. Now wasn't the time to mention Harry's offer in London. There would be plenty of opportunities when Emma returned from her interview in New York.

He reached into his shirt pocket and brought out a paper bag.

"Ye Olde Candy Shoppe got in those chocolate cashew bonbons." He handed her the bag. "I saved some for you."

Three Days Before New Year's Eve
Snowberry, Vermont

Fletcher paced around the library of The Smuggler's Inn and pulled his mind back to the present. The sun was setting over the fields, and the church steeple gleamed in the distance. It didn't matter whether he and Megan got married in New York or Vermont, as long as they were together.

He might not have all the answers. Some days it was still hard to comprehend that he was divorced, and no matter how hard he tried, Lola could be a complete mystery. But he knew one thing: He and Megan had to communicate with each other. There couldn't be any secrets between them, or their marriage would fail before it started.

Thirteen

EMMA SAT AT A TABLE at the Snowshoe Café on Main Street and toyed with a bowl of baked-potato soup. It was late afternoon, and Emma had been sitting there for hours.

Every now and then the waitress looked meaningfully at her and Emma ordered something else: French country bread, or a cup of hot tea with lemon. But she wasn't hungry, so the plates piled up like snowflakes on the cars outside the window.

She had started the day with a brisk walk through the forest, followed by a breakfast of poached eggs and Vermont sausage. But when she came downstairs to find Lola, Betty said Lola had gone out, and there wasn't going to be any kids' club this afternoon.

Emma hid her disappointment and mumbled something about catching up on her work. She spent half an hour playing listlessly on the piano, but Betty kept poking her head in and asking if she wanted a muffin. Emma finally gathered her laptop and headed into the village.

She told herself it was good that Lola was busy; she had to finish the ad copy for Lancôme's new lipstick. But she imagined Lola and Fletcher and Megan sharing fondue at some cozy restaurant, and felt oddly alone.

The waitress glared at her, and Emma tried to examine her feelings. She often tagged along with Bronwyn and the girls on outings. And she didn't mind being the single woman at Bronwyn and Carlton's dinner parties when she was between boyfriends.

She had to be honest with herself. She couldn't stop thinking about Fletcher. But he hadn't given her any reason to believe they were anything but old friends. He was infatuated with Megan. In six months they'd be married, and Fletcher would completely forget about running into Emma at Christmas.

But this morning when she was jogging through the forest, she wondered if Bronwyn was right. Could Fletcher and Megan really be in love if they had only known each other for a few months? What if Emma was meant to come to Vermont to find Fletcher, and synchronicity really existed?

There was a new email notification on her laptop from her boss, Helen, and she opened it.

Dear Emma,

Normally I hate to send or receive work emails during Christmas week. So feel free to ignore this and go back to snorkeling or watching hula dancers or whatever you and Scott are doing in Maui.

I just received word that Lancôme was so pleased with your ads for the deep lash mascara, they are assigning you a new product. It's top secret, but it's some kind of age-defying serum, and it's yours from the test kitchen until it hits the stores.

Put a couple of daiquiris on your expense account to celebrate, and I can't wait to hear about your vacation. There's a betting pool in the office whether you'll come back wearing a diamond ring. If I win, I'll be able to afford the January sales at Bloomingdale's.

Best, Helen

Emma closed the laptop and groaned. She should have told Helen she had broken up with Scott and wasn't going to Maui. Now a swarm of copywriters and account executives would gather around her desk, inspecting her suntan and her ring finger.

Her very own product! She should ask the waitress for a slice of maple walnut pie to celebrate. Instead she felt slightly hollow, like the day she'd been promoted to copywriter. It had been January three years ago, and she had just broken up with a writer named Paul. She had been so thrilled about the promotion; she'd called Bronwyn to tell her the good news. But Bronwyn had been at a toddler gymnastics class and Emma's parents were on a cruise, and she couldn't think of anyone else to tell. She picked up some salmon chowder and went home and watched *The Real Housewives of New York City*.

She could call Bronwyn now with the news. But Bronwyn might be busy making sure Liv didn't sneak her mermaid shampoo and bubblegum toothpaste in her carry-on.

Emma remembered when she had taken the bus to New York from Colby for her first job interview. She was so excited to see the landmarks she had read about: the Statue of Liberty, the Botanical Gardens, the New York Public Library. But halfway through her first day in Manhattan, all she wanted was to hear Fletcher's voice on the other end of her phone. Without that, the jugglers in

Union Square and the parade that happened to pass through Midtown seemed as drab as the Greyhound bus station.

April, 2008
New York

Emma glanced at her flip phone and slipped it dejectedly in her purse. She had been in New York for twenty-four hours; her head throbbed and her feet ached and all she wanted was to go back to Colby.

Her interview at Ogilvy & Mather had been yesterday afternoon. She'd been so nervous, she spent an hour pacing up and down outside the office building. She might never have worked up the courage to enter the revolving glass doors if a police officer hadn't asked if there was something wrong.

The interview went better than she expected, and she left flushed with optimism. Then she pulled out her *Lonely Planet* and vowed to do everything it suggested. She started at Grand Central Station, and it was one of the most magical places she had ever seen: the pale blue ceiling was painted with elaborate murals, and she could have spent hours in the food hall sipping espresso at Café Grumpy and sampling red velvet cupcakes at Magnolia Bakery.

By the time she left Grand Central Station, it was almost dusk, and she was suddenly anxious about walking alone. But the guidebook said she had to fit in a quick tour of the Guggenheim before it closed. She ate dinner at a falafel place on Sixth Avenue, and by the time she reached the hostel, she was convinced New York was the best city in the world.

She tried to call Fletcher, but his phone went straight to voice-mail. She tried again four more times because the Australian tourists at the hostel kept her awake until midnight with their rowdy discussion about the differences between rugby and football. She even tried the phone in his dorm, but some guy answered groggily and said he hadn't seen Fletcher all night.

This morning she had woken early, determined to fit in more sightseeing before going back to the bus terminal. But she didn't enjoy the bagel with strawberry cream cheese at Ess-A-Bagel because Fletcher still hadn't returned her calls, and she almost got thrown out of the Met for answering her phone. She was sure it was Fletcher, but it had been her suitemate asking where she kept her curling iron.

Now it was afternoon, and she was standing in Central Park wondering where Fletcher could be. On Thursdays he only had one class, and even if he was studying in the library, he could have stepped outside and taken her call.

There was a food cart selling hot dogs, and she decided to buy one because there was nothing worse than the Velveeta sandwiches they sold at the bus terminal. She handed the vendor three dollars, and there was a ringing sound in her purse.

She reached for her phone, but the hot dog slipped and splattered mustard all over her bag. By the time she found her phone the ringing had stopped, and the phone read: INCOMING CALL UN-KNOWN.

It couldn't have been Fletcher; his number would have printed out. She started eating the hot dog when her phone rang again.

"Hello?" She flipped it open.

"Emma, it's Fletcher," he answered. "I'm sorry I haven't called. One of the actors got pneumonia, so I spent last night begging every guy in the drama department to play Hamlet's father. Today they offered me an extra shift at work, and my phone fell out of my pocket while I was bicycling to Ye Olde Candy Shoppe. The phone in the dorm wasn't working because someone left it off the hook, so I'm calling from the phone in my advisor's office." He paused to take a breath. "How is New York?"

Rain was beginning to fall, and people scurried for cover. There was a mustard stain on Emma's blouse, and the hot dog bun was soggy. But none of that mattered because she was standing in Central Park looking at the Manhattan skyline, and Fletcher was on the other end of the phone.

"New York is the most amazing place I've ever been," she said, and had never felt so happy. "I can't wait to show it to you."

Emma hung up and hurried out of the park before the rain ruined her new pumps. There was a line of people waiting at the bus stop, and her phone rang again. She thought it was Fletcher, but instead there was an unfamiliar male voice.

"Is this Emma?" the man asked. "This is Walter Barrows. We met yesterday afternoon."

"Of course." Emma tried to keep the phone dry. Walter was a senior copywriter at Ogilvy & Mather, and was on the team that had interviewed her.

"This is a little premature because we have to get approval from the higher-ups, but we wanted you to know how impressed we were," he said. "You should be hearing the good news from HR shortly."

"Are you serious?" She gulped. "Do I have the job?"

"It's not official, and anything can happen in advertising," he said, but there was a smile in his voice. "However, if I were you, I'd be scouring the classifieds for an apartment."

Emma was tempted to call Fletcher. But Walter had said it wasn't final, and she didn't want to jinx it. The bus pulled up and she hopped on board. The next time she ate a hot dog in New York, she would be a junior copywriter at Ogilvy & Mather. Fletcher would be assistant director for some off-off-Broadway play, and they'd meet for lunch in Central Park. There was a break in the clouds, and her smile was as wide as the rainbow in the sky.

Three Days Before New Year's Eve
Snowberry, Vermont

Emma tried to ignore the waitress at the Snowshoe Café clearing the next table, and wondered what would have happened if she'd called Fletcher back all those years ago. But that was ancient history, and so much had happened.

She caught her reflection in the window and was angry with herself for thinking she and Fletcher had a chance. Fletcher was engaged, and she wasn't going to start pining for him like a teenager reading the diary of her first crush.

The café door opened and a small figure entered the space. Her face was hidden by a hooded jacket, but Emma recognized Lola's pink tights and lace-up boots.

"Lola! What are you doing here?" Emma asked.

"Betty said you came into the village." Lola pushed back the hood and plopped down across from Emma.

"Does your father know you're here?"

"He was in the library, and I didn't want to disturb him," Lola answered. "I had to see you. It's important."

"You can't wander around Snowberry by yourself," Emma said.

"I grew up in London, and now my father lives in the East Village." Lola rolled her eyes. "I'm perfectly capable of walking one block to Main Street. This is life or death—it couldn't wait."

"Life or death?" Emma grinned, and felt foolish at how happy she was to see Lola.

"Maybe not exactly life or death, but you'll understand when I tell you what happened."

"It's going to have to wait until we leave." Emma pointed to the waitress. "I've been sitting here too long, and I'm going to get kicked out unless I order something."

"That's fine with me." Lola picked up the menu. "I haven't eaten since lunchtime, and I'd do anything for a burger and a shake."

"So I took a hot bath, and then I was about to go into my dad's room to get my sweater," Lola began after the waitress delivered a turkey burger with a side of sweet potato fries. "I didn't even know Megan was there; I thought she was at the beauty parlor."

"Megan went to the beauty parlor yesterday," Emma said, trying to follow the story.

"There was an inner tubing accident. Megan's leather jacket was ruined, and her hair got wet," Lola explained. "Honestly, Megan's hair looked good with a little frizz, but she likes it pin-straight. Anyway, I heard her talking—"

"Don't tell me you eavesdropped again," Emma interrupted.

"I didn't mean to." Lola crossed her hands over her chest. "At first, I thought she and my dad were talking, but then she mentioned his name and I realized she was on the phone." Lola looked at Emma. "Megan said she couldn't believe Fletcher made her spend Christmas week in Vermont, and she was going to miss the most important theater party of the year."

"She was probably just complaining to a girlfriend," Emma said uneasily. "Sometimes my friend Bronwyn talks about her husband, Carlton, and they have a wonderful marriage."

"Does your friend say things like 'he cares more about his bratty daughter than about me,' and 'I always dreamed of getting married at the Plaza, and I'm not going to settle for a garden wedding at some country inn in the wilds of Vermont'?" Lola squeezed ketchup onto her burger.

"You must have heard her wrong," Emma assured her.

"They do those hearing checks at school where they ring a bell. I have perfect hearing." Lola's face was serious. "Then she said she'd better get the lead in the play, or marrying Fletcher is a bad idea."

Emma's cheeks paled and her heart beat faster.

"Megan is a beautiful woman with a Yale degree. She wouldn't marry your father to get a part in a play."

"The person on the phone must have said something, because Megan *did* say he seemed sexy in the beginning," Lola said, and stuck out her tongue. "You don't know the theater—actors do crazy things to get roles all the time. My godfather told me about an understudy who filled the dressing room with roses even though the lead actress was allergic. The understudy claimed she didn't know, but every night someone whisked away the flowers the actress received because even looking at them gave her hives."

"Lola," Emma said sharply. "Whatever goes on between your father and Megan is none of our business. All couples have arguments. If it's something serious, they'll tell you."

"How can my father say anything when he doesn't know himself?" Lola asked. "He can't marry Megan if she's using him to get a part in a play."

"You're nine years old. You can't stop them."

"Will you stop talking about my age? Emma Watson was only eleven when she starred in the first Harry Potter," Lola said impatiently. "My father is one of the two people I love most in the world. I can't let anyone hurt him."

Emma wished she could talk to Bronwyn, or even Betty. This was serious, and she had no idea how to answer.

"You can't say anything to your father. You don't have any proof, and Megan would deny it." Emma fiddled with her napkin. "Spreading gossip is wrong, and it's only going to get you into trouble."

"I hadn't thought of that." Lola ate a handful of fries. "Cammi's stepfather is an entertainment attorney, and one of his clients is some big music producer. *US Magazine* wrote something bad about him, and he sued for millions of dollars," she said thoughtfully. "He told Cammi if being a divorce attorney doesn't work out, she should switch to entertainment law."

"I have a feeling Cammi will do well at whatever she tries," Emma chuckled, feeling more relaxed. "Fletcher and Megan will work it out. Why don't we find Betty and work on the program?"

"We can't do that now, I have to help my father," Lola protested.

"You just agreed there's nothing you can do," Emma reminded her.

"You said people shouldn't listen to gossip," Lola said and took a large bite of her burger. "Could you please pay the check? There's somewhere we have to go."

"What are we doing in here?" Emma hissed at Lola.

They were standing in the waiting area of Nancy's Nail & Hair Salon. It was the opposite of the salons in Manhattan: one vinyl sofa faced a chipped coffee table, and Christmas cards were arranged on the Formica reception desk.

Lola peeked at the back of the salon, where women were sitting under old-fashioned hair dryers. Her eyes widened and she approached the desk.

"We'd like to get our nails done," Lola said to the receptionist.

"I can fit you both in tomorrow at nine in the morning." The woman flipped through her book.

"It has to be now—it's for a Christmas party, " Lola said, and turned to Emma. "You get your nails done, and I'll watch."

Emma had no idea what Lola was up to. But Lola's jaw was set in a determined line, so Emma gave up and played along.

"Could you squeeze me in?" Emma asked the woman.

"I suppose," the woman sighed heavily. "Gretchen will take you back."

"You still haven't told me why we're here," Emma whispered when they were seated behind a curtain. Lola flipped through *People* magazine, and a dark-haired woman dunked Emma's fingers in a bowl of sudsy water.

"Look, it's a photo of Haley Thomas, the actress who is going to play the lead in *Father of the Bride*." Lola waved the magazine in front of Emma. "She's only twenty-two, and she's already won two Tonys."

"I thought Megan was going to play the lead," Emma said, and winced. The water was too hot, and Emma wished the woman wouldn't squeeze her fingers.

"Haley has the same manager as Alec Baldwin. If they fire Haley, Alec might quit too," Lola said loudly. "The producers would kill if they lost Alec Baldwin—he's the reason the play will open on Broadway."

"I'm sure your father knows what he's doing," Emma said uncertainly. "He wouldn't jeopardize the production."

"Graham told me a story about when he was going to produce a revival of *Jesus Christ Superstar* with Jay-Z and Beyoncé. The director decided to replace Jay-Z with some rap sensation who happened to be a friend."

"I didn't know Beyoncé was going to be in *Jesus Christ Superstar*," Emma said.

"When they fired Jay-Z, she quit so fast you could feel the wind in the theater after the door slammed behind them," Lola said knowingly. "The biggest star is the one with the control."

There was a crashing sound on the other side of the curtain, and Lola closed the magazine. She moved closer to Emma and pointed to the row of nail polishes.

"You should try the Christmas Burgundy," she said, reading the name on the bottle. "It would look so pretty with your complexion."

"What was that about?" Emma asked when they left the nail salon. Her nails looked lovely under the streetlight, and she thought she'd buy a bottle for Bronwyn as a present.

"Megan was on the other side of the curtain," Lola said.

"How do you know?" Emma gasped.

"I passed the salon when I was coming to see you." Lola skipped along the pavement.

Emma stopped in front of a dress shop. The salesgirl was filling the window with balloons, and there was a gold banner that read HAPPY 2020.

"Lola, please don't tell me you made that up for Megan to hear!" Emma turned to Lola. "If they fire Haley, Alec Baldwin might quit too. And the story about Jay-Z and Beyoncé?"

"I can't remember what I said. Anyway, it doesn't matter whether I did or not." Lola pressed her face against the glass. "I was talking to you in private. It's not my fault if Megan heard us. You're the one who said people shouldn't listen to gossip."

When they got back to The Smuggler's Inn, Lola ran upstairs to find Fletcher, and Emma poked her head in the kitchen.

"There you are. I was hoping you'd be back soon." Betty was standing at the stove. "I took a pork rib eye out of the oven, and wanted someone to taste it. It's on tonight's menu, and I'm afraid I used too much pepper."

"I'd be happy to," Emma said. The counter was scattered with platters of sautéed spinach and sweet corn, along with a cheese board and toasted nuts.

"Stephen was here, and I got inspired." Betty followed her gaze. "He's quite the chef. He gave me some new recipes, and showed me how to roast nuts in the oven."

"Stephen was here?" Emma raised her eyebrows.

"He dropped off some things for the talent show, and brought me a poinsettia," she said, waving at the counter. "We discovered the craziest coincidence: his daughter lives in the same town in New

Jersey as my son! He offered to give me a ride the next time he visits her."

"That's very kind of him," Emma said slowly.

"I miss John terribly, but it's nice to talk to a man." Betty flushed. "I can't help but feel this was all meant to be: not the possibility of losing the inn, but doing the talent show and reconnecting with Stephen."

"Do you believe in that sort of thing?" Emma prodded. "In synchronicity?"

"When I was in the theater, everyone believed in chance happenings. If you didn't, you couldn't go to endless auditions that never amounted to anything except wearing out new pairs of shoes." Betty picked up an oven mitt. "But then one day you got the part in a TV commercial because the girl they wanted had food poisoning, and the director recognized you from the subway when you were reading one of his favorite books." She paused. "If you had been reading anything else, he may not have remembered you, and might have given the job to someone else."

"I hadn't looked at it like that before," Emma mused. "Life has always moved in a straight line for me: go to a college and find a career you love. Then hopefully get married and start a family."

"That's important, but you have to allow for a little magic." Betty scooped up gravy. "If you didn't, life would get quite boring, after all."

After Emma left the kitchen, she went to her room and opened her laptop. The screen flashed, and she pressed the FaceTime icon.

"Emma? Hold on, let me take this thing off." Bronwyn

appeared on the screen. A silk sleep mask covered her eyes, and she was wearing some kind of pajama top.

"Were you asleep?" Emma wondered. "It's six o'clock in the evening."

"I'm adjusting to vacation time." Bronwyn pulled the mask over her forehead. "We leave for The Breakers in the morning."

"Palm Beach is in the same time zone."

"Vacation time is different. The girls get up at six in the morning so they can check out the soaps in the hotel bathtub. They're so worn out from spending the day at kids' club, they pass out before dinner." She patted her hair. "They wake up around midnight starving, so I have to call room service and pay a fortune for two hot dogs and glasses of chocolate milk. I can't wait until Carlton arrives. He's so good at taking care of the girls at night if they get restless so I can sleep."

"I'm sorry, I shouldn't have woken you," Emma said.

"It's fine; I was having a nightmare that Zac Efron was sitting by the pool at The Breakers."

"How could that be a nightmare? He's gorgeous," Emma laughed.

"In the dream I forgot to put on sunscreen," Bronwyn sighed. "I envy women with darker complexions. My skin is that kind of milky white that sounds romantic in a Barbara Cartland novel, but I have to lather on so much protection I look as sexy as Liv when she's covered with diaper ointment."

"I was wondering," Emma began. "Do you really think synchronicity exists?"

"Did something happen with Fletcher?" Bronwyn was completely alert.

"Lola overheard Megan talking to someone on the phone," Emma answered. "Megan was saying that if she doesn't get the lead in the play, she'd wish she hadn't agreed to marry Fletcher."

"I told you!" Bronwyn jumped up. "Megan is going to flounce back to New York and you'll take her place at the dining table before Fletcher notices she's gone."

"Even if Megan leaves, Fletcher hasn't shown any interest in me," Emma said, shaking her head. "And Lola could be wrong about the whole thing—she's not Megan's biggest fan."

"Synchronicity is never wrong," Bronwyn said. "You only have to read Jung to understand. He documents dozens of cases where a convergence of events resulted in a unique outcome."

"I'm not talking about something you studied in college," Emma urged. "Have you seen it happen in real life?"

"I must have told you the story about how Carlton and I met," Bronwyn reflected. "I was at Bloomingdale's, buying sheets for my new apartment. I ended up on the seventh floor instead of the eighth, and then I got on the down escalator by mistake and tried to climb back up. Carlton was on the same escalator going down and he looked at me like I was crazy. Two weeks later we bumped into each other at a Starbucks in Midtown. I had been trying out a new skin product and my cheeks were covered in spots because I had an allergic reaction. A month after that, we were at the same dinner party. He said I was the most memorable person he hadn't actually met, and from that night we were inseparable."

"That's a great story, but I just don't know," Emma said doubtfully. "Fletcher has an ex-wife and a daughter and a demanding career. Even if he was single, there isn't any room in his life for me."

"Fletcher found time to fall in love and get engaged to a woman he barely knew," Bronwyn reminded her. "Reuniting with you will be like slipping on a favorite pair of kid gloves."

"What if you're wrong? Fletcher and Megan are probably just having a tiff, and it will blow over." Emma sighed. "They'll come down to dinner together and Megan will look even more beautiful because she spent another afternoon at the beauty parlor. She'll keep her hand on Fletcher's arm to show she's not angry, and Fletcher won't notice anyone else in the dining room." She groaned. "I should skip dinner and stay in my room."

"Synchronicity can only take you so far, and then you have to do the work," Bronwyn said sternly into the camera. "Take a bath and wash your hair. Put the curling iron on low so you get a few sexy waves. And use that Lancôme deep lash mascara you sent me—it really works." She studied Emma. "Wear something that matches your fingernails. They look gorgeous."

"I got my nails done; it's called Christmas Burgundy." Emma glanced at her nails and felt a little brighter.

"Your burgundy silk blouse would go perfectly. And wear the charcoal jeans," Bronwyn suggested. "How many women our age can wear slim-fit jeans? You have great thighs, and you should show them off."

Emma pressed the END button and gazed out the window. It was dark outside; the stars were diamond buttons on a swath of black velvet.

There were so many unbelievable things she took for granted every day: that when she dialed Bronwyn's number, her voice could be heard across a phone line as if she were in the same room. When she put sliced apples and pie crust in the oven, it miraculously came out as an apple pie. Why shouldn't she believe in synchronicity?

Fletcher's watch lay on the desk, and she rubbed it as if it were a magic genie. She couldn't stay in her room when Betty was serving pork rib eye and all those delicious cheeses. And why shouldn't she wear something festive to dinner? It was Christmas week; it was nice to feel pretty while she was on vacation.

Fourteen

FLETCHER STOOD IN FRONT OF the bathroom mirror and lathered his cheeks with shaving lotion. Megan would be back from the beauty parlor soon, and they would all go downstairs to dinner.

Sometimes a scotch and a hot shower was all he needed to put things in perspective. He and Megan didn't have any problems that couldn't be worked out. And he could tell Lola was happy. She had knocked on his door earlier and said Betty was making pork rib eye and she hoped he was hungry.

The guestroom door opened and he peered into the mirror. Megan was wearing a wool dress and black leggings. Her long legs were showcased by suede boots, and her blond hair fell smoothly down her back.

"Dinner is in half an hour; Betty is cooking up a feast," he called happily. "You don't need to change, you look stunning the way you are."

"When were you going to tell me it would be impossible to let

Haley out of her contract because you'd lose Alec Baldwin, too?"
Megan appeared in the bathroom mirror.

Fletcher's stomach dropped and he put down his razor.

"Where did you hear that?" He turned around.

"It doesn't matter where I heard it. What's important is if it's true," Megan said.

"I told you I had to check with the producers before I could offer you the lead, and that they have the final say," he reminded her.

"But you never said it was virtually impossible!" Megan exclaimed. "You never mentioned that my getting the part was about as likely as Oprah Winfrey wandering into The Smuggler's Inn. Even I understand that the producers can't do anything to upset Alec Baldwin," she said furiously. "You let me believe I had a chance when there was none at all."

"I did try to tell you." He touched her hand. "But the older sister is a great part, and there will be leads in other plays."

"Don't patronize me," she said, snatching away her hand. "When I was younger, directors thought I was too sophisticated to play the ingénue. Soon I'll be thirty, and I'll be too old to be anything but the best friend or some other supporting role. I've spent the last four years humiliating myself at auditions alongside actresses who've never read a book because I want to be a star, not so I can be on the second page of the program."

"You're only twenty-six—there's plenty of time to be a star."

"Maybe in dreary England where they still perform *Twelfth Night* every season, but not in New York. Celebrity is all about youth, and there will come a time when the blond highlights won't distract from the creases on my forehead or the lines around my mouth."

"What are you saying?" Fletcher asked.

"My career is important to me, and I thought it was to you too." She walked into the bedroom and opened the closet. "I'm going back to New York for Jordan Roth's New Year's Eve party. Are you coming?"

Fletcher grabbed a towel and wiped the shaving cream from his cheeks. Megan unzipped her suitcase, and Fletcher felt sorry for her. How could she not see that she was one of the most beautiful women he'd ever met, and that a few wrinkles wouldn't change that?

"I can't leave," Fletcher said. "I promised Lola and Betty I'd help with the talent show."

"Do you remember when we met in that taxi going downtown?" Megan stood up straight. "You were desperate to get to the theater, and I thought I'd found someone like me: someone who wouldn't let a bad back or a sudden downpour or no taxis stand in the way of keeping the most important job in the world. Then we talked in that bar after my performance and I'd never felt so understood. I loved you, Fletcher, and I thought you loved me. But you're putting the problems of someone you barely know before our future."

"I'm doing it for Lola, not Betty," Fletcher corrected. "And we agreed there would be other theater parties."

"You've changed, Fletcher," Megan insisted. "How can you consider getting married in Vermont? Holding our wedding at the Plaza will be one of the best things that happens to our careers. And what about what I want? I've always dreamed of a big church wedding."

"When I was at Tiffany's picking out the ring, I wasn't thinking about the play," Fletcher said stiffly. "And why shouldn't we get married in Vermont instead of New York? We can still get married in a church. Directing the summer festival is tempting. It would be good for Lola to be in the fresh air, and New York is dead in August."

"It can't always be about what's good for Lola. What about what's good for me? I can't imagine wearing a satin Vera Wang gown in a church in Snowberry. If we want fresh air, we can go to the Hamptons, or hope to get invited onto someone's yacht," Megan said, bristling. "Do you really think I'd spend the summer acting with a bunch of has-beens, picking apples for fun and checking my skin for ticks?"

"A lot of renowned actors do summer stock," Fletcher insisted. "When I was at college, I saw Robert Redford perform at a theater in Maine."

"Maybe after I won a couple of Tonys and an Oscar, but not now," Megan said vehemently. "You need to take a look at our future."

"What do you mean?" he asked.

"When you proposed in front of the fountain at Lincoln Center, I imagined attending opening nights and maybe tackling Hollywood together. I was prepared for the hard stuff, too: helping you read scripts and sitting through your rehearsals, even when I only had a few lines. I even enjoyed Lola—she was with her mom most of the time, and when she's around, she's entertaining. But I'm not sure what your priorities are anymore."

"I didn't realize I had to have priorities. I thought it was enough to be in love," Fletcher said before he could stop himself.

"That's the thing about love—you have to actually care about what the other person wants," Megan retorted.

Megan zipped up the suitcase and walked to the door. Her

boots made a clip-clopping sound on the hardwood floor, and every step was a pain in Fletcher's chest.

"It seems we both need to do some thinking. I'm going to Jordan's party. Goodbye, Fletcher, and happy new year." She turned the handle. "I'll give your regards to Jordan, and I hope the talent show is a success."

The door slammed shut, and Fletcher was alone in the room. The navy blazer he was going to wear to dinner lay on the bed next to his dress shirt. He had been going to ask Megan whether the blazer was too formal, and if he should wear his new sweater.

How could he go down to dinner now? Lola would ask where Megan was, and Fletcher would have to say she went back to New York.

He picked up his phone and dialed Graham's number.

"Fletcher," Graham answered. "I'm talking to you more than when you're on the other end of Notting Hill. You're lucky you caught me; I'm having pre–New Year's Eve drinks with a woman I met last night. We were both waiting for the valet, and she accused me of getting into her Mini Cooper. It turns out we had the same car, right down to the racing stripes."

"New Year's Eve isn't for three more nights," Fletcher said.

"If we like each other, we'll progress to dinner, and then the ball at Claridge's on New Year's Eve," Graham explained. "Claridge's is two hundred pounds a ticket, and we agreed it would be foolish to spend that much money unless we're certain we enjoy each other's company."

"She sounds perfect for you," Fletcher chuckled. "Let me guess, she's an analyst, or something else to do with numbers."

"Securities specialist at the Bank of London," Graham clarified. "Why did you call? Is something wrong?"

"Megan left," Fletcher said. "She went back to New York."

"What do you mean, she left?" Graham asked.

"She discovered that the producers would never let Haley go because they'd lose Alec Baldwin too," Fletcher said miserably. "She accused me of leading her on, letting her think she could have the lead in the play."

"Why didn't you tell her the truth?" Graham inquired.

"I tried, but she wouldn't listen. She had this idea that the director could do whatever he wanted." He sighed. "She should never have asked in the first place."

"There's no harm in asking. You begged to direct *As You Like It* when you were barely more than a kid with a few college credits in Shakespeare," Graham reminded him. "It took two more seasons until you were allowed to direct your first play."

"Megan isn't used to being told no," Fletcher said. "She's going to attend Jordan's party alone."

"Are you sure this hasn't something to do with Emma?" Graham prodded. "You spent all day with her yesterday, and—"

"I swear, Emma has nothing to do with this!" Fletcher exclaimed. "Megan said I need to figure out what my priorities are."

There was a silence, and Fletcher wondered if they had lost the connection.

"I'm sorry, Fletcher, but I have to agree with Megan on this," Graham said finally. "For your sake and Lola's, deciding what you want is a very good idea."

Fletcher hung up, and there was a pain between his shoulders as sharp as the icicles hanging from the roof of The Smuggler's Inn. It would be so easy to slip down to the library and bring the bottle of scotch upstairs.

He walked back into the bathroom and lathered his cheeks

with shaving lotion. The least he could do was join Lola for dinner. She was counting on him, and he wouldn't disappoint her.

"Fletcher, Lola, you both look so festive tonight," Betty said, greeting them in the dining room. Fletcher had decided on the new sweater, and Lola was wearing a green velvet dress with red tights. "Where's Megan?"

"She had to go back to New York," he said quickly. "It was an emergency. There was a leak in her apartment."

He told himself he was protecting Lola by lying about the reason Megan left. If he and Megan worked things out, Lola would have worried for nothing. But in reality, he was embarrassed to admit the real reason Megan had gone back to New York.

"It's odd that the doorman didn't take care of the leak," Lola said to Betty. "Megan lives in a fancy apartment building with a doorman like Cammi's father. Cammi's father gives his doorman a Christmas bonus, and the doorman would do anything for him; every time Cammi's grandmother stops by unannounced, the doorman says Cammi's father isn't home."

"Maybe Megan's doorman can't be so easily bribed," Fletcher said under his breath. He took Lola's hand and beamed at Betty. "We just need a table for two."

"I'm afraid all the small tables are taken; I had to turn a couple away." Betty surveyed the room. "Everyone is dining at the inn tonight. I'm glad; I have a special announcement."

Fletcher and Lola sat at a round table, and Fletcher tried to ignore the extra place setting. The room looked so festive, with silver and gold lights twinkling on the Christmas tree and logs crackling in the fireplace.

Betty walked to the front of the room and tapped a fork against a wine glass.

"I want to thank everyone for joining us tonight. I left the kitchen door open so the smell of pork rib eye would entice you, and it seemed to work." She let out a little laugh. "Christmas week has always been my favorite time of the year, because it's a chance to slow down and be with the ones you love. I'm so happy you decided to spend this week at The Smuggler's Inn. There won't be a talent show tonight because I want everyone to rest up for the talent show on New Year's Eve. It's going to be at the Snowberry Playhouse, and I hope you can all join us." She paused and her eyes grew misty. "Events like this make me realize the value of good friends. I'm so grateful to Fletcher and Lola and Emma for helping to save the inn." She waved her hands. "Now, please eat, before the pumpkin soup with sour cream gets cold."

"Emma is here!" Lola swiveled in her chair and pointed to a table in the corner. "We have to ask her to join us."

"No, we don't." Fletcher turned around.

"She's sitting alone, and Betty needs more tables," Lola argued. "If Emma dines with us, Betty can give the table to someone else."

Before Fletcher could protest, Lola darted across the space. Fletcher sipped his water and wished he had followed his original plan of taking the bottle of scotch to his room.

Emma approached the table and Fletcher almost didn't recognize her. Her hair was softly curled, and she was wearing tight-fitting charcoal-colored jeans.

"Hello." She smiled at Fletcher. "Lola made it sound important that I sit with you, but I don't want to interrupt."

"There's nothing to interrupt." Lola sat down. "Megan went back to New York. There was a fire in her apartment."

"It was a leak, not a fire," Fletcher corrected, and wondered why he was so irritable. It wasn't Lola's or Emma's fault that Megan wasn't here.

"I'd love to join you, if it's all right." Emma pulled out a chair. "I eat too much when there's no one to talk to, and I'm going to get fat."

"You look lovely," Fletcher offered, and there was a catch in his throat. "You have the same figure you had in college."

"I doubt that. When I was twenty, I could eat anything," she said and smiled at Lola. "Your father worked at Ye Olde Candy Shoppe, and he'd bring me bags of saltwater taffy."

"Dad's right, you don't have to worry about getting fat." Lola studied Emma critically. "But you're not too skinny like Megan. She's like the models in my mom's fashion magazines. They eat lettuce with a squeeze of lemon for dinner, and they never eat ice cream."

"Megan eats ice cream all the time," Fletcher said, and was suddenly desperate for a drink. Discussing his fiancée who had just stormed off to New York with his daughter and his old girlfriend was more than he could handle.

"If you excuse me, I need something in the library." Fletcher pushed back his chair.

Lola looked at Fletcher and pointed to a cabinet next to the Christmas tree.

"You don't have to drink the scotch in the library. Betty keeps a bottle in the dining room."

"I'm sorry, I didn't mean to be rude," he said when he returned to the table. His chest was warm from the scotch and he felt more in control. "I had a difficult afternoon. There are some issues with the play, but they'll be worked out."

"I'm the same way," Emma said, cutting into her potato. While Fletcher was getting the scotch, the soup had been replaced with pork rib eye, sautéed spinach, and baked potato in its own jacket. "I thought I wouldn't do any work in Snowberry, but there's always new emails."

"Working isn't any fun on vacation." Lola wrinkled her nose. "You should come to see the sled dog races with us tomorrow morning."

"I don't think that's a good idea," Fletcher cut in.

"Why not?" Lola asked. "You said the sleigh was big enough for all of us."

"I've got to make the sets for the talent show. There isn't time to watch the races," Fletcher said too loudly. "And even if there was time, a bunch of dogs yapping in the freezing cold doesn't sound like fun."

An awkward silence settled over the table, and Fletcher felt terrible. He shouldn't have raised his voice, and he shouldn't have snapped at Lola. But the misery of Megan leaving, combined with having to make small talk with Emma, made him feel as gutted as the remains of the baked potato on his plate.

"If you'll excuse me, I promised Betty I'd help with the gingerbread mousse." Emma stood and smiled at Lola. "You should take your father to see the carolers. It's a perfect night to sip apple cider and listen to them sing 'Twelve Days of Christmas.'"

"We already heard the carolers," Lola said stubbornly. "I thought we were going to work on the program after dinner."

"I really have to get some work done," Emma said apologetically.

"And you're lucky to have your dad to yourself at Christmas. You should do something festive."

Fletcher paced around the library and listened to the sound of laughter coming from the dining room. He didn't really want to be in the library; he didn't even want any more scotch. But after the gingerbread mousse, Lola had run upstairs to Skype Cassandra, and Fletcher had no desire to linger with the other guests.

He couldn't remember being so out of sorts. Graham had always marveled at how he stayed calm in any situation. Once a famous actress had run off to Rome the week before the play opened. On opening night, the actress was at the theater waiting for the curtain to go up, and Graham wondered how Fletcher had found her when there were dozens of hotels in Rome. Fletcher explained that only a few hotels could provide the actress the pampering she expected: warm towels spritzed with her favorite perfume, and a pot of tea with brown sugar before bed to help her vocal cords.

No wonder Emma and Lola had left; he'd behaved like a little boy at dinner. But he had glanced from Megan's place setting to Lola's expectant face and felt like a complete failure. At least when he and Cassandra divorced, they'd sat Lola down and explained that it wasn't anyone's fault. He had let his fiancée drive off in the middle of their vacation, and there was no one to blame but himself.

He opened the door of the library and ducked down the hall. The sound of music came from the conservatory and he peered inside. A glass chandelier dangled from the ceiling; one corner of the room was taken up by a Christmas tree, and the fireplace was hung with stockings. Outside the window, the sky was lit with stars.

But none of that registered—not the toy trains arranged under the tree, or the candles flickering on the mantel, or even the sweet scent of mistletoe. All he noticed was a girl sitting at the piano. Her head was bowed, and she wore a burgundy blouse that was as bright as fireflies.

The girl glanced up, and he realized it wasn't a girl at all—it was Emma. She caught his eye and he felt suddenly thrown off-balance, like when he'd first arrived in New York and was always getting on the wrong subway.

"I'm sorry, I didn't know anyone was here," he said, stumbling over his words.

"I finished helping Betty in the kitchen, and didn't feel like going upstairs," Emma answered.

"The piano was always a bigger draw than schoolwork." Fletcher entered the room. "You still play beautifully."

"I'm out of practice," Emma said, shaking her head. "There's not much call for a copywriter to play John Lennon's 'Imagine,' and I could as easily fit a piano into my apartment as an elephant."

Fletcher stood next to the piano and put his hands in his pockets.

"I'm sorry about my behavior at dinner," he began. "Lola was being stubborn, and I—"

"You don't have to apologize," Emma interrupted. "I'm sure a leak in Megan's apartment was upsetting."

"There wasn't a leak, or a fire," Fletcher admitted. "Megan left because she was angry."

"I see . . ." Emma's voice trailed off.

Fletcher didn't know why he wanted to defend himself to

someone he hadn't seen in eleven years. But somehow he couldn't keep silent.

"Megan is very focused on her career," he began. "She was upset that I wanted to help with the talent show instead of attending a theater party in Manhattan."

"You don't need to tell me," Emma said, putting up her hand.

"You and Lola have become friends." He kept talking. "I shouldn't have lied to Lola. I guess I was embarrassed. What kind of guy lets his fiancée leave during a Christmas holiday?"

"I'm sure it wasn't your fault, and Lola loves you no matter what." She looked at Fletcher. "You have a wonderful daughter."

There was something so easy about talking to Emma. He remembered long nights of worrying what they would do after graduation: whether Fletcher could expect to land a theater job, and if Emma would be able to afford to live in Manhattan on whatever salary she earned straight out of college.

"It's been so long since we saw each other," he blurted out.

"We just had dinner. And we spent all day yesterday passing out programs."

"I mean really saw each other," he said, his voice quiet. "More than ten years."

"I really have to do some work." She got up from the piano. "Maybe you should go for a walk. Don't be too hard on yourself." She paused, and he remembered how her smile used to make him happy. "You and Megan are engaged. I'm sure it will all work out."

"Emma," he said, stopping her.

"Yes?" She turned around.

"I don't know if it will work out," he answered. "Megan accused me of not caring about our careers. She said I need to figure out my priorities."

Emma was silent, and he wished he hadn't said anything. His and Megan's relationship had nothing to do with Emma.

"Then you probably should," Emma said finally. "Good night, Fletcher. I'll see you tomorrow."

Fletcher walked down the steps of The Smuggler's Inn and headed toward Main Street. It was the kind of crisp cold he remembered from winter nights at Colby. The clear sky and swath of stars always made it seem warmer from his dorm window, but when he crossed the field to the campus theater or hurried to the library to collect Emma, the freezing air would bite into his clothes.

He just needed to do a few laps around the village green before he went upstairs to Lola. What a miserable evening; first he'd lost Megan, then he'd snapped at Lola, and now he'd poured out his troubles to Emma.

The carolers stood on the stage in front of him, and he wished he had brought Lola. They could have made snowmen and shared molasses cookies.

But he couldn't treat his daughter like a teddy bear he held when something was wrong. He was a grown man; he had to sort things out for himself.

The carolers sang the first verse of "Silent Night"; all around him, families crowded the stage. Christmas lights were strung across the village green, and a vendor was selling cinnamon rolls.

Megan and Graham and even Emma had said he needed to figure out his priorities. He wanted a happy family and a career he enjoyed. And he wanted to spend Christmas with the people he loved.

Fifteen

Two Days Before New Year's Eve
Snowberry, Vermont

EMMA STOOD AT THE SIDEBOARD in the dining room and filled her plate with sausages and scrambled eggs. There was a bowl of granola and pitchers of milk and orange juice.

It was mid-morning, and a few guests were lingering over coffee and the newspaper. A fire crackled in the fireplace, and a soft snow was falling. She was about to sit down when she noticed a small figure sitting at a table by the door. Lola's face was hidden behind a book, her wavy red hair caught by a red ribbon.

"Good morning." Emma approached her. "Do you mind if I join you?"

"Hi." Lola put down the book. "You have to try the English muffins, they're delicious. Betty even bought me some English marmalade from the Snowberry General Store. It's much better than American jam." She sighed theatrically. "Sometimes I miss England so much, especially at Christmas. There's no place like London during the holidays."

"You have to give New York a chance." Emma sat down and glanced at Lola's book. "What are you reading?"

"It's called *Understanding Your Parents During the Divorce*." Lola slid it across the table. "I read a review in the newspaper. Sometimes adults going through a divorce act crazy, and you can't take it personally. Like when my parents don't tell me the truth."

"What do you mean?" Emma asked, forking scrambled eggs onto whole-wheat toast.

"I Skyped my mother last night, and she still didn't mention the new baby," Lola said. "She was standing in the kitchen next to a jar of pickles and an open bag of potato chips. My mother hates pickles, and she would never eat potato chips; she says they're just grease and salt. It must be pregnancy cravings. There was an article in one of my mother's magazines about a pregnant woman who eats two peanut-butter-and-banana sandwiches every night before bed. Ugh, that sounds so mushy."

"I'm sure your mother will tell you soon," Emma said gently. "Maybe she wants to wait until you get home."

"And my father lied to me about the reason Megan left." Lola's face fell.

"How do you know?" Emma asked. "Don't tell me you were listening outside the door."

"I didn't mean to! I swear, it must be fate that makes me overhear all these important conversations. It never happened before I arrived in Snowberry. I was looking for my dad and heard him talking to my godfather on the phone. He was telling Graham why Megan went back to New York, and it wasn't because of a leak in her apartment," Lola said dejectedly. "My father sounded really upset, and whatever Graham said didn't make it better."

"You really have to stop listening to other people's conversations," Emma commented.

"I couldn't just barge into the room, and it was too interesting to leave." Lola ate a bite of muffin. "I don't understand why my father lied. I don't care that Megan left; I know she doesn't like me."

"Of course Megan likes you. And . . . men have their pride," Emma said slowly. "Maybe your dad doesn't want you to think less of him."

"This book says grown-ups are supposed to be wallpaper," Lola sighed. "You don't notice them at all because you're busy being a kid. Even Betty told a fib. She said we had to wait until later to do the programs because she had to go to the market. But when she came into the dining room, she was wearing a white blouse and smelled of perfume. No one wears white to squeeze vegetables, and she wouldn't be able to smell the fruit over her own perfume. She was probably meeting Stephen."

"Maybe you should concentrate on yourself and not worry about the adults," Emma counseled her.

"Someone has to worry about my father. He didn't even realize Megan wanted to marry him to help her career." She pushed back her chair. "I'm going upstairs to finish writing my postcards."

Lola ran upstairs, and Emma cut into her sausage. There was the sound of footsteps, and Fletcher was standing in the doorway, holding a shopping bag.

"Good morning," she said when he approached the table. "You missed Lola; she went upstairs."

"Do you mind if I join you?" he asked. "It's snowing outside, and I could use a cup of coffee."

Emma nodded and Fletcher walked to the sideboard. She noticed how handsome he looked; a scarf was wrapped around his neck, and he was wearing a gray overcoat.

"I went out early and bought Lola a present," he said when he returned. He reached into the bag and brought out a small box. "I bought you something too. It's not much; there weren't a lot of stores open in Snowberry this early."

Emma unwrapped the paper and took out a faux-fur key chain.

"The shopkeeper said holding the key chain is a wonderful way to warm up your hands while you're driving. But then I realized you live in New York, and probably don't drive a car," he said apologetically. "I got Lola a faux-fur bookmark. Half the things in the store were faux fur; there was even a faux-fur laptop case."

"It's perfect, thank you," Emma said, laughing. "You didn't have to get me anything."

"I wanted to thank you for taking care of Lola at kids' club. This is your vacation too, and you've spent almost every afternoon with my daughter," Fletcher said. "And I also wanted to apologize for behaving badly at dinner. Ten years in the theater, and I can't drink more than one scotch. Graham says that's what's holding back my career—many directors only do their best work after they become hopeless alcoholics."

"I've enjoyed spending time with Lola—and your career is doing wonderfully," Emma insisted. "You're having a play produced on Broadway."

"None of that seems important. I'm worried about Lola." Fletcher stirred his coffee. "Megan and Lola and I were going to be a family. Now Megan is gone, and Lola will be disappointed."

"I wouldn't worry about Lola," Emma said. "She seems quite happy."

"It's not easy for a child to go through a divorce. I thought I'd be married forever," he said absently. "But then there was a new girl from Connecticut in Lola's class at school in England. The parents were divorced; the father was designing a museum in London, and the mother worked for some British fashion brand.

"Cassandra began spending less time at the theater; she wanted Lola to have a normal childhood. She started doing things together with the father and the little girl. It began innocently enough: taking the girls to pantomimes in the park, having them around for fish and chips while I was at the theater. The next thing you know, Cassandra and Chuck were in love."

"I'm sorry," Emma said quietly.

"The funny thing was, I had to follow Cassandra to America. Chuck's contract was only for a year, and then he moved back to Connecticut. His ex-wife still lives in London, and Chuck sees his daughter in the summer and on holidays. So Lola's part of this tidy family in Connecticut, but when she's with me we're like a rowboat in Central Park that's missing an oar."

Emma thought about Cassandra having another baby, and wondered how Fletcher would react. But it wasn't her place to tell him, and she wasn't about to cause him more pain.

"I'm sure Lola doesn't see it that way," Emma said. "All she talks about is how she's going to be the biggest star on Broadway."

"Lola likes being with you." Fletcher looked at Emma. "I was wondering if you'd join us at the Vermont Teddy Bear factory this morning."

"I thought you had to work on the sets at the playhouse," Emma reminded him.

"Stephen texted and said he had to run some errands and wouldn't be back until this afternoon."

"Betty put off doing the programs until after lunch, too," Emma said, grinning. "I think there's a budding romance."

"I promised Lola we'd do something fun, and it's too chilly to watch the sled dog races," Fletcher explained. "Please—it would be more fun if you were there."

Fletcher had given her a present, and now he was asking her on an outing. But she didn't know if Megan had left for good, and she didn't want to get hurt.

Fletcher waited for her reply, and she realized she was being ridiculous. They'd spent hours in the village distributing posters, and she hadn't given it another thought. It was only the Vermont Teddy Bear factory, and Fletcher was probably just asking as friends.

"Why not?" Emma shrugged. "I can't be the only person at The Smuggler's Inn working when everyone is playing hooky."

"I'll tell Lola." Fletcher stood up and smiled. "And thank you for listening; I feel much better."

Emma sat at the desk in her room and clicked on her computer. The FaceTime icon blinked and Bronwyn's face appeared. She was wearing a floppy hat and the most incredible sunglasses Emma had ever seen. They were a bronze color, with small rhinestones that glinted at the camera.

"I wasn't sure if you were still on the plane," Emma said. "And where did you get those sunglasses?"

"We arrived half an hour ago," Bronwyn said. "These were in the window at the hotel gift shop. Do you think they're too much?" She peered into the camera. "You should see the women walking through the lobby; they're all incredibly fit, and have perfect tans. I caught my reflection in the revolving doors and saw a pale New York mother who hasn't been in a gym since 2014. I had to buy something to make myself feel better."

"How will they make you feel when you get the room bill?" Emma laughed.

"It's vacation. And Carlton feels so badly about not being here yet, he said I should spoil myself and the girls." Bronwyn smiled. "He really is sweet. The suite was full of flowers when we arrived, and he had the concierge deliver buckets and spades for the girls. They were so thrilled, they couldn't wait to get to the beach."

"You and Carlton are lucky to have each other," Emma agreed. "Fletcher invited me to go to the Vermont Teddy Bear factory."

"The Vermont Teddy Bear factory?" Bronwyn peeled the price tag off her hat. "That sounds as romantic as Carlton asking me to check the blister on his foot after a tennis match. Where's Megan? The last time we talked, Fletcher and Megan were having a tiff, and you were going to wear your most drop-dead outfit to dinner."

"Megan left," Emma answered.

"'Left' as in, she went back a few days early because she had a family emergency? Or 'left' as in, 'I get the Pottery Barn sofa, and you can have the engagement ring back if you really want it'?"

"Fletcher made some excuse that Megan had a leak in her apartment. But Lola is positive it's because she couldn't have the lead in the play," Emma said. "Fletcher was pretty upset. He told me all about his divorce. He thinks it's his fault Cassandra fell in love with another man."

"He discussed Megan and his ex-wife?" Bronwyn said.

"What's wrong with that?" Emma asked.

"He's putting you in the friend zone. He'll come over when you're in New York in rumpled sweats and a baseball cap to hide the fact that he hasn't showered in a week." Bronwyn shuddered. "Your television will be permanently on the History channel, where he'll watch soldiers blowing each other up to remind himself he's still a man. You don't want Fletcher to tell you his problems. You want him to take you to dinner at sexy French restaurants, where you talk about the imbalance of power in America, or whatever single people do on dates until it's time to get in each other's pants."

"I don't have to eat at French restaurants, and I don't want to sleep with Fletcher," Emma said, horrified. "I feel bad for him. He's worried about Lola."

"Of course you want to sleep with him!" Bronwyn exclaimed. "That's why you drove four hours to Vermont. Not *just* to sleep with him, though from his pictures on Facebook, he's pretty hunky. You want a romantic relationship, and that's not going to happen if you're a shoulder to cry on."

"We like listening to each other's problems. Fletcher and I understand each other. That was one of the great things about our relationship."

"Along with the sex. And being in love, and planning a life after graduation," Bronwyn pointed out. "You can't have one without the others."

"I can listen to his problems if we have sex?" Emma asked.

"A little whining while you snuggle is perfectly acceptable," Bronwyn recommended. "When I can get Carlton to stay awake long enough, he's been quite helpful in telling me how to get Marjorie Black to pay her account. Marjorie doesn't want her husband to know she gets microneedling, but he took away her credit cards because she spends more money than a Kardashian."

"Why does this have to be so complicated?" Emma wondered. "When we were in college, we shared everything, and we were happy."

"Everything is more complicated as we get older." Bronwyn studied her reflection in the camera. "These sunglasses make my skin look yellow. I should exchange them for the pair in black. Black is the safest color if you don't have a tan."

Fletcher and Emma and Lola entered the Vermont Teddy Bear factory, and a guide pointed them to the group forming in the lobby.

"I didn't want to go on another boring tour, but this is the opposite of the glassblowing factory," Lola said excitedly. "Did you see the signs when we entered the gates? The tour is led by 'certified bear ambassadors.' There's a gift shop that sells every kind of bear, and we can visit the teddy bear hospital and meet Doctor Traci."

"Doctor Traci?" Emma asked. They were standing in the lobby of an ivy-covered building that resembled something found on a college campus. There were photos of children clutching teddy bears, and a framed diploma stating each bear had a lifetime guarantee.

"Didn't you read the brochure?" Lola asked. She was bundled up against the cold in a purple sweater dress and striped leggings. "Doctor Traci can fix anything. When you bring in your bear, you fill out a form giving the patient's name and age and fur color. I wonder if we could bring Paddington. I'd love to get his toggles sewn on."

A man in a brown uniform wearing teddy bear ears clapped his hands, and Emma and Fletcher and Lola joined the circle.

"Let's start by thanking our parents for bringing us," the man intoned. "You're about to experience the best hour of your lives: We're going to show you how teddy bears are made, and introduce you to some new bears. At the end of the tour you'll make your own bear." He beamed at the group. "Who's ready to become a student at SnowBeary Academy?"

A cheer rose from the children, and Emma stole a look at Fletcher. The pained expression he'd had at breakfast had been replaced by a warm smile.

"Are you ready?" Fletcher took Lola's hand. "We want to get in the front, so we don't miss seeing how they sew on the eyes and nose."

They followed the man through a maze of rooms stuffed with teddy bears. There were bears wearing ski goggles and holding snowboards, and bears dressed as firemen. There was a bear in a pink ballgown and slippers, and a whole section of Christmas bears with reindeer sweaters and red-and-green scarfs.

The tour guide turned them over to Doctor Traci, who led them through the bear hospital and showed them where the patients were brought in. She explained that with careful stitching, most patients made a complete recovery. If they didn't, the child could pick out a new bear free of charge.

"Maybe I should make a bear for Cammi," Lola said when the tour was nearly complete. "They come in four different colors, and for an extra charge they use premium fur."

"Isn't Cammi almost eleven?" Fletcher asked. "She might be too old for teddy bears."

"You're never too old for teddy bears," Lola replied. "I was wondering if I could have a new bear. I mean, I've had Paddington forever." Lola looked at Emma proudly. "Paddington even shook hands with the Queen."

"Your teddy bear met the Queen?" Emma repeated.

"I was invited to a reception at Buckingham Palace a few years ago," Fletcher recalled. "Lola begged me to take Paddington. He was inside my coat; the security guards thought he was some kind of bomb, and wanted to take out his stuffing," Fletcher said wryly.

"I had to beg them not to touch him, or Lola would have been devastated."

Lola went to join the children making bears, and Emma scanned the shelves for teddy bears for Liv and Sarah.

"Children get so attached to their stuffed animals," Emma said to Fletcher. "Last year I went to Disney World with Bronwyn and her children. Sarah left her stuffed giraffe on the ride from *A Bug's Life*. Bronwyn had to stay at the resort with the girls while I combed every ride in the park until I found it."

"You went to Disney World with Bronwyn and her daughters?" Fletcher repeated.

"It was supposed to be a family vacation, but Carlton had a last-minute business trip." Emma nodded. "I didn't mind. But then Liv got an ear infection and spent the last night screaming. Poor Bronwyn. The only thing that quieted Liv down was singing 'It's a Small World After All' while watching the fish tank in the lobby."

"Being around small children is hard work," Fletcher said. "If you enjoy them so much, why haven't you had any of your own?"

Emma was caught off-guard by his question. She put down the orange teddy bear she was holding and turned around. "I told you, I'm not good at relationships. I'll think I've found the right guy, and then at about three hundred and sixty-four days I'll realize I was wrong."

"Every time?" Fletcher asked. "Surely there was one who would have lasted."

"Philip was getting a master's degree in microbiology at NYU, and I thought he was the one," Emma remembered. "But for Christmas he surprised me with a one-way ticket to Angola. He'd received some kind of grant and expected me to come along. I'm sure Angola is fascinating and I admire his work, but I couldn't imagine three years in the jungle without Internet or running water. And then there was Jason," Emma continued. "We made it all the way through New Year's, and I was certain he was going to propose. He called Bronwyn and asked her to take me on a girls' weekend. Bronwyn and I were sure he was going to show up in the Berkshires with a diamond ring, but it turned out an old girlfriend was coming to New York, and he wanted the coast to be clear." Emma flinched at the memory. "Bronwyn helped me clear out his things from my apartment and we donated them to the Salvation Army."

"It sounds like Bronwyn isn't someone you want to cross," Fletcher chuckled.

"She'd do anything for me, and I'd do the same." Emma nodded.

Fletcher was looking at Emma intently. "You've grown even more beautiful over the years, and you have this quiet confidence. I wonder what—"

"Look what I made!" Lola barreled into the room, holding two teddy bears. "California Bear is for Cammi when she grows up and moves to Beverly Hills"—Lola pointed to the bear wearing sunglasses and carrying a pair of roller blades—"and this is Broadway Bear. If you push a button, it plays the theme song from *Annie*."

Emma glanced at Fletcher, but he was flipping through the brochure. Whatever he was going to say had been forgotten.

"I bet these bears are starving," Fletcher said. "Why don't we take them to the Bear Cafeteria and share bear brownies and hot chocolate with whipped cream?"

"That sounds great," Lola agreed. "I can tell you and Emma an idea I had for a Broadway musical. It would be about a bear like Paddington, who arrives at Grand Central Station and can't find his new family."

"That is a good idea." Fletcher took Lola's hand.

"I love the SnowBeary Academy," Lola beamed, reaching out to Emma with her other hand and walking toward the cafeteria. "This is the best morning I've ever had."

Emma sat on the bench in The Smuggler's Inn mudroom and tried to unzip her boots. Lola had run upstairs with her new teddy bears, and Fletcher was taking off his jacket.

"Are you all right?" Fletcher noticed her yanking at the zipper.

"It's stuck," Emma explained. "I have terrible luck with boots."

Fletcher crouched beside her and fiddled with the zipper. He was so close; Emma recognized the scent of his cologne. Suddenly the zipper budged, and the boot slipped off her foot.

"Thank you—I would have been wrestling with it for ages," she said, taking off her other boot.

"Thank you for coming this morning," Fletcher said, nodding. "Lola and I are having dinner tonight at Le Soufflé in Dorset. Would you join us?"

"I don't think so." Emma shook her head. "I should catch up on my work."

"It can't be that urgent," Fletcher urged. "Please come. It's hard to share a soufflé with just two people."

Fletcher looked at her with the blue eyes she knew so well. Why shouldn't she have dinner with Fletcher and Lola, and there were only two more days in Snowberry before New Year's Eve.

"All right—I'll go." Emma nodded.

"Excellent." Fletcher smiled. "I'm going upstairs to brush up on my French. I don't want to embarrass Lola by ordering the wrong kind of soufflé."

Emma entered her room and dropped the teddy bears for Liv and Sarah on the bed. Bronwyn had said she shouldn't enter the friend zone, but touring SnowBeary Academy with Fletcher and Lola had been fun. And Fletcher had asked her out to dinner.

She looked in her closet for something to wear, and was surprised by how excited she was. For a moment, she didn't care what Bronwyn thought. She enjoyed being with Fletcher and Lola, and that was all that mattered.

Sixteen

Two Days Before New Year's Eve
Snowberry, Vermont

FLETCHER STOOD IN THE SNOWBERRY Playhouse, studying the stage. He had worked all afternoon, creating a podium and stringing up fairy lights. A Christmas tree had been donated by the Snowberry Tree Farm, and there was a rocking chair in case any of the performers wanted to sit down.

Megan hadn't called or texted since she left for New York. He could call his therapist, Margaret, but would she be able to help? It was up to him and Megan to work through their problems.

He punched in Megan's number and waited; it went straight to voicemail.

"Megan, it's me, Fletcher," he said into the phone. "I just wanted to check that you got back to New York safely. Please call me; we need to talk."

He pressed END, and debated sending a text. But you couldn't solve relationship problems in a small bubble on a screen.

He closed his phone and his mind wandered to this morning with Emma and Lola at the Vermont Teddy Bear factory. It had been a perfect morning. And it wasn't just because Emma was so easy to talk to, or because Lola had seemed like all the other children instead of a little girl who'd moved across the ocean because her parents got divorced. It was also unzipping Emma's boots in the mudroom. He hadn't meant to ask her to dinner, but suddenly—being so close to her—he'd wanted to see her again.

Fletcher took out his tape measure to measure the stage and recalled his last college production at Colby. Would everything have turned out differently if he hadn't worked night and day, with barely any time to see Emma?

May, 2008
Waterville, Maine

Fletcher wiped the sweat from his forehead and glanced at his watch. It was six o'clock at night, and he hadn't stopped all day except to eat a sandwich at lunchtime. Even that had been unsatisfying. His food allowance at the college cafeteria had run out, so he kept a loaf of white bread and a container of SPAM in his dorm room. It would have tasted decent with mayonnaise, but that would have meant paying for a mini fridge, and he was trying to save every penny.

This was the last production of his college career, and he was directing a full-length performance of *Romeo and Juliet*. He had hoped it would have been one of the easier plays; most students read *Romeo and Juliet* in high school, and everyone could relate to the star-crossed lovers. But the set designer had finished his exams early and gone home, so Fletcher was stuck painting backgrounds and building furniture.

In the hours that he wasn't at the theater, he stood behind the counter of Ye Olde Candy Shoppe. He'd asked the owner for extra shifts, and so for the last three weekends, he'd doled out licorice sticks until there were cramps in his hands and he could barely read the numbers on the cash register.

It would all be worth it when he marched into the travel agent's office in Waterville and bought Emma a plane ticket to London. It was only two weeks until graduation, and he wondered again if he should have told her about Harry's offer. But what if he couldn't earn enough for the plane ticket? It would be better to explain the whole story when she was holding the British Airways ticket in her hand, along with a photo of the garden flat in Notting Hill he'd found for them to rent. Besides, what if Emma got the job offer in New York? He didn't want to say anything until he was certain he could make London work if she agreed to join him.

Fletcher remembered when the large airmail envelope had appeared in his mailbox two weeks ago. Inside was a one-way ticket to London, with a letter from Harry Stone.

Dear Fletcher,

It was a pleasure meeting you at Colby. I was quite serious about the job offer as assistant director at the Old Vic. I've been looking for someone who can make Shakespeare appeal to the younger crowd, and you're perfect for the position.

Next season we're attempting *Two Gentlemen from Verona*, and if that doesn't entice you, I'm considering doing Somerset Maugham's *The Sacred Flame*. It's a wonderful play about World War 1, and you'll welcome the chance to dress the actors in English uniforms and not have them speak Shakespearean English.

I have enclosed a paid one-way ticket to London. My son William has decided to stay in America after graduation, so I can also offer you the downstairs bedroom in our flat for as long as you need it. I am hoping you will respond with your arrival time at Heathrow Airport.

Cheers,
Harry Stone

Would Emma come with him to England? She'd had an interview with Ogilvy & Mather in New York a couple of weeks ago, but she hadn't heard anything. There were bound to be job opportunities in London. They could live there for a couple of years, and then come back to New York.

Fletcher had almost told her about Harry's offer, but what was the point? She couldn't afford a plane ticket, and they couldn't live in William Stone's downstairs bedroom. He had to present her with everything already paid for, and hope that being together was more important than her dream of living in New York.

There were footsteps, and he turned around. Emma stood in the doorway, carrying a picnic basket. She was wearing a cotton blouse and floral skirt, and Fletcher was reminded of her beauty.

"Hi there," he greeted her. "I'd come and kiss you, but any sharp movement might result in a permanent back sprain."

"You're the director," Emma said, noticing the hammer and nails he was holding. "You're not supposed to build the set."

"The director does everything. Yesterday I had to write the last paragraph of the lead actor's history paper so he doesn't fail and get kicked out of school before the play. And tomorrow I have to find a car to pick up the accompanist's hay fever medicine, because he has allergies and I'm afraid he'll sneeze his music off the stand."

"You can't write another student's paper. You'll get expelled." Emma walked down to the stage and kissed him.

"It was only five sentences. It will be okay." He kissed her back. "Whatever is in the basket smells too good; it might make me do something I'll regret."

"We can't make love here," Emma laughed. "Someone might find us."

"That sounds tempting. But I was thinking of taking a break and eating everything in the picnic basket. Then the set won't be ready for the dress rehearsal."

"You have to eat." She handed him sourdough bread piled with ham and Swiss cheese. There was a thermos of tomato soup and two slices of chocolate cake.

"God, you know my weaknesses," Fletcher groaned, taking a bite of the sandwich.

"I certainly hope so," Emma said happily, biting into her own sandwich. "If I don't know them all yet, I plan on learning them in the future."

This was the perfect time to tell Emma about Harry's letter.

But he still had to work four more shifts at Ye Olde Candy Shoppe to be able to afford her plane ticket. All he had to do was keep the secret for another week, and then he would tell her everything.

"Any word from Ogilvy & Mather?" he asked casually.

Emma stopped chewing and her face clouded over. She wiped her mouth, and her lovely shoulders moved up and down.

"Nothing yet." She shook her head. "I should be setting up other interviews, but I just keep hoping they'll call."

"It's hard to schedule interviews from Maine. It's better to wait until we graduate," Fletcher said quickly. "Anyway, I'm sure you'll get the job."

"What if I don't?" Emma said, uncertain. "My parents are coming for graduation. If I don't have a job, they'll whisk me back to Wisconsin and make me work as a receptionist in my uncle's dentist office."

"Let's not think about that now. You are about to finish your thesis, tomorrow night is the dress rehearsal, and soon this will all be over." He gestured to the rest of the theater. "We don't want to look back on this time in ten years and regret we didn't enjoy it."

"In ten years?" Emma looked up from her sandwich.

"When you're a hugely successful copywriter and I'm directing plays that receive amazing reviews, and neither of us think anything of buying champagne and caviar."

"I don't see us as champagne-and-caviar kind of people." Emma smiled.

"Neither do I." Fletcher took a bite of chocolate cake. "A lot can change in ten years. Except for the way I feel about you; that will never change."

"It better not," Emma returned, wiping frosting from her lips. "Because then I'll be stuck with a case of unrequited love. I know from reading *Wuthering Heights* that it's the most painful thing in the world."

Two Days Before New Year's Eve
Snowberry, Vermont

The door of the Snowberry Playhouse opened and Fletcher heard footsteps. For a moment he thought it was Emma, but Stephen appeared in the aisle.

"You're still here," Stephen said. "You were holding that tape measure when I left."

"Stringing fairy lights took longer than I thought," Fletcher agreed. "I'm almost done for tonight."

"I just came from The Smuggler's Inn." Stephen joined him at the front of the theater. "Betty and Emma and Lola have been brainstorming all afternoon. They suggested we have someone dress as Santa Claus and hand out presents. Lola said, the more festive we make it, the more money people will donate."

"She's right," Fletcher chuckled. "Christmas is the season of giving."

"Lola is a special girl," Stephen mused. "I wish you would consider directing the summer festival; Lola would love it. I'm in talks with Nathan Lane to play Bottom in *A Midsummer Night's Dream*."

"I love Nathan Lane! That's fantastic," Fletcher said, marveling at the thought of directing one of his favorite Broadway actors.

The Snowberry Playhouse would be too hot in the summer, and he'd go to bed every night covered with mosquito bites. But Vermont would be lush with foliage, and Lola could ride horses and swim in the lake.

"I will think about it," Fletcher said firmly. "Right now I have to get back to The Smuggler's Inn. I'm taking Lola out for soufflé. If I don't shower, they might not let me into the restaurant."

Fletcher knocked on the door of Lola's room. It was seven o'clock, and their dinner reservations were in half an hour.

"What are you doing?" Fletcher asked when he finally opened the door. "You're not dressed."

"I *am* dressed." Lola looked up from arranging teddy bears on the bed. "I'm wearing jeans and the shirt I made at Color Me Mine."

"You're not dressed for dinner." Fletcher caught his own reflection in the mirror. He was wearing a leather jacket and twill slacks. "Le Soufflé is pretty fancy, and it's freezing outside. You need a coat and mittens."

"I can't go to dinner. Betty and I are having a teddy bear party."

"A teddy bear party?" Fletcher perched on the bed.

"Betty has an attic full of teddy bears. We're going to stitch them up and donate them to SnowBeary Academy. They give them to families who can't afford to buy their own bears," Lola explained. "Then we're going to have a welcome dinner for my new bears, Tiffani and Tasmin. Tiffani is California Bear, because girls in California all have names like Tiffani that end in the letter *I*. And Tasmin is Broadway Bear, because when I have a little girl I want to name her Tasmin."

"Aren't you a little young to think about having children?" Fletcher asked with a smile.

"Yes, but time flies. Next month I'll be ten, and before you know it I'll graduate from high school." Lola snapped her fingers. "I bet that's how you feel when you're with Emma."

"What do you mean?" Fletcher asked.

"That it was only yesterday you were both in college, and now you're in your thirties." Lola's nose twitched the way it did when she was concentrating on something. "Has Emma changed? Did she always have such long lashes, and was her hair always shiny?"

"I have no idea—I hadn't noticed," Fletcher said abruptly. "I better tell Emma dinner is canceled."

"You can't cancel dinner!" Lola jumped up. "I mean . . . that wouldn't be polite. You two can go without me."

"I don't think so." Fletcher pictured sitting across from Emma at a candlelit table. "The three of us can go another night."

"There's only two more nights, and we'll be busy with the talent show," Lola said urgently. "Emma was looking forward to it."

"Emma said she was looking forward to it?" Fletcher repeated.

"Emma's never had soufflé, and she always wanted to try it." Lola sank back onto the bed with a smile on her face. "Can you imagine never having had soufflé? I'm so glad you and Mom took me to Paris. Cammi has never been to Europe."

"I'll tell you what—why don't you and Betty and the teddy bears join us?" Fletcher suggested.

"You want the teddy bears to eat at Le Soufflé?" Lola's eyes were wide. "I guess we could. But Betty and I would have to eat with the bears. There wouldn't be room for everyone at the same table."

"It's a deal." Fletcher shook Lola's hand. "You go tell Betty and round up the teddy bears, and I'll tell Emma about the change of plans."

Fletcher waited in the parlor of The Smuggler's Inn, fiddling with a shot glass. What would he and Emma talk about without Lola's constant chatter? And what if Megan called or texted? She hadn't returned his call, and there was a photo of her on Instagram getting into a town car. She was wearing a cocktail dress and diamond teardrop earrings that he had never seen before.

There was the sound of heels on a hardwood floor, and Fletcher looked up. Emma stood at the top of the staircase in a navy coat. Her hair was pinned back, and she was wearing gold earrings.

"Where's Lola?" she asked when she reached the living room.

"She's getting Betty and the teddy bears. I hope you don't mind." His eyes twinkled. "They were going to have a tea party, and I asked them to join us instead."

"Why should I mind?" Emma laughed. "I loved the whole morning at the teddy bear factory."

"I hoped you'd say that." Fletcher grinned. "Don't worry—Lola insisted that she and Betty and the bears have their own table."

"I'm glad we came," Fletcher said to Emma, scooping up a spoon-ful of goat cheese soufflé with fig jam. The table was set with a silver bread basket, and there was a bowl of spinach salad with wal-nuts and slices of orange. Betty and Lola and the teddy bears were sitting at a round table on the other side of the restaurant.

The dining room of Le Soufflé was like something out of a French guidebook. The stone floor was strewn with woven rugs, and brass pots were hung from the ceiling. The waiter had suggested a French cabernet to accompany the soufflé, and Fletcher sipped his wine and enjoyed the warmth rising from the fireplace.

"I'm glad too," Emma replied, glancing across the room to where Lola was feeding soufflé to a teddy bear. "Betty and Lola have grown very fond of each other. Betty bought Lola's favorite English toffees from the General Store, and Lola drew a map of places for Betty to see if she ever visits London."

"I was at the playhouse this afternoon and ran into Stephen," Fletcher added. "He thinks it would be wonderful for Lola to spend the summer in Vermont."

"Are you considering it?" Emma asked. "I thought Megan wanted to get married at the Plaza."

"I don't know if that's going to happen." Fletcher took out his phone and flipped to the photo of Megan on Instagram. "Megan has only been gone for a day, and she seems to have forgotten us. She was all dressed up and getting into a town car."

"That is a gorgeous dress," Emma said, glancing at the phone. "But she could have been going anywhere."

"I know Megan's jewelry, and I've never seen those diamond earrings before," Fletcher remarked.

"Are you saying someone bought them for her?" Emma asked.

"I don't know. It doesn't really matter. What's important is Lola," he replied. "Megan has to see that Lola comes first; that's what having children is about."

"But you haven't broken it off?" Emma asked. "There is a chance you'll work things out."

"Megan and I haven't spoken since she left," Fletcher admitted. "My friend Graham will shoot me if we end the engagement. Megan is educated and beautiful and talented." He smiled wryly. "He thinks she's a miracle, and I would be a fool to mess it up."

"I know what you mean," Emma said, drinking her wine. "Bronwyn would be furious if she knew we were talking about Megan and Lola."

"Why would she be angry?" Fletcher asked.

Emma blushed the color of the wine. She took another sip and leaned forward. "I shouldn't tell you this, and I may have drank my wine too fast, but she's worried that if we don't discuss other things you'll think that I'm boring."

Fletcher noticed the impish smile on Emma's lips and laughed.

"You're not the sort of woman who could ever be boring," he responded. "But we can talk about something else."

"I don't mind," Emma said, suddenly serious. "I liked hearing about your problems in college. Don't you remember? The theater was more interesting than repressed sexuality in nineteenth-century English literature."

"I don't know. I enjoyed it when you read *Lady Chatterley's Lover* out loud," Fletcher returned. He reached across the table and touched Emma's hand before he could stop himself. "It is good to see you; you make me happy."

Emma busied herself dipping French bread into the soufflé, and there was an awkward silence.

"Tell me about yourself," Fletcher said, changing the subject. "All I know is that you live in New York, and you don't mind being with a screaming two-year-old at Disney World."

"I adore being a godmother," Emma acknowledged. "But I enjoy other things; I love window-shopping on Fifth Avenue, and attending outdoor concerts in Central Park." She paused. "And I like my job. Writing copy to sell cosmetics might sound frivolous, but it's never boring, and I'm quite good at it."

"I'm sure you are." He leaned back in his chair. "And it doesn't sound frivolous. I stand in the back of a theater and watch people act out stories that have nothing to do with real life. At least you help women feel good about themselves."

"I hadn't thought about it like that," Emma mused. "You're doing what you always wanted to do: helping a theater full of people escape their lives for a couple of hours."

"We both are where we wanted to be." Fletcher finished his wine. "Except for the fact that my fiancée would rather be at some theater party than a romantic Vermont inn, and your boyfriend is sitting on a beach in Maui without you."

"Except for those two things, yes," Emma said, and the impish smile was back on her face. "Life turned out just the way we planned."

After dinner, Betty and Lola and the teddy bears took a sleigh back to The Smuggler's Inn, and Fletcher and Emma strolled through the village of Dorset. They saw a covered bridge and clapboard houses strung with Christmas lights, and the Christmas tree in the village square. Behind them, the snowy hills were dotted with barns.

"I should have made Betty and Lola stay," Fletcher said. "Dorset is so pretty at night."

"Apparently the teddy bears have a bedtime that can't be missed." Emma grinned. "But actually, I think we've been set up."

"What do you mean?"

"Lola is concerned that without Megan, you'll get lonely," Emma explained. "And she knows we were friends in college."

Fletcher let that sink in. "She asked me if I thought you'd changed," he recalled. "She wondered if your eyes always had such thick lashes, and if your hair was always so shiny."

Emma was quiet. Fletcher heard the clip-clopping of horses. A sleigh drove by with a young couple huddled under blankets.

"I said I hadn't noticed, but that's not true." He stopped walking and gazed at Emma. The night air was crisp, and it suddenly felt so romantic: the velvet sky and stars like diamonds, the Christmas tree lit with colored lights.

"I did notice. You're even more beautiful than in college. Your cheekbones are more defined, and your eyes are even bigger than I remember." He touched her cheek.

Emma was completely still, and Fletcher wanted nothing more than to kiss her. But red and green lights lit up the sky, with the sound of something popping.

"What's that?" Emma jumped away.

"It's fireworks." Fletcher gazed at the silver rockets sizzling above them. "The village of Dorset has a fireworks display every night between Christmas and New Year's. There's a parade and free Christmas cookies. I thought Lola would enjoy it, but we can stay and watch them."

Emma looked at Fletcher and there was something new in her eyes.

"I should go back to the inn," she said, shaking her head. "I need to finish some work."

"During Christmas week?" Fletcher said wonderingly. "Nothing can be that urgent."

Emma tightened her coat and smiled. "That's what Lola said, but it really can't wait. Thank you for a lovely evening."

Fletcher unwound his scarf and draped it on the bed in his room. It wasn't late, but he didn't feel like sipping brandy in the library. And he didn't want to talk to anyone. Thankfully, Betty and Lola were in the attic putting the teddy bears to bed when he arrived.

Would he have kissed Emma if the fireworks hadn't started? How would she have responded? Her work couldn't have been so urgent; she merely wanted an excuse to end the evening. Was that because she didn't enjoy his company, or did she have feelings for him and was afraid to act on them?

And then there was Megan. He couldn't just follow her Instagram feed; he had to make a decision about their relationship. Either they had to talk things out, or admit it was over.

He picked up his phone and called Megan's number.

"Hello." Her voice came over the line.

"I'm glad I caught you—it's Fletcher."

"I know it's you," Megan said. "Why are you calling? Did you decide to come back to New York?"

"You know I can't do that." Fletcher gripped the phone. "And besides, what if I had? It seems you were out all night."

"Have you been spying on my Instagram?" Megan demanded.

"You didn't respond to my voicemail, and it came up on my feed." Fletcher paused. "But if you think it's spying, I've answered my own question."

"What do you mean?" Megan asked.

"Couples in love don't spy on each other," Fletcher returned. "Maybe you were right—I needed to get my priorities straight. We tried to want the same things, but it didn't work. I have to put Lola first, and you can't see beyond your own ambitions."

"You've made yourself perfectly clear," Megan snapped. "I'll leave the engagement ring on the kitchen counter, with all your passwords. It's late, and I'm going to bed."

Fletcher hung up and paced around the room. Thank god the scotch was all the way downstairs in the library; it would have been too easy to reach for a glass. But then he thought about Emma in her red dress with the fireworks going off behind her, and realized he didn't need a scotch at all. Perhaps there was some kind of magic Christmas spell over The Smuggler's Inn, because right this moment, he'd never felt better.

Seventeen

One Day Before New Year's Eve
Snowberry, Vermont

EMMA SAT AT THE DESK in her room and tapped at the computer keyboard. It was mid-morning, and the sky was a cobalt blue usually reserved for photos of glamorous ski resorts in magazines. Emma always envied the models in those photos, their cheeks bronze from skiing; they held coffee mugs as big as cereal bowls, looking happy and relaxed.

Instead of sitting by an après-ski fire, she was sitting alone in her room, thinking up copy to sell lipstick. She hadn't been completely honest with Fletcher last night. Her boss Helen wasn't expecting the copy until next week. But Emma had been afraid that Fletcher might try to kiss her, and she needed an excuse to go back to The Smuggler's Inn.

Had Fletcher been trying to kiss her? He'd stood so close, and then the fireworks had started and she'd jumped. She couldn't kiss him; he was still engaged to Megan. But it had been a lovely evening; the moment had felt so heady, with the twinkling lights on the Christmas tree and the diamond-painted sky.

There was a knock at the door, and Emma wondered if it was Fletcher.

"Can I come in?" Lola poked her head inside.

"What a pretty dress," Emma commented when Lola entered the room, wearing a red pinafore with a Peter Pan collar and oversized pockets.

"My mother made it." Lola perched on the bed. "We were supposed to Skype this morning, but I overslept. By the time I called, she was out."

"You overslept?" Emma repeated. "I thought all children woke up at the crack of dawn. Bronwyn has to wear a sleep mask because Sarah comes in at six in the morning and opens the curtains."

"I went to bed late." Lola stifled a yawn. "Stephen showed up as we were finishing putting the teddy bears to bed. He told Betty they needed to go over the donations, but that's not why he came. Knowing how many T-shirts with pictures of moose the Stowe Mercantile Company is donating could have waited until morning."

"Why do you think Stephen was there?" Emma asked.

"To see Betty. Betty got all flustered and went to the bathroom to reapply her lipstick. Who puts on lipstick before they go to bed?" Lola wrinkled her nose. "I wouldn't have minded, but he interrupted our bedtime stories for the teddy bears. We hadn't finished reading *Peter Rabbit*."

"Maybe he was in the neighborhood and decided to stop by," Emma suggested.

"We're in Vermont. You need to put on a coat and mittens just to walk outside," Lola reminded Emma. "Then Betty asked if he'd join her for a cup of coffee, and I knew he'd be there a while."

"Why would you think that?" Emma wondered.

"Betty doesn't drink coffee at night; it keeps her awake," Lola finished knowingly.

"Stephen seems very nice," Emma said, smiling.

"I'm glad for Betty; she misses being someone's wife," Lola agreed. "When I went to bed, the light in my dad's room was off. He must have got back early."

"We came back to The Smuggler's Inn right after we walked around Dorset." Emma felt herself blushing. "I had to do some work."

"I thought you and Dad would have lingered. Dorset is so pretty at night, and they have fireworks in the village square. Betty showed me in a brochure."

"Lola, were you trying to set us up?" Emma said suspiciously.

"I'm nine years old." Lola fiddled with her pockets. "I don't know what you mean."

"Just because Megan left, it doesn't mean they've broken up." Emma ignored her comment. "And even if they do, your father and I are just friends."

"Of course they've broken up," Lola insisted. "And I know my father likes you. He gets this distracted look when I mention your name."

Emma turned back to her laptop. "I don't have time to talk about it. I have to finish some work."

"What's the ad for?" Lola pointed at the photo of a model wearing a hooded jacket. The only color on her face was a bright red lipstick.

"It's a new lipstick called Christmas Red. I've been staring at it for hours, and I can't think of a thing to write."

"What do you usually do when you're stuck?" Lola asked.

"Walk past the windows on Fifth Avenue, or take the escalator up and down Bloomingdale's," Emma mused. "But you won't see women in designer heels strutting down Main Street in Snowberry, and the General Store doesn't sell couture."

"You could visit the outlet stores in Manchester," Lola suggested. "Betty says they carry all the big names, like Ralph Lauren. She's going to take me there if we're here next summer. I'll be ten and a half, and she said she'd buy me some pretty perfume."

"The outlet stores—that is a good idea." Emma grabbed her jacket.

"You're going now?" Lola asked. "Betty wanted to go over the contestants' song selections."

"It can wait until after lunch," Emma said sweetly. "It won't make a difference if they're performing 'Jingle Bells' or 'God Rest Ye Merry Gentlemen.'"

A taxi deposited Emma at the outlet stores, and she zipped up her jacket. Manchester was charming, with its quaint brick buildings and iron park benches covered in snow. A giant sleigh was parked in the middle of the village square, and a banner welcomed visitors to the friendliest town in southern Vermont.

Lola had been right: there was a whole row of designer stores. The window of Ralph Lauren held piles of ski sweaters, the mannequins in Armani were draped in cocktail dresses for New Year's Eve, and Eddie Bauer had displays of hats and mittens.

In the past when Emma strolled through the department stores, ideas had flowed faster than she could jot them down. She recalled an ad she'd created for Lancôme Splash-proof Mascara; it had a photo of a couple playing tennis, with the copy: STEP UP YOUR GAME WITH LANCÔME SPLASH-PROOF MASCARA. The woman in the ad wore a pleated tennis dress, and the man had a sweater draped around his shoulders. A butler stood on the sidelines, holding two champagne flutes.

There was the ad that had proved so popular for Sunkissed perfume, with two couples on a yacht and the copy: SUNKISSED: FOR WHEN YOU'RE RUBBING SHOULDERS WITH THE JET SET. Emma had gotten the idea from the Donna Karan cruise collection at Saks.

But now she trudged past the pleated slacks at Theory and the quilted jackets at Kate Spade and her mind stayed completely blank. She was about to give up and get a cup of coffee when she noticed a familiar figure wearing a dark overcoat. Emma recognized Fletcher.

"Fletcher?" she called. He turned, looking so handsome with his collar pulled up against his cheeks.

"Emma." He approached her. "This is a surprise."

Emma suddenly wondered if Lola was up to mischief again. "Don't tell me Lola told you . . ."

"I left the inn before Lola woke up." He shook his head. "I needed to do some shopping. Why are you here?"

"I've been trying to write copy for a new lipstick," Emma explained. "Usually seeing beautiful clothes gives me inspiration, but it's not working. I was about to get a cup of coffee and go back to the inn."

"Why don't we have coffee together?" Fletcher suggested.

"I suppose so." Emma shrugged. "I'm not getting anything done, and Lola and Betty and I aren't meeting until after lunch."

"Excellent!" He beamed. "You can help me shop first. I need a tuxedo for New Year's Eve. I just remembered that my only tuxedo never made it over from England."

Emma was about to ask why he needed a tuxedo, and stopped.

Perhaps Megan had called this morning and begged him to go to the New Year's Eve party.

"I don't know if I have time," Emma said, her resolve wavering.

"Please? I'm terrible at choosing my own clothes." Fletcher took her arm. "Don't you remember how in college I had to attend a dinner for the theater department, and couldn't find anything to wear?"

Emma recalled combing the thrift stores together for a dinner jacket. All the jackets Fletcher tried on had been too narrow, with ragged stitching. Then Emma had noticed a midnight-blue jacket with red piping. Fletcher slipped it on and Emma thought he resembled an old-fashioned matinee movie idol.

"All right," she said reluctantly.

They strolled through Brooks Brothers and admired the starched shirts and silk bow ties. At Armani, Fletcher tried on a black tuxedo that made him look like a young Gregory Peck. Emma matched it with a camel-colored scarf and tasseled loafers.

"Thank you. If you weren't here, I'd still be struggling to find a shirt with proper cuffs," he said, collecting their parcels. "Let's buy something for you." He wandered to the women's section and pointed to a red dress. "This would look wonderful with your hair."

"Why do I need a dress?" Emma asked, puzzled.

"Betty wants everyone to dress up," Fletcher said. "Maybe you brought something with you. We could buy a pretty wrap. Stephen said the theater will be heated, but every time I've been there, it's freezing."

"You bought the tuxedo to wear to the talent show?" Emma inquired.

"Why else would I buy it?" Fletcher asked. "Betty and Lola think if everyone is feeling festive, they'll be willing to donate more money."

Why hadn't Betty told her the attire was going to be formal? But she couldn't think about that now; she was heady with relief that Fletcher wasn't returning to New York.

"I thought Megan called, and you were going to the party in New York after all." She looked at Fletcher.

"I called Megan last night," Fletcher said slowly. "She's going to leave the engagement ring on the kitchen counter, along with the extra key and the passwords to Netflix and Hulu."

"I'm sorry," Emma replied.

"It's for the best," Fletcher said. "I had already decided to take Stephen up on his offer this summer, and I couldn't have planned a wedding from Vermont."

"Oh, I see," Emma said, and felt oddly disappointed. "Lola will be thrilled. All she talks about is learning to fish. And Betty wants to teach her to make ice cream."

"That's not the only reason I broke it off." Fletcher was still talking. "There's something else."

"Something else?" Emma whispered.

"I want to ask you to be my date for the talent show," Fletcher said. "And I don't want anything standing between us."

Fletcher touched her arm and the air rushed out of Emma's lungs. She looked up and her face broke into a smile.

"I'd love to be your date," she said and laughed. "But you're right. I don't have anything to wear."

"Then we're in the right place." Fletcher smiled. "I'll sit here, and you can try on some dresses."

"Won't that be boring?" Emma wondered.

"I am a father, and Lola does like to shop." He grinned. "I'm used to spending an hour in a department store."

Emma tried on a green velvet dress and a silver gown with a

shirred bodice. She finally settled on a red silk dress and paired it with a gold wrap.

"I feel more festive already," Emma said after the saleswoman returned her credit card. "I should get back to the inn. Betty and Lola and I still have work to do."

"I'd share a cab, but I have to pick up some props for the play-house," Fletcher said when they walked outside. The snow was thick on the pavement and the whole world was a bright white. "Would you like to have dinner tonight?"

"I'd love to." Emma nodded happily. "Tell Lola to pick some-where that serves soups and salads. If I eat any more burgers or waffles, I'm going to get fat."

"I wasn't planning on bringing Lola," Fletcher said. "I thought it could be the two of us."

Emma looked at Fletcher and felt a flutter of excitement mixed with nerves.

"The two of us sounds perfect," she agreed before she could chicken out. "I'll see you later."

Emma hung the red dress in her closet and perched on the bed. She wanted to show it to Bronwyn, but when she FaceTimed her there was no answer. Bronwyn would have clapped her hands and pointed out that synchronicity was working. First Emma had found Fletcher's watch in the jewelry store in the East Village. Then Me-gan and Fletcher had had a falling-out, and now Fletcher had asked Emma to dinner. Even running into Fletcher at the outlet stores this morning was synchronicity.

Was it possible that she and Fletcher had a future? Being with Fletcher was the same as when they were in college: completely comfortable and thrilling all at once. None of the guys she'd dated over the years made her feel the same: not Theo, who'd graduated from Harvard with a Boston accent like a Kennedy; or Enrico, who came from Cuba and was part owner in a trendy nightclub; or Sylvan, who had the thickest eyelashes and loved to cook.

When Emma told her the news, Bronwyn would start picking out flower girl dresses for Liv and Sarah to wear to Emma and Fletcher's wedding. But Emma had never told Bronwyn the real reason she and Fletcher had split up. It wasn't just the five thousand miles that had separated them when he left for London and she moved to New York. It was what happened before.

She picked up Fletcher's watch and remembered the night one week before graduation, when the campus was filled with seniors eager to start their new lives, and the future was as bright as the spotlights on the stage.

May, 2008
Waterville, Maine

Emma entered Fletcher's dorm room, surveying the bed strewn with textbooks and the pile of T-shirts waiting to be taken to the laundry.

Tonight was the opening of *Romeo and Juliet,* and Fletcher had asked Emma to bring a copy of the script he left on his desk. She caught her reflection in his closet mirror and was pleased she had dressed up. The green dress accentuated the tan she'd gotten while studying on the lawn, and the low-heeled sandals made her bare legs look sexy.

It was Fletcher's last play, and Emma had reserved a table at Cucina's in Waterville to celebrate. She'd called ahead for a bottle of their least expensive champagne, and she was going to present him with the watch she'd bought him as a graduation present.

She could finally tell Fletcher the good news that had been bubbling inside her like the oatmeal she made on the hot plate in her dorm room.

Ever since her interview with Ogilvy & Mather in New York two weeks ago, she had been on pins and needles. For the first few days, every time her phone buzzed, she was sure it was Walter. But he didn't call, and her excitement turned to panic. She even mustered up the courage to call him, and Walter's secretary said she'd give him the message.

Another week passed, and she was certain she hadn't gotten the job. It was too late to set up interviews, and she would have to wait until graduation. She was glad she hadn't said anything to Fletcher. He was swamped with rehearsals for *Romeo and Juliet,* and didn't need to be burdened with her worries.

Then yesterday Walter had called and apologized. He'd had an emergency appendectomy, and was finally back in the office. Everyone loved Emma, and they wanted her to start right after graduation: assistant copywriter with a salary of $32,000 a year, plus health benefits.

Emma had hung up the phone and bicycled straight into Waterville. She spent almost all the money her parents had sent for graduation: she bought the green dress, the watch for Fletcher, and a pair of pumps for her new job. For once she didn't worry about the price tags. In three weeks she'd be a working girl in Manhattan.

The script lay on the desk and she picked it up. An envelope fell to the floor and an airline ticket slipped out. Emma turned it over and read Fletcher's name. It was a one-way ticket to London, and there was a letter from someone named Harry Stone.

Emma scanned the letter and sank to the floor. Why hadn't Fletcher told her about Harry's offer? She had assumed he was going to look for a theater job in New York. Even Boston or Philadelphia would have been all right, because they could have visited each other on weekends. But London! Fletcher would get on that British Airways flight two days after graduation, and she'd never see him again.

She could ask him about it at dinner, but Fletcher would know she was snooping. She would have to wait for him to bring it up. She slipped the ticket back in the envelope and grabbed the script. How was she going to pretend nothing had happened, when their whole future together was in jeopardy?

Emma sat across from Fletcher at Cucina's and dipped garlic bread into melted butter. Everything about the restaurant was perfect: the table was lit by flickering candles, the fettuccine marinara with sea scallops and lobster was delicious, and even the champagne was passable. But every time she tried to swallow, her stomach tightened, and she had to force herself to take another bite.

"You didn't have to order all this," Fletcher said, waving at the caprese salad in a silver bowl and the sides of sautéed vegetables. "We could have shared a burger at the Proper Pig."

"It's your last play at Colby." Emma clutched her champagne flute. "When will we celebrate opening night again?"

"It did go well, didn't it?" Fletcher said happily. "I was afraid the actress playing Juliet would forget her lines. She had the stomach flu and missed the last week of rehearsals. But she remembered every word, and the actor playing Romeo was better than I hoped. Ryan is from California, and I thought he'd come across as a surfer instead of the scion of a noble Venetian family."

"Everyone was wonderful, and it was because of you," Emma agreed. "You're the star of the theater department. Producers are going to line up offering you a job."

Fletcher put down his fork, and Emma thought he was going to tell her about the letter. He'd say he told Harry he couldn't accept the job because he wanted to stay in New York, and she'd tell him about the offer from Ogilvy & Mather.

"I met a British producer, and he said my plays made Shakespeare accessible to young people." Fletcher's eyes were bright. "It's wonderful when someone understands what you're trying to do. It makes all the late nights and slices of cold pizza worthwhile."

Fletcher had never looked so excited, like a child on Christmas morning. Emma suddenly understood why he hadn't told her about the letter. He desperately wanted to accept Harry's offer, and was afraid Emma would stop him. She had to tell him she knew about the job offer. But how could she do it without Fletcher knowing that she'd seen the letter?

"Wouldn't it be exciting if you got a theater job in London?" she returned. "You'd learn so much and be so successful. Covent Garden is one of the theater capitals of the world."

Fletcher started to say something and changed his mind. He concentrated on dipping lobster into steaming butter. "That's about as likely to happen as pigs flying. There are a lot of talented assistant directors in England, and I'm just an American college kid that staged a decent production of *As You Like It*. I'll have to settle for something off-off-Broadway in New York, or maybe Chicago or Philadelphia."

Emma looked down at her plate so Fletcher couldn't see the hurt in her eyes. If Fletcher wasn't going to tell her about the letter, it was obvious he was planning on going to London without her. He'd call from some bedsit in London and say long distance romances didn't work, and it was better if they broke up.

"I want to hear about you," Fletcher returned. "You said you had exciting news."

"I finally heard from Ogilvy & Mather. I got the job."

"I knew you'd get it." He beamed. "You're going to be working on Madison Avenue and eating expense-account lunches at swanky restaurants in Midtown."

Emma gulped her champagne and had never felt so betrayed. How could Fletcher lie to her? She didn't want him to think she was pining for him in New York. It was better if there was a way to make a clean break. But if she broke up with him now, what would be the reason? She tried to think of a place that didn't have a proper theater scene, somewhere Fletcher couldn't possibly follow her.

"Actually, they hired someone else for that position. This is a better opportunity—it's assistant copywriter at Ogilvy & Mather in Milwaukee."

"Milwaukee?" Fletcher said, stumbling over the word. "Your dream is to live in New York."

"There will only be two people on the account, so there's a better chance of promotion," she said quickly. "I can probably transfer to New York in a year. Plus, my aunt lives in Milwaukee. I could stay with her and save money."

"What about us?" Fletcher asked.

"If you're in New York or Philadelphia, I can visit on weekends," she said shakily. "This is a wonderful chance; I can't pass it up."

"Of course you can't." Fletcher looked at Emma and sipped his champagne. "You're going to be the best copywriter Ogilvy & Mather, Milwaukee, ever had."

The waiter brought caramel flan for dessert, and they reminisced about college: The winter mornings when it was minus ten degrees, so by the time they walked to class, they thought they'd never be warm again. The last few weeks when everyone was so anxious to leave, the dining hall was like Grand Central Station at rush hour.

It was only after they both returned to campus and made up an excuse not to spend the night—Emma had to revise her senior thesis, and Fletcher wanted to make notes for tomorrow's matinee—that Emma let the grief wash over her. She sank onto the bed in her dorm room and felt something hard in her pocket.

She took the watch out of the case and turned it over. It had taken her hours to come up with the inscription: TO FLETCHER, YOU HAVE MY HEART. EMMA.

She hadn't given him the watch at dinner. Now she didn't know if she ever would.

One Day Before New Year's Eve
Snowberry, Vermont

Emma sat on the bed in her room at The Smuggler's Inn and wondered what would have happened all those years ago if she hadn't lied to Fletcher about the job in Milwaukee. But she had felt so betrayed. If Fletcher loved her, he would have told her about the opportunity in London; instead, he'd just planned on disappearing.

She walked to the closet and wondered what shoes she should wear with the red dress. Maybe she should run to the beauty parlor and get her hair done: proper curls, so she looked elegant and sexy.

Fletcher and Megan were no longer engaged, and tonight she and Fletcher were going to have a romantic dinner. She slipped on her coat and grabbed her purse. Bronwyn would say it was all synchronicity, and nothing could go wrong.

Eighteen

FLETCHER RUBBED SHAVING LOTION ON his cheeks and buttoned up his shirt. He was meeting Emma for dinner in half an hour, and he was as nervous as a teenage boy before the prom.

It had been so odd running into Emma in Manchester this morning, after he called Megan last night. He was beginning to believe that fate kept bringing them together. Being with Emma was like sipping a cappuccino after going weeks without coffee: warm and sweet and electrifying at the same time.

Could they start seeing each other again? They were both single, and they enjoyed each other's company. It didn't have to be anything serious; they could explore the East Village, or Emma could show him her neighborhood.

Then why was he so anxious he'd missed a button? There was a knock at the door, and he opened it. Lola stood in the doorway, wearing a blue jacket and sheepskin boots.

"I knocked on your door earlier," he said when Lola entered his room. "I was wondering when you and Betty would get back."

"We had a wonderful afternoon." Lola plopped on the bed. "We delivered homemade fudge to all the vendors who are donating to the talent show. Then Betty showed me the covered bridge where her children fished every summer. They caught trout this big." Lola held out her hands.

"I bet you can catch one even bigger." Fletcher fixed the buttons on his shirt. "Maybe Stephen can set you up with a fishing pole. And you'll need plenty of mosquito repellent; I heard the mosquitoes in Vermont in the summer eat better than the people."

Lola glanced at Fletcher and her eyes were wide as saucers.

"Do you mean it?" She clapped her hands. "Are we going to spend summer in Vermont?"

"I haven't told Stephen yet," Fletcher said. "I wanted to check with you first. And of course we need to talk to your mom."

"It would be the best summer of my life!" Lola gushed. "What did Megan say? Are you going to get married at The Smuggler's Inn?"

"That's the other thing I want to talk about," Fletcher said. "Megan and I aren't getting married after all. We decided to end the engagement."

"That diamond ring never suited her anyway," Lola insisted. "That ring is better suited to someone with smaller hands."

"I never noticed," Fletcher laughed. It felt good to be laughing with Lola, as if a weight had been lifted from his shoulders. "I'll keep that in mind the next time I give a woman a ring."

"Cammi's mother's wedding ring is as big as an Easter egg because her new husband is loaded," Lola continued. "Mom's new ring is pretty small, but it does have a pretty emerald." Lola clamped her hand over her mouth. "I shouldn't have said that. You don't like it when I talk about Mom and Chuck."

"You have to talk about them," Fletcher said. "You live with Mom most of the time, and Chuck is her husband."

"You really don't mind?" Lola fiddled with her coat toggle. "Because there's something you should know. Emma said Mom should tell you, but I hate keeping secrets. It makes me feel like I swallowed a balloon that's going to burst."

"What kind of secret?" Fletcher said sharply. "And what does this have to do with Emma?"

"I discovered it by accident and didn't know if I should tell you," Lola said. "Emma was worried how you'd react to Mom and Chuck having a baby."

The room seemed to sway and Fletcher put his hand on a chair to steady himself.

"When did your mother tell you she was pregnant?"

"That's the thing—she hasn't told me," Lola rushed on. "We were talking on Skype and Chuck asked how her doctor's appointment went and whether he should buy pink or blue cigars."

"Your mother doesn't know that you know?" Fletcher tried to process the information.

Lola's eyes filled with tears. "Maybe she doesn't care how I feel. All she's worried about is the new baby."

"Of course she cares how you feel." Fletcher hugged her. "Emma's right, she probably wants to tell us in person. It's exciting news; you're going to be a wonderful big sister."

"Do you think so?" Emma asked expectantly. "Babies are cute. Susannah at school has a baby sister, and she blows bubbles. I was thinking of giving the baby my Paddington Bear. I could send it to SnowBeary Academy and Doctor Traci can sew on his coat toggles."

"That's a good idea," Fletcher agreed. "We'll dig out your Beatrix Potter books, and you can teach the baby about Peter Rabbit."

"I used to love it when you pretended you were Farmer McGregor." Lola looked at Fletcher. "I won't mind if you have a baby someday."

"I doubt that will happen, now that I'm not engaged," Fletcher said gruffly.

"There's always Emma," Lola remarked. "She just came back from the beauty parlor. She said you were going out to dinner."

Fletcher flushed. He should have asked Lola to join them. Even though he wanted to be alone with Emma, Lola came first.

"I was going to ask if you wanted to come," Fletcher said quickly.

"Emma already did, but I said no." Lola shrugged. "Stephen asked me and Betty to see the Christmas parade in Chester. Santa Claus pulls a sleigh with real reindeer, and they serve gingerbread snaps." She rubbed her stomach. "I love gingerbread snaps, I could eat a whole box."

"Emma already asked you?" Fletcher repeated curiously. "Well, we'll both be disappointed. But I don't mind being replaced by live reindeer."

"I'm sure you'll have a nice dinner; you have a lot to catch up on." Lola eyed Fletcher's button-down shirt and newly shaved cheeks. "It's kind of odd, though."

"What's odd?" Fletcher wondered.

"When Cammi comes over, she usually wears jeans and a T-shirt," Lola said. "You're all dressed up, and Emma got her hair done."

"What are you saying?" Fletcher asked.

"Old friends wear their most comfortable things around each other. It looks like you and Emma are going on a date."

"Emma and I are going to dinner, that's all." Fletcher kissed

Lola on the forehead and turned to the closet. "If I don't finish getting dressed, I'll be late."

Lola went downstairs to join Betty, and Fletcher reached for a sweater. He was about to grab his coat when his phone rang.

"Graham, how are you?" Fletcher answered. "I read the review of *A Winter's Tale* in *The Guardian*. You hit it out of the park."

"I love a glowing review, but it's giving my leading lady a very big head," Graham said, and sighed. "Annika is demanding heated slippers and a glass of Pimm's after every performance."

"The budget can afford it; you must be making a mint." Fletcher glanced at the time on his phone. "I can't talk long, I'm late for an appointment."

"You mean you're late for dinner with Emma," Graham corrected.

"Who told you that?" Fletcher wondered.

"I couldn't get hold of you, so I called The Smuggler's Inn. A woman answered and said you were out. She put Lola on the phone, and Lola told me you were going to dinner with Emma."

"You talked to Lola?"

"She *is* my goddaughter," Graham reminded him. "It's bad enough that you took her five thousand miles away. At least I can talk to her on the phone."

"Lola adores you," Fletcher agreed. "She was just here, and she didn't mention talking to you."

"Like you didn't tell me Megan went back to New York?" Graham returned. "I suppose I could have predicted it, the way your week was going. And now you're already planning a romantic dinner with Emma."

"Maybe you were right about the magic Christmas spell over The Smuggler's Inn," Fletcher commented. "I thought when I broke off the engagement, I'd be completely wrecked. But I feel like a new man."

"You're talking about the oldest spell in the books," Graham chuckled. "It's called love."

"I don't know about that. Emma and I are just friends," Fletcher said hastily. "I'd rather have a steak and baked potato with Emma, then retreat to my room with a bottle of scotch and a carton of Ben & Jerry's Minter Wonderland ice cream."

"You and Emma have never been just friends," Graham rejoined. "When I met you, you were ten pounds thinner because you'd hardly eaten since you arrived in London. We went out for fish and chips and you barely touched them."

"They were too greasy," Fletcher recalled. "They were wrapped in newspaper, and the newspaper was covered in oil."

"And when we went back to your flat, you had photos of Emma in a scrapbook," Graham continued.

"There was one photo of Emma on the opening night of *Romeo and Juliet*," Fletcher said. "Was I supposed to cut her out of the photo?"

"Remember how Cassandra found the watch Emma gave you the day before your wedding?" Graham kept talking. "I always wondered why you kept it. Maybe you didn't want to get married."

"I loved Cassandra, and I have Lola," Fletcher said. "I wouldn't have traded my marriage for anything."

"Emma appears in Vermont, and a few days later you and Megan break off your engagement," Graham continued. "You're like a dog with a bone. You've never really let Emma go."

"I suppose you have a point," Fletcher said warily.

"I just want you to be careful. You've closed off a space in your heart that no one else can reach," Graham said. "I'm a theater producer; I know how easy it is to glamorize the past. Don't let nostalgia for your first love get in the way of common sense. You're my best friend, and I don't want you to get hurt. We're getting old, Fletcher. Our hearts don't mend easily."

Fletcher hung up the phone and glanced in the mirror. Graham was wrong; he wasn't glamorizing the past. But maybe Graham had a point. He couldn't take Emma to a diner in Snowberry, like the ones they'd frequented in college. If there was any chance of their relationship progressing, they had to try something different.

Suddenly he had an idea. He took off the wool sweater and put on the silk tie that Megan had packed in his suitcase. Then he slipped on his coat and draped a scarf around his neck. He and Emma were going to have a night neither of them would forget.

Emma was standing in the parlor when he walked downstairs. She turned and his heart hammered in his chest. Her hair was freshly curled, and she was wearing a belted coat that made her look like a movie star.

"What have you done to your hair?" he asked. "And that coat! You look stunning."

"Do you like it?" She touched her hair. "Betty lent me the coat, it's vintage Halston. She said it would keep me warm if we're walking around Snowberry."

"Your hair is lovely, and the coat suits you," Fletcher rejoined. "But we're not going to dinner in Snowberry."

"Where are we going?" Emma asked.

"It's a surprise." He held out his arm. "I promise, we're going to have a good time."

"Stowe!" Emma exclaimed when the taxi dropped them off in front of a sign that curved above stone pillars.

Fletcher tipped the driver and climbed out after her. Above them, cable cars transported visitors to restaurants on the slopes, and lit torches guided nighttime skiers down the mountain. There was a Christmas tree as large as anything he had seen at Harrods, and lampposts decorated with silver bows.

"I've never been to Stowe, but the guidebooks say it's a must-see destination in Vermont," he explained. "There are half a dozen gourmet restaurants, and they have almost as many designer boutiques as Fifth Avenue. Plus we can take the cable car up the mountain and see the Green Mountains at night."

"It's gorgeous," Emma said as they passed shop windows with mannequins outfitted in expensive ski gear. Even the salespeople were different from those in Snowberry: the saleswoman at the Stowe Mercantile Company was dressed in a chic ski sweater and leather slacks.

There was a chocolate shop that sold truffles with gold icing, and a cheese store where they offered samples of goat cheese accompanied by spoonfuls of caviar. The liquor shop resembled the inside of some fabulous wine cellar, and there were three jewelry stores with cases of gold watches and diamond brooches.

"It reminds me of the ski resorts in Switzerland," Fletcher said when they explored the ski shop. Fletcher tried on a pair of wraparound sunglasses that made him feel like a downhill racer, and Emma stroked a ski jacket lined with mink.

"I would never wear fur, but it's dreamy to touch," she sighed. "I feel like we're at one of those chic ski resorts in the movies where everyone sits around sipping Campari. I've never been to Europe; it would be lovely to visit Gstaad or St. Moritz."

"You've never been to Europe?" Fletcher asked quizzically.

"It's too expensive on a copywriter's salary in Manhattan if you want to afford a decent apartment." She shrugged. "I will some-day. I've promised myself a trip to Rome when I get my next raise."

"All those boyfriends," Fletcher teased. "And no one took you on a romantic weekend in Venice, or a whirlwind trip to Portugal?"

"Evan planned New Year's in Paris a few years ago: three nights at the Ritz and a New Year's Eve cruise on a barge on the Seine. I only found out because the concierge at the Ritz called when I was clearing my things from his apartment and left a message on the answering machine," she said with a smile. "I broke up with him the day after Christmas. He was sweet, but he was a massive base-ball fan, and I couldn't sit in front of the television watching a ball being hit around a field." She looked at Fletcher. "I hope that doesn't sound too demanding. I just want to grow old with someone who has similar interests." Her eyes sparkled. "Someone who loves big dogs and wants a whole army of grandchildren so we can always look forward to their visits."

"You'll be a wonderful grandmother," Fletcher said, playing along. "You'll be the kind who plays touch football and lets them watch *The Bachelor* when they're stressed from college entrance exams."

"I'll be too old to play football by the time I have grandchil-dren. If I have them at all," Emma said doubtfully. "At least I have Liv and Sarah. Once a month I spend the day with them and we go to the Natural History Museum. Liv usually falls asleep, and she's so heavy I can hardly carry her. But Sarah loves the dinosaurs."

"That's the thing about being a parent—sometimes you don't

know how you keep going," Fletcher said. "Then they put their hand in yours, and it's the best feeling in the world."

"You're doing a great job with Lola," Emma returned. "She has so much self-confidence, and she's very kind. She spent hours sewing ears on the teddy bears so Betty could donate them to charity."

"I have a confession to make." Fletcher took Emma's hand. "I didn't want to talk about Lola tonight. I wanted this evening to be about us."

"About us?" Emma looked at Fletcher.

"I didn't want to sit in a diner in Snowberry and talk about college or Megan or even Lola," Fletcher said earnestly. "I wanted to show you how much I've accomplished. You know, the big Broadway director who's spent winters in fashionable ski resorts and knows the names of different kinds of caviar. But that's not who I am. I love being Lola's father, and if we're even thinking about a future, you have to recognize how important she is to me."

"Are we thinking about a future?" Emma asked. She was standing so close to Fletcher, and suddenly all he wanted was to kiss her.

"I can't seem to think about anything else." He touched her cheek tentatively. "It's been a long time, and we've both lived different lives. Do you think we can give it a chance?"

Emma was quiet, and he was afraid he'd said too much. He should have taken it slowly and pretended it was a casual evening between friends. But then she reached up and kissed him. Her lips tasted of chocolate, and he put his arms around her.

"I'd like some kind of future together," Emma whispered when they parted.

"You would?" Fletcher said, and realized his heart was pounding.

"Very much," Emma agreed, and smiled. "But right now I'd

do anything to go somewhere warm and have dinner. Do you think we can find a place to eat?"

"I made reservations at a Michelin-starred restaurant, but I could only get a table an hour from now," Fletcher said, hesitating.

"Would you mind if we ditched it and ate here instead?" Emma pointed to the only storefront that didn't have a gold canopy or brass awnings.

"The Stowe Waffle and Pancake House?" Fletcher laughed, peeking through the window at the waitress carrying an old-fashioned coffee pot.

"When I get back to New York, I probably won't eat maple syrup again," Emma grinned. "But right now a pancake sounds perfect."

Fletcher ordered a "lumberjack crêpe" with local ham and cheddar, while Emma had a hazelnut pancake with organic bananas. After dinner they strolled through Stowe and watched the ski patrol ski down the mountain. Children waved sparklers and ate complimentary sugar cookies.

"Would you like to go up in the cable car?" Fletcher asked. "The view at night is supposed to be spectacular."

"I've never been in a cable car before." Emma eyed the red box suspended from an iron rod.

"I've never been either," Fletcher admitted.

"I thought cable cars were all the rage in European ski resorts," Emma said.

"We always had Lola with us, and she was too small." Fletcher shrugged.

"Why not?" Emma decided. "It's about time I tried something adventurous."

Fletcher took her hand and they walked toward the cable car entrance. Above them the mountain loomed like a giant in one of Lola's books of fairy tales.

"I'll buy the tickets. I would love to do something new together." Fletcher felt a stab of anticipation. Emma looked so lovely with her brown eyes and her coat belted around her waist.

Emma's face broke into a smile and she nodded. "So would I."

The cable car lurched into the air, and Emma leaned against the hard wooden seat.

"It's even more beautiful than I imagined," she breathed. The sky was so close she could count the stars, and the village of Stowe was lit up with fairy lights. She could see the giant Christmas tree and the snow-covered steeples.

"I agree, I've never seen anything more beautiful." Fletcher took her hand.

"You're not even looking at the scenery," Emma said, glancing over at him.

"You're right," he said, pulling her close. "Because I can't stop looking at the beauty beside me."

Fletcher kissed her, and his mouth was warm and sweet. She kissed him back, and a shiver of delight ran down her spine.

The cable car kept moving, and finally she pulled away.

"You have to look at the scenery," she said, laughing. "We can kiss anywhere, but how many times will we ride a cable car in Stowe?"

Fletcher draped his scarf over a chair in his room and sank onto the bed. Lola was already asleep, and the lights in the upstairs hallway were dimmed.

The evening with Emma had been magical: eating crêpes at the Stowe Waffle and Pancake House, and taking the cable car to the top of the mountain. The valley had spread out below them, and the villages were like charms on a charm bracelet. And he wished the kiss could have gone on forever!

Then they'd shared a nightcap in the library of The Smuggler's Inn, and Fletcher longed to ask Emma to his room. But it was too soon, and he didn't want to do anything to disturb the tentative romance growing between them.

Fletcher walked to the closet and hung up his coat. Tomorrow was the talent show. He had to spend the morning putting finishing touches on the set. Lola was so excited about performing, she said it felt like Christmas all over again.

Outside a light snow was falling, and it looked so peaceful. He was in Vermont with Lola and Emma and it was almost New Year's Eve. Lola was right: it felt exactly like Christmas, and he couldn't wait until tomorrow.

Nineteen

New Year's Eve
Snowberry, Vermont

EMMA RAN A BRUSH THROUGH her hair and pulled on a sweater. The weather report said it was going to snow all day, and she didn't want to catch a cold. Tonight was the talent show and she had to see if Betty needed help with the donations, and help Lola rehearse her song.

Last night with Fletcher had been the best evening she could remember. At first she had been nervous that they wouldn't know what to say and the whole night would be awkward. But Fletcher had surprised her by taking her to Stowe, and it had felt so glamorous to browse in the designer stores and mingle with the tourists dressed in fur hats and après-ski boots. Then when Emma suggested eating at the pancake and waffle house, Fletcher had canceled their reservation at a Michelin-starred restaurant and agreed to eat crêpes and drink coffee that had probably been sitting in the coffee pot since lunchtime.

Riding the cable car had been a wonderful idea. She was worried it might be scary swinging from the side of a mountain in a box that resembled a toy car. But Fletcher kept her hand in his and the mountain was lit with twinkling lights, and it was one of the most beautiful views she had ever seen. And their kiss was like something out of a romantic movie. It had taken all her willpower not to invite Fletcher into her room, but she didn't want to rush things.

She flipped open her laptop and pressed the FaceTime icon. The image blurred and Bronwyn appeared on the screen. Bronwyn was wearing an expensive-looking floral robe and she was sitting on a balcony with a palm tree and the ocean behind her.

"I tried FaceTiming you last night, but you didn't answer." Bronwyn closed her magazine. "I'm reading the real estate section of *Palm Beach Life*. I'm thinking of moving to Palm Beach. You can buy a four-bedroom oceanfront condo for the price of a two-bedroom apartment on the Upper West Side. The Wind & Sand has a private beach club and on-site babysitters."

"You can't move to Palm Beach," Emma said patiently. "You have a successful dermatology practice, and Carlton is a stockbroker at a major firm in Manhattan."

"I could open a practice here. These women lather themselves with tanning oil when they're young, and they're surprised when their skin starts looking like a withered orange. And Carlton can commute. I met a guy who hops on his private jet every Monday and flies back to Palm Beach for the weekend. His wife sees more of him than she did when they lived in Westchester, and their children know how to sail."

"Sarah is only five, and she already takes dance and martial arts," Emma pointed out. "She doesn't need to learn how to sail."

"Look behind me." Bronwyn waved her hand. "That's the Atlantic Ocean, and it's warm enough to go swimming. And see that yellow thing?" She pointed at the sky. "That's the sun; we won't see it in New York until March. And just when we decide to go to work without a jacket, there will be a freak snowstorm. Even God doesn't think people should live in New York."

"You can't move to Palm Beach because you're my best friend and I'd miss you," Emma interjected. "I haven't spoken to you in days. I have so much to tell you."

"I miss you too. I've hardly spoken to an adult since we arrived," Bronwyn admitted. "Carlton spends most of the day riding around in a golf cart, and none of the women talk to each other. They lie at the pool with cucumbers covering their eyelids, like plastic figures in a modern art installation."

"The day before yesterday Fletcher and Lola and I took a tour of SnowBeary Academy," Emma began. "It was so much fun— you and Carlton should bring the girls. There's a bear hospital and a gift shop that sells bear food."

"I told you not to go to the teddy bear factory," Bronwyn groaned. "Now when Fletcher thinks about you, he's going to picture a roomful of children sobbing because their teddy bear lost an ear. I know. When Trixie chewed up Pinkie, Liv cried harder than I did at my grandfather's funeral."

"Then he asked me to dinner that night and we went to Le Soufflé," Emma said, ignoring her. "Afterward we walked over a covered bridge in Dorset."

"Covered bridges are romantic." Bronwyn perked up. "Did you kiss?"

"Fletcher was about to kiss me, but then there were fireworks, and I pulled away—"

"Almost isn't good enough," Bronwyn interrupted. "Tonight is New Year's Eve, and tomorrow you go back to New York. Your apartment is going to look pretty gloomy when you see Scott's Instagram photos of Maui. I have to remember to unfollow him; he keeps posting photos of luaus with tropical fruits and pigs sizzling on a stick. Even I'm jealous, and I'm sitting under a coconut tree."

"You didn't let me finish," Emma replied. "Yesterday morning I went to the outlet stores in Manchester and ran into Fletcher. I helped him pick out a tuxedo, and he asked me to dinner."

"Synchronicity at work." Bronwyn nodded. "Go on, I'm dying with anticipation."

"It was the most wonderful evening!" Emma said, flushing. "We went to Stowe and browsed in the boutiques and rode the cable car to the top of the mountain. He kissed me and it was the best kiss I can remember. Then we came back to The Smuggler's Inn and had a nightcap in the library."

"Did you go up to his room and have incredible sex?" Bronwyn asked eagerly. "I can't remember what it's like to sleep with someone new. You've slept with Fletcher before, but you both must have learned stuff in the last eleven years."

"I didn't sleep with him!" Emma exclaimed. "Lola was right next door. And anyway, there isn't any hurry. We both want to take it slowly."

"I agree, rushing into sex is like finding out if the baby is a boy or a girl before it's born." Bronwyn nodded. "It's better to keep the mystery going and have something to look forward to."

"I have to thank you," Emma returned. "If you hadn't convinced me to come to Vermont, Fletcher and I would never have reunited."

"I had little to do with it," Bronwyn insisted. "From the moment you found that watch, everything was put into motion. You were bound to end up with Fletcher; that's what synchronicity is all about."

"Fletcher's watch!" Emma remembered. "I have to tell him I found it at the jewelry store in the East Village. He thinks that my being at The Smuggler's Inn is a coincidence."

"You don't have to tell him," Bronwyn said warily.

"Of course I do," Emma replied. "If we're going to have a relationship, there can't be any secrets between us. And why shouldn't I tell him? You're the one who keeps saying it's synchronicity, and it all worked exactly as planned."

"Some people might not see it that way," Bronwyn faltered. "He might think you were stalking him."

"Stalking him?"

"You know, finding out where he was on Facebook and then booking a room at the same inn."

"But that's exactly what you did," Emma reminded her.

"And look how well it turned out!" Bronwyn said breezily. "It's like when I get a skin peel. Carlton doesn't need to see me with green goop all over my face. It's better if he only witnesses the results: his wife with baby-faced cheeks like Selena Gomez or Ariana Grande."

"Keeping secrets doesn't sound like a good idea," Emma said uncomfortably.

"I'm a married woman, I know how men work," Bronwyn said wisely. "I have to get ready for New Year's Eve. The Breakers puts on a New Year's Eve ball that would make Marie Antoinette feel at home. Carlton gave me the most beautiful gold necklace as a New Year's Eve present with a card saying he won the lottery when he married me." She paused. "Maybe I won't move to Palm Beach after all. I don't want Carlton to commute."

Emma closed her computer and picked up Fletcher's watch. Bronwyn was right: Fletcher might think it was odd that she'd followed him to Vermont. But could she keep it a secret? And what about Lola? Lola was so inquisitive; if she asked how Emma ended up at The Smuggler's Inn, Emma would have to tell her the truth.

The snow was coming down harder outside, and she grabbed a coat. Sometimes she had to listen to her best friend, and sometimes she had to listen to herself.

Betty was in the kitchen when Emma went downstairs. A pot of oatmeal was simmering on the stove, and there was a platter of crisp bacon. Betty had sliced a loaf of bread, and the room smelled of toast and butter.

"Good morning." Betty looked up. She was wearing high-waisted slacks and a red sweater. "I love snowy mornings; they make me want to stay inside with a cup of tea and a good book."

"It's coming down pretty hard," Emma said, nodding. "The weather report says it's going to snow all day."

"That's why I made all this food," Betty said, and waved at the platters of sausages and stacks of pancakes. "Guests don't like to venture into the village in this weather. I hope it eases up for the talent show."

"Don't worry, everyone will come," Emma assured her. "Flyers are up all over town."

"I know, and I'm so grateful." Betty nodded. "Lola is more excited about the talent show than she was about last night's live reindeer."

"How was your evening?" Emma asked. "Lola was asleep when I got home."

"We had so much fun. We sang Christmas carols and Stephen took us on a skimobile." Betty stirred the oatmeal. "He asked me to go on a cruise with him in February. I haven't been on a cruise in years. I love Vermont in the winter, but it will be nice to remember that the whole world isn't bright white."

"That sounds romantic," Emma said teasingly.

"John has only been gone for eight months, and this thing with Stephen is quite sudden," Betty faltered. "But John and I knew Stephen and his wife for years. And you can't stop having feelings for someone. What if it doesn't happen again?"

"I suppose you're right." Emma thought of her and Fletcher. "But what if it's not the right time?"

"Falling in love is like being pregnant. It's often inconvenient, but it's the best thing in the world." Betty looked at Emma. "Lola told me that you and Fletcher had dinner alone."

"We went to Stowe and it was wonderful." Emma's cheeks turned red. "It's just . . ."

"You and Fletcher enjoy each other's company. And you're both single," Betty said, stopping her. "I don't see the problem."

"Fletcher and I dated in college, and I've never felt like this about anyone else," Emma admitted. "But what if it doesn't work out and we both get hurt? And Lola has been through so much—maybe she's not ready to share Fletcher again."

"We never know what life will bring us. I thought John and I would be sitting on that porch in matching rocking chairs when we were eighty. But I wouldn't give up the time we had just because I'm alone now," Betty counseled. "And Lola is like any other child. She just wants to be loved."

"I suppose you're right," Emma said, nodding. "I have to go. I'm meeting Fletcher at the playhouse."

"You're going out in this?" Betty waved at the thick flakes sticking to the window.

"I have to tell him something important." Emma walked toward the mudroom.

"You must be falling in love." Betty smiled and turned off the oatmeal. "I'm not going farther than the fireplace in the living room."

Emma hurried into the playhouse lobby and stamped the snow from her boots. Even a sweater and her thickest coat hadn't kept her warm. She rubbed the watchcase in her pocket and opened the door to the theater.

Fletcher was kneeling on the stage, hammering a star to the podium. He was wearing a flannel shirt and corduroys, and Emma's heart turned over. Just seeing him and remembering last night's kiss ignited the feelings inside her. She moved closer and he looked up in surprise.

"Emma!" He jumped up. "What are you doing here? It's really coming down out there. I thought you and Lola would be at the inn all day, playing board games and rehearsing for the show."

"Lola is asleep. I'm going to practice with her this afternoon." Emma approached the stage. "I wanted to see you. It all looks wonderful."

"It does, doesn't it?" Fletcher said, beaming. A gold banner was strung across the stage, and the floor was littered with confetti. Silver stars hung from the ceiling, and a red carpet was spread across the wood planks.

"Betty is thrilled, and Lola is so excited," Emma said warmly. "Thank you for going to all this trouble."

"I'm the lucky one." Fletcher approached her. "If Lola hadn't had the idea for the talent show, you and I may never have gotten together. I had the best time last night. I can't wait to show each other New York."

Fletcher put his arms around her and drew her close. Emma kissed him, and suddenly she wondered if she should leave the watch in her pocket after all.

"You said you wanted to see me," Fletcher said when they parted. "Was it something important?"

Emma took a deep breath and reached into her pocket. "I wanted to show you this."

Fletcher snapped open the case and took out the watch. He turned it over and looked at Emma.

"It's the watch you gave me in college. Where did you get it?" he asked.

"At a secondhand jewelry store in the East Village. I took in a bracelet that Scott gave me for Christmas. I was going to sell it and donate the money to the Salvation Army, but then I saw this in the jewelry case. I couldn't believe it. What was your watch doing here after ten years?"

"It must have been quite a shock," Fletcher agreed.

"I showed it to my friend, Bronwyn, and she said it was synchronicity," Emma explained. "She learned about it in a psych class in college. It means a meaningful coincidence that plays an important role in our lives. She said I was meant to find the watch, and to ignore it was to lose the possibility of happiness."

"Go on. I don't quite follow," Fletcher said, frowning.

"I thought it was silly, but she looked you up on Facebook and discovered you were living in New York," Emma hurried on. "You were a Broadway director with an ex-wife in Connecticut, and you were spending Christmas week at The Smuggler's Inn in Snowberry, Vermont. She booked me eight nights as a Christmas present." Emma paused. "She didn't know you had a fiancée and a daughter."

Fletcher paced around the stage and Emma's heart hammered uncomfortably.

"You drove all the way to Vermont to stay at a country inn because you thought I was here?" He turned to Emma.

"You haven't met Bronwyn. She wouldn't take no for an answer." Emma smiled. "She said it would be good for me to get out of New York. I was so embarrassed when I saw Megan, I was going to turn around and go home. But then I met Betty, and Lola suggested we do the talent show, and it seemed more fun to stay."

Fletcher walked over to Emma and took her hand. "I don't know if I believe in synchronicity, but I'm glad you're here."

"You're not angry that I didn't tell you in the first place?" She looked at him.

"I can see how it would have been hard to explain," he chuckled. "I don't even know how the watch ended up at the jewelry store. When Megan moved some of her stuff into my place, she asked if she could get rid of a few things in my drawer. She must have read the inscription and decided she didn't want a reminder of old girlfriends," he said thoughtfully. "I still remember when I found the watch in my suitcase after I arrived in London. I called to thank you, but you never answered. I even tried calling your parents, but they never returned my call. Finally I gave up and put it in a drawer."

Emma froze. She'd never told Fletcher the truth about her job at Ogilvy & Mather in New York. Should she tell him now? If she did, it might ruin everything. But she convinced herself there couldn't be any secrets between them. He had been so understanding about her finding the watch and following him to Vermont, and it had all happened so long ago.

"I never understood why you didn't give it to me in person," he finished. "I looked for you at graduation, but you disappeared."

"I tried to give it to you. I went to your dorm the morning of graduation, but you weren't there," she answered. "I chickened out and put it in your suitcase."

"What do you mean, you chickened out?" Fletcher asked. "And why didn't you return my calls? I tried to find a number for you in Milwaukee, but Ogilvy & Mather wouldn't give me any information."

"That's because I wasn't in Milwaukee. I was working at Ogilvy & Mather in New York."

Fletcher moved away, and Emma felt a chill run down her spine.

"What did you say?" he gasped.

"The night of the opening of *Romeo and Juliet,* you asked me to deliver your script. I knocked over an envelope on your desk and a one-way ticket to London fell out. I read the letter and it was a job offer at the Old Vic. I waited for you to mention it at dinner, but you never did." She looked at Fletcher. "Do you remember? I said something about you getting a job in London and you said that would never happen. I was so hurt that you lied to me, I pretended my job was in Milwaukee." She gulped. "There's no theater scene, and I knew you wouldn't follow me. Ogilvy & Mather did hire me, but to be an assistant copywriter in New York."

"I don't understand," Fletcher said, puzzled. "Why would you lie to me?"

"I felt so betrayed. I didn't want you to call from London and break up with me. I thought if I said I was going to be in Milwaukee, it would be a clean break." She blinked back tears. "That's why I disappeared after graduation. I was afraid I couldn't go through with it. I'd say something and ruin everything."

"You did ruin everything! I was in love with you." Fletcher's eyes flashed. "I didn't tell you at dinner because I was saving up money for your airfare, and wanted it to be a surprise. I only accepted Harry's offer because I thought you didn't care about our relationship. All you talked about was the job in Milwaukee, and there wasn't anything there for me. I thought, if your career was more important to you than our relationship, I may as well move across the Atlantic."

"You wanted it to be a surprise?" Emma gasped.

"I'd been working extra shifts to save money for weeks. I suppose I could have told you then, but I wanted to make sure I could afford the ticket. I never dreamed of going to London without you." He started pacing. "I spent the first few weeks in London with a terrible cold, because it rained all June and I didn't have a raincoat. My room in Harry's house was the size of a closet, and his other children lived at home so I didn't have a moment alone. I was tempted to chuck the whole thing and come back to America, but I couldn't see the point."

"Maybe destiny was working then, and it was good you didn't know the truth," Emma said reflectively. "If you had come home, you would have missed out on a brilliant career."

"I couldn't care less about destiny! It didn't feel good when I was lonelier than I had ever been in my life," Fletcher grumbled. "If I hadn't met Graham, I might have thrown myself into the Thames or drowned my sorrows in whiskey. If you knew about the letter, you should have told me. I would have explained everything."

"I'm sorry," Emma said. "I didn't mean for you to get hurt."

Fletcher looked up and it was if he didn't see her.

"I'm going to go," he said hoarsely.

"What do you mean?" Emma asked.

"I have to put Lola first," he said. "I'm sorry. But there isn't room in my life for this kind of drama."

"I see," Emma said, nodding. Her body felt as if it was encased in ice. She knotted her coat around her waist and turned to the door. "I'll go. You're still working on the set and you don't want to disappoint anyone. I've done enough of that myself."

Luckily Betty was talking on the phone when Emma entered The Smuggler's Inn. Emma ran past the kitchen and raced upstairs, unbuttoning her coat. She didn't want to talk to anyone; she didn't want to do anything except let the cold realization of what happened with Fletcher seep through her bones.

She shouldn't have lied to Fletcher, but it had been for the right reasons. And it had been eleven years ago. Fletcher was the one who said their relationship should be a new beginning. Everyone made mistakes; it was part of being young and inexperienced.

Lola would sense the friction between Emma and Fletcher, and she didn't want to spoil the talent show. She eyed her suitcase and wondered if she should leave while the roads were still passable. She could write a note and say it was some kind of emergency, that Liv or Sarah was sick and Bronwyn needed her. But could she abandon Lola, when Megan had just done the same?

It was all too confusing, and Emma didn't know which way to turn. She opened the drawers and emptied sweaters and slacks on the bed. Lola wasn't her concern anymore. Emma was alone, and all she wanted was to get as far from Fletcher and The Smuggler's Inn as possible.

Twenty

FLETCHER PACED AROUND THE LIBRARY of The Smuggler's Inn and sipped his scotch. It was mid-afternoon, and he was only allowing himself one drink. He glanced at the bottle on the sideboard and wished he could keep refilling his glass until everything was as blurry as the snow falling outside the window.

After Emma left the playhouse, he'd attempted to work on the set. But he narrowly missed hitting his thumb with the hammer, and then the podium almost toppled on top of him. He finally gave up and came back to the inn.

Betty was in the kitchen when he arrived, and she showed him the note that Emma had left for Betty in her room. Her friend Bronwyn was sick, and Emma had to go and help with the girls. She was sorry to leave before the talent show, but she was afraid she'd get stuck in the snow. There was a postscript asking Betty to apologize to Lola, and hoping Betty could accompany Lola on the piano.

Fletcher read it twice before handing it to Betty. He asked if

Emma had left a note for him. Betty looked at him with something odd in her eyes and said that it was the only letter she'd found.

Now Fletcher replayed their conversation at the playhouse in his head and wondered if he'd overreacted. Emma had lied to him all those years ago; she hadn't given him a chance to make a decision about their future.

Would things have been different if he'd told Emma about Harry's offer instead of waiting until he could afford to buy her a plane ticket? But on the other hand, if she'd had any faith in their relationship, she would have known he wouldn't go anywhere without her.

Then there was Lola. How could he put all his energy into raising Lola if he and Emma were already arguing? Maybe Graham was right, and the idea of rekindling things with Emma had been crazy in the first place.

He put the glass on the side table and walked into the hallway. Music floated from the conservatory and he peeked through the door. Lola was sitting at the piano, wearing a striped pinafore and turning the pages of a songbook.

"Where is everyone?" Lola said, looking up. "Betty isn't in the kitchen, and I haven't seen Emma all day. She was supposed to help me rehearse; the talent show starts in three hours."

"Betty went into the village with Stephen," Fletcher said, entering the conservatory. "Emma had an emergency. She went back to New York."

"Emma wouldn't do that to me!" Lola's eyes widened. "She knows the talent show is the most important thing in the world."

"I'm sure it was unavoidable," Fletcher said uncomfortably.

"Her friend got sick and she had to help take care of her goddaughters."

"I have to call her and beg her to come back." Lola was suddenly a little girl. There were tears in her eyes, and her mouth wobbled.

"There's probably no phone reception in this weather." Fletcher waved at the snow falling outside. "I'm sure Emma is as upset as you are. What if I help you practice? What are you singing?"

"The talent show won't be the same without Emma," Lola said stubbornly. "But I do need someone to practice with." She flipped through the songbook. "Emma picked out the song. It's called 'So This Is Christmas.'"

"Emma picked it out?" Fletcher repeated.

"She told me the whole story. It was when she was at college and the boy she was in love with surprised her with a night at a romantic inn and made a CD of her favorite Christmas songs," Lola gushed. "Isn't that dreamy? He finally told her he loved her and it was the best Christmas she ever had."

"That's a wonderful story." Fletcher remembered the night they'd spent at the Village Inn during Christmas of their senior year. Fletcher had rented every Christmas movie that was set in New York, and had made a CD of Christmas songs.

Lola ran through the song three times, stopping to rub her throat.

"What do you think?" she asked. "I was afraid I couldn't hit the high notes."

"You were superb," Fletcher said truthfully. "You've never sung better."

"I wanted to sing it for Cammi over Skype, she's a good critic,"

Lola continued. "But she got in trouble and her mother took away her computer and grounded her for a month."

"What did she get in trouble for?" Fletcher asked, grateful to change the subject from the talent show and Emma.

"She let her guinea pig out and he chewed her mother's fur coat. Cammi said it served her mother right for owning fur, because you shouldn't kill animals," Lola reported. "Cammi was afraid her mother would never forgive her. I told her everyone makes mistakes. Once the punishment is over, everything will go back to normal. No one stays mad forever."

"What did you say?" Fletcher asked sharply.

"Which part?" Lola wondered. "Apparently it was a mink that Cammi's stepfather brought back from Paris."

"Not about the coat, about making mistakes and being punished," Fletcher urged her.

"That's the great thing about being a parent," Lola replied. "You can teach your kid lessons while showing you love them at the same time. Once I left the lid on the peanut butter jar loose and when Mom picked it up, it shattered on the kitchen floor. She sent me to my room and took away television for one night," Lola finished. "I know she loves me; she just didn't want it to happen again. Now I screw the lids on jars as tightly as possible. And forgiveness isn't just important between parents and children, it's something you have to do as an adult. I read a series about forgiveness in mom's *Good Housekeeping*. Every month it highlights a different story. Last month it was about a woman who couldn't forgive her husband for leaving the door open and their dog, Fluffy, running away. The husband had a broken arm and he couldn't carry the groceries and close the door at the same time. It was only open for a minute but Fluffy bolted before they could stop him. The magazine pointed out that it was his wife's fault too: she could have offered to carry the groceries or Fluffy could have been better trained. Anyway, Fluffy was found and he was fine."

Why hadn't Fletcher been able to forgive Emma? She'd lied about the job in Milwaukee, but it was only because she'd felt betrayed. Everyone made mistakes, and if he loved her, he had to forgive her. The snow was thick on the windowpane and he wondered if it was too late. But he couldn't sit at The Smuggler's Inn. He'd let Emma go once without a fight; he wouldn't do it again.

"I have to go somewhere." He jumped up.

"Now?" Lola said in alarm. "It's snowing, and the talent show starts soon."

"Don't worry, I'll be back in plenty of time." He gave her a hug. "You really are the best thing I've ever done. I'm lucky to be your father."

Fletcher drove down Route 100 and peered through the windshield. The snow was falling so hard, he could barely see a few feet in front of him. As soon as he had inched the car out of The Smuggler's Inn driveway, he knew it was foolish. Emma was probably on the interstate by now, heading back to New York.

Something kept him moving forward. He passed the only open diner and scanned the parking lot, hoping she'd stopped for a cup of coffee. But she wasn't at the diner, and the guy at the gas station hadn't seen her.

He had to give up; he couldn't risk getting stuck and missing the talent show. He turned the car and headed back to Snowberry. Suddenly his car swerved as he noticed a Honda on the side of the road. Its windshield wipers were waving furiously and the windows were covered in snow.

He parked behind it and rapped on the window. The door opened gingerly and Emma poked her face out.

"Fletcher! What are you doing here?" she gasped.

"Are you all right?" He ignored her question. "Your lips are blue, we need to get you to a doctor."

"I'm fine, the car slipped off the road and I couldn't get it to budge," she said uncertainly. "I called triple A and they'll be along soon."

"You're not waiting in this car, it's freezing in here," he exclaimed. "We'll leave it here and take my car back to the inn."

"I can't make you go to all that trouble," she said stiffly. "And you haven't told me what you're doing out here."

"We'll talk about it in my car." He said gently, opening the door.

Emma followed Fletcher into his car and slid into the passenger seat. He turned on the engine and put the heat on high. Emma stopped shivering and the color returned to her cheeks.

"Thank you." Emma rubbed her hands. "I guess I was colder than I thought."

"Betty showed me the note, but I didn't believe it." Fletcher looked at Emma. "You told me Bronwyn is in Palm Beach with her husband and children. Unless she came down with some tropical disease, I don't see how she needed your help."

"I made that up. I couldn't stay; I didn't want to spoil the talent show for Lola," Emma acknowledged. "But I couldn't go through with it. Lola was counting on me accompanying her on the piano. I turned around, and the car skidded and landed in a ditch."

"Is that the only reason you were coming back to The Smuggler's Inn?" Fletcher asked.

"What other reason could there be?" she wondered. "You made it pretty clear that you needed to put Lola first, and that our relationship wouldn't work. I thought you wanted me to leave."

"Whatever I made you think, I was wrong," he said, and gulped. "I came out to find you because I couldn't let you go."

"You came out in this snowstorm to find me?" she gasped.

"I thought I was doing the right thing by turning you away. Even if I had feelings for you, I had to put Lola first. But then Lola told me this story about Cammi getting grounded, and I realized that a parent has to teach forgiveness." He looked at Emma. "You lied because your feelings were hurt. But I made a mistake too. I should have told you about Harry's offer instead of keeping the plane ticket a surprise."

"We were both young and inexperienced," Emma offered. "I didn't leave a note for you or Lola because I didn't want to lie to you both," she explained. "I thought I could just disappear and we'd never see each other."

Fletcher leaned forward and kissed her. "We've been apart for eleven years. Now that we've found each other, I'd like to try again."

Emma kissed him back. He put his arm around her and crushed her against his chest.

"I would like that too," she whispered, and glanced at the clock on the dashboard. "But now we have to hurry. The talent show starts soon, and we can't be late for Lola's number."

Fletcher put the car in drive. The wheels spun, and for a moment he thought they were stuck. Then Emma touched his arm and the car edged onto the road.

"Don't worry, I won't let us miss the show," he said. "Lola's counting on both of us, and we won't let her down."

Fletcher stood in the back of the Snowberry Playhouse and thought everything looked perfect. A gold banner reading WELCOME 2020! was strung across the stage, and below it was a Christmas tree decorated with ornaments. The women in the audience were wearing glimmering cocktail dresses, the men were dressed in dinner jackets, and the hall was filled with the scent of perfume and men's cologne.

Emma sat at the piano in her red dress with the gold stole draped over her shoulders, and Fletcher thought she'd never looked so beautiful. Lola was wearing one of Cassandra's most outrageous creations, a patchwork velvet jumper over a turtleneck and neon yellow tights. Her hair was festooned with a red bow, and she was wearing black Mary Janes.

As Fletcher waited for Lola to start, he recalled the nights he'd stood anxiously in the back of the Old Vic, like when the female lead in *The Taming of the Shrew* had a Scottish accent and he was afraid no one would understand her lines. Even when Daniel Day-Lewis had been in the audience of *King Lear,* he hadn't been as nervous as he was now. Lola was going to sing in front of all these people, and he didn't want anything to go wrong.

Stephen appeared on the stage and announced the next act. Lola strode to the podium and took the microphone as if it were an old friend.

The opening strains of "So This Is Christmas" came from the piano, and Fletcher let the music carry him away. He recalled the first time he'd heard Lola sing at a child's birthday party, when he'd realized she had a special talent. Emma looked up from the piano in his direction, and he thought his heart might burst.

The song ended and everyone stood up and clapped. The applause continued, and the smile on Lola's face was as wide as the Ferris wheel in Hyde Park.

The curtain came down and Fletcher was about to return to his seat. Suddenly Lola hurtled down the aisle and flung her arms around Fletcher's waist.

"How did I do?" she asked. Her eyes sparkled and her cheeks were flushed. "Do you think I could be a Broadway star when I grow up?"

"You don't have to wait until you grow up." Fletcher picked her up and twirled her around. "You're a star now."

It was the last act and everyone returned to their seats. Betty appeared on the stage, wearing a silver evening gown. The spotlight illuminated the diamond earrings in her ears.

"What a wonderful night we've had," Betty said into the microphone. "In all my years of celebrating New Year's Eve in Snowberry, I can't remember one I've enjoyed more." She looked out into the theater. "Before I announce the winners, I want to thank everyone for being here. Less than a week ago, I thought I might lose the inn, and a special girl suggested how I might keep it. I was skeptical, but that's because I forgot about Christmas miracles. You've all shown me so much love and support. No matter whose name is in this envelope"—she waved the envelope—"I'm the biggest winner tonight."

Everyone clapped, and Emma slipped into the seat beside Fletcher. He squeezed her hand and there was a rustling onstage.

"We have a tie for second place," Betty read from the card. "Marie Gould for her rendition of 'God Rest Ye Merry Gentlemen' and Tom Addams for his piano recital of Brahms's 'Lullaby.'"

Everyone applauded, and Fletcher saw the look of hope mingled with disappointment on Lola's face. He put one arm around her and waited for Betty to continue.

"Our grand prize winner is a young lady with a voice we'll hear many times in the future." Betty peered at the clock on the wall. "It's almost midnight, so I'm not going to waste any more time announcing Lola Conway as tonight's winner of a week's stay at The Smuggler's Inn!"

Lola jumped up and dashed onto the stage. Betty squeezed her tightly and Stephen joined them at the podium.

"I want to thank Betty and Stephen and everyone involved with the talent show," Lola said into the microphone. "But mostly I want to thank my father for bringing me to The Smuggler's Inn and Emma for helping me practice. I'm almost ten, and I thought I had to stop believing in Santa Claus. But I think I'm going to keep believing. What else besides a Christmas miracle could be responsible for all the good things that happened this week in Snowberry?"

Lola returned to her seat and showed the trophy to Fletcher and Emma. Betty came and joined them and Lola was so excited she kept humming "Jingle Bells" while people stopped by to congratulate her. Then Betty and Lola joined Stephen and they passed out sparkly eyeglasses and bags of confetti.

The overhead lights dimmed and the hall was only lit by the twinkling lights on the stage. Everyone glanced up at the ceiling and gold and silver balloons floated to the ground. "Auld Lang

Syne" played over the loudspeaker and everyone clapped and cheered. People blew streamers and Fletcher pulled Emma closer.

"Happy New Year," he breathed, kissing her. Emma kissed him back. Fletcher whispered in her ear, "Lola's right; everything about this week has been a Christmas miracle."

Twenty-one

New Year's Day
Snowberry, Vermont

EMMA FOLDED BLOUSES INTO HER suitcase. It was New Year's Day, and she was driving back to New York. Triple A fixed the battery and she and Fletcher had picked her car up this morning. Fletcher and Lola were leaving at the same time, and they were going to caravan. Outside the window, the sky was a crisp blue, and the fields were blanketed in fresh snow.

Last night after the talent show had been a whirlwind. The snow had finally stopped, and she and Fletcher and Lola went to the diner and shared an ice cream sundae. Lola put her trophy in the middle of the table and was so excited, Fletcher had to keep reminding her to take bites of the vanilla ice cream and chocolate syrup.

When they returned to The Smuggler's Inn, Lola went to her room to Skype Cassandra, and Emma and Fletcher lingered in the parlor. Betty had discreetly left out a bottle of sherry, and they talked for hours. Fletcher told Emma about being a director, Emma described her work as a copywriter, and they talked about London and New York.

Then they went upstairs and kissed in the hallway for so long, Emma's mouth was numb. Emma was tempted to ask Fletcher into her room, but decided against it. They were both exhausted from the talent show, and there was no reason to rush into making love.

There would be plenty of opportunities; they both agreed they wanted to start seeing each other regularly. Fletcher asked her to attend the opening of a Broadway show, and Emma invited him to a dinner party at Bronwyn and Carlton's. They planned a trip to the Natural History Museum with Lola, and Emma suggested an English pub Fletcher might like in Midtown.

There was a knock at the door and Emma answered it.

"I wondered if you needed help packing." Lola entered the room. "Betty is making a late breakfast before we leave. She said we need a proper Vermont breakfast: pancakes with maple syrup and cheddar cheese omelets and sausages."

"I'm still full from last night," Emma groaned, tucking a book into her suitcase. "What did your mother say when you showed her your trophy?"

"She was thrilled. We're going to keep it next to her Oliver award for costume design—that's like the British Tonys," Lola said knowledgeably. "Stephen's friend at the *Southern Vermont Gazette* is writing an article about the talent show, and he's going to use my photo. I hope my hair looks all right; it gets frizzy under the lights."

"Spoken like a true actress," Emma laughed. "Trust me, you looked lovely. You stole the talent show."

"Betty said we raised enough money to save the inn," Lola said eagerly. "She's going to make the talent show an annual event, and next Christmas she'll donate the proceeds to charity."

"Your mother should be proud of you," Emma returned. "Learning how to help others is one of the most important lessons of all."

"She said we could do something special to celebrate." Lola fiddled with her hair. "I told her I'd like some new boots, and maybe we could get something for the baby at the same time."

"You said you knew about the baby!" Emma exclaimed.

"I didn't mean to; it slipped out." Lola perched on the bed. "But I'm glad it did. I hate keeping secrets. At first she seemed upset, but then I told her I couldn't wait to read the baby my Beatrix Potter books." Lola looked at Emma. "The funniest thing happened— my mother started crying. She said there was something in her eye and that she needed tissues. But when she came back, her eyes were watery and she was sniffling."

"I'm sure she was relieved," Emma offered. "There's nothing she wants more than for you to be happy."

"How can I not be happy? I won a trophy, and someday I'm going to be on Broadway." Lola noticed Emma's belongings scattered on the bedspread. She picked up a black jewelry case and opened it. "Why do you have a man's watch?"

"It's a present," Emma said quickly, holding out her hand.

"It's engraved with Dad's name." Lola's eyes widened. "*To Fletcher, you have my heart. Emma.*"

"I gave it to your dad a long time ago," Emma admitted. "Then the craziest thing happened. I found it in a jewelry store in New York on Christmas Eve."

"You mean you and Dad were more than just friends in college?" Lola asked.

"I guess you could say that," Emma said, nodding. "It was a long time ago."

"I could tell you liked each other!" Lola exclaimed. "I have an instinct about these things."

"I do like your father." Emma looked at Lola. "I hope that's all right with you."

"It's the best news ever." Lola nodded happily. "We can do so many fun things in New York, like visit Dylan's Candy Bar and climb to the top of the Empire State Building."

"Slow down," Emma laughed. "You have to go to school and I have to work. But we'll make a list and work our way through it."

"I'll meet you downstairs." Lola jumped off the bed. "I can smell the pancakes from the top of the staircase. Broadway actresses always eat big breakfasts after a performance." She tossed her hair over her shoulders. "Using your vocal cords makes you hungry."

"There you are," Betty said when Emma entered the dining room. The table was set with a floral tablecloth and a potted chrysanthemum. There was a pitcher of orange juice and a plate of homemade muffins. Fletcher was sitting at one end of the table, digging into scrambled eggs. Lola was next to him, pouring syrup onto an enormous stack of pancakes.

"It smells delicious, but that ice cream sundae last night almost finished me off." Emma pulled out a chair across from Fletcher. "I'll start with coffee."

"You need more than coffee." Betty placed a cup in front of her. "You have a long drive to New York. I packed turkey sandwiches, so you don't have to eat at some highway stop where the sandwiches come in vending machines and the cheese tastes like plastic."

"I will miss Vermont cheeses; there's nothing like them in Manhattan. I'll miss everything about The Smuggler's Inn." Emma looked at Betty. "Especially having a new friend."

"I'm the one who should be grateful." Betty sat down. "The talent show raised enough money to pay the taxes, and the phone is ringing off the hook with new reservations. Stephen and I are planning a trip to New York in January. He has to check on some investments and I'll buy some cruise wear." Betty glanced from Emma to Lola. "Maybe you can join me for afternoon tea at the Plaza."

"We'd love to." Emma smiled.

"And Dad and I will be in Snowberry all summer," Lola announced, eating a bite of sausage. "Stephen said I can be a fairy in *A Midsummer Night's Dream*. I'm going to take tap lessons at the local dance studio. A Broadway actress has to be well-rounded."

"Will you be joining us this summer?" Betty asked Emma.

"We talked about it last night." Emma glanced at Fletcher. "I can work from home on Fridays, so I'm going to come for long weekends."

"Emma will stop me from spending all my time at the theater." Fletcher smiled. "Without her to drag me away from the playhouse, I'd be the only person in Snowberry who doesn't have a tan by Labor Day."

"Emma showed me the watch she gave Dad when they were in college," Lola announced to the table. "She found it in a used jewelry store on Christmas Eve." She sighed. "It's like the romantic movies that Cammi's mother watches when she's supposed to be making dinner."

"I was going to give it to you as a late Christmas present," Emma said to Fletcher. "That is, if you'll wear it."

"Of course I'll wear it." Fletcher nodded and reached into a shopping bag. "I bought you a Christmas present." He handed her a box wrapped in red paper.

Emma opened it. Inside was a silver charm bracelet, with one charm: a maple leaf.

"I found it at the Snowberry General Store," Fletcher said. "Every time you return to Vermont, you can add a new charm."

"It's lovely." Emma fastened it around her wrist. "Thank you."

"I bought you a present too," Fletcher said, handing Lola a parcel wrapped in Christmas-themed paper.

Lola tore off the paper and discovered an American Girl doll. She had wavy red hair and carried a tennis racquet.

"It's an American Girl doll, because now you're an American girl," Fletcher said to Lola.

"I love it—I can't wait to show it to Cammi." Lola hugged her father. "Cammi says the American Girl Café is the coolest restaurant in New York."

"She's carrying the tennis racquet to remind you to be a child," Fletcher said, hugging her back. "Not everything in life revolves around the theater."

"This is the best Christmas ever," Lola gushed. "I made new friends and won a trophy, and learned how to stitch teddy bears back together."

"It *is* the best Christmas," Fletcher said, smiling at Emma. "And there's so much to look forward to: summer in Vermont, and the opening of the play on Broadway. I can't wait until next year when we all celebrate Christmas at The Smuggler's Inn."

Emma looked at Lola with her wild red hair, and Fletcher in his turtleneck and ski sweater, and was completely confident that in 365 days she'd be sitting between them toasting the new year.

If anyone had told her a week ago that she'd be having break-fast with Fletcher and his daughter at a Vermont inn with snow-flakes sticking to the windowsill and logs crackling in the fireplace, she would have said they were crazy. But, as Bronwyn would have pointed out, that was the thing about synchronicity: it appeared in your life when you least expected it, and made your dreams come true.

"I agree," she said, returning Fletcher's smile. "Next Christmas is going to be perfect."

Acknowledgments

Thank you to my wonderful editor, Lauren Jablonski, and agent, Melissa Flashman, and to the incredible team at St. Martin's Press: Meghan Harrington, Jordan Hanley, Brant Janeway, and always to Jennifer Weis and Jennifer Enderlin.

Thank you to my dear friends Tracy Soderberg Whitney, Sara Sullivan, Kelly Berke, Laura Narbutas, and Pat Hazelton Hull. And thank you to my children for all the joy in my life: Alex, Andrew, Heather, Madeleine, and Thomas.

Read on for a look ahead to

A MAGICAL NEW YORK CHRISTMAS —

the next heartwarming Christmas novel
by Anita Hughes, now available in
trade paperback from St. Martin's Griffin!

There really was nothing like the Plaza Hotel in New York at Christmas. The Pulitzer Fountain on Fifth Avenue was strung with silver lights, and the valets resembled chocolate soldiers in their red velvet coats and gold caps. But it was the lobby itself— white and gold columns wrapped in satin bows and glass tables scattered with presents—that took Sabrina's breath away.

She reminded herself she wasn't a tourist about to go ice-skating in Rockefeller Center or see a show at Radio City Music Hall. She was here to work. But her heels clicked faster on the marble and when she saw the Christmas tree, yards and yards of lights and ornaments reaching to the ceiling, she couldn't squelch her excitement.

"Hi, I'm here to see Mr. Prescott," she said as she approached the concierge desk.

"We're happy to have Mr. Prescott back at the Plaza." The man tapped on his computer. He glanced up at Sabrina. "You must be Miss Post. A butler will show you up to his suite."

"Oh, that's not necessary." Sabrina shifted and wondered what the concierge thought of her outfit. The skirt was a designer knockoff that she'd had since her first postcollege job but the blouse was a recent purchase. The salesgirl had said it could be worn anywhere from the office to a holiday party, but that probably didn't include the Plaza Hotel, where other guests wore cashmere sweaters and the softest Burberry slacks.

"What's not necessary elsewhere is standard at the Plaza." The concierge snapped his fingers and a butler appeared as if by magic.

Sabrina tried to think of something to say to the butler in the elevator but she was too nervous. There were six hundred dollars in her bank account and if she didn't get this job, she'd be eating beans the whole week between Christmas and New Year's. Not to mention the rent on her apartment in Queens. Her parents would be happy to send the rent check as a Christmas present. But it had been four years since Sabrina received her journalism degree, and it was time she was financially independent. Then she thought of one of her favorite books, Dickens's *A Christmas Carol,* which she had been reading on the subway. There was a reason Dickens wrote about poverty in his books: writers were usually on the verge of being broke.

"Mr. Prescott is in the Vanderbilt Suite," the butler said when the elevator doors opened. "Would you like me to announce your arrival?"

"No, thank you," Sabrina commented. If he escorted her any farther he would expect a tip, and he probably wouldn't accept the laundromat token in her purse.

The hallway was decorated in grays and yellows with thick beige carpeting and gold-framed paintings on the walls.

"Miss Post," Grayson Prescott said when she rang the doorbell. "Please come in."

Sabrina had googled him, of course. Grayson Prescott had

sold more than a billion dollars' worth of paintings during his career as a private art dealer and he was credited with sparking Beyoncé and Jay-Z's interest in the work of Damien Hirst. His clients ranged from Bill Gates to Mary-Kate Olsen and there wasn't a private collection from the Hamptons to Beverly Hills that Grayson hadn't been involved with.

"Can I get you something to drink? The orange juice is delicious." He waved at the minibar and Sabrina thought he looked younger than his eighty years. He had a full head of white hair and his eyes were clear and blue. He was over six feet tall and Sabrina could imagine him in one of those faded newspaper photos of college quarterbacks in the 1950s—all square shoulders and thick chests.

"I'm fine, thank you." Sabrina shook her head.

"Please, I won't feel as guilty if you join me." He poured her a glass. "The prices at the Plaza always make me feel that way. The last time I had the Wagyu beef at the Palm Court, I had such a guilty conscience I wrote a check for the same amount to the Red Cross."

Sabrina accepted the orange juice and took a small sip.

"You came highly recommended by an old friend, Chester White. I gather you're his goddaughter."

"Our families have known each other for years," Sabrina said with a nod. "I grew up in New Jersey and my parents are both professors."

"Anyone Chester recommends is good enough for me." Grayson leaned back in his chair. "I hadn't heard of ghostwriters before, let alone thought I needed one. When I signed with my publisher, I imagined writing a memoir would be fun. Who doesn't want to believe his life might be interesting to others? But then Leo's emails changed from rants about the Giants game with a polite sentence asking how the book was coming to pointed letters saying he needs the first draft by January."

"I'm sure I can do a good job." Sabrina was earnest. "I spent the last week researching your career. I was impressed with your early appreciation of Kenneth Noland. You sold one of his pieces to Robert De Niro when the only place they had been displayed was in Noland's guest bathroom."

"It was a clever place to hang it. Most dinner party guests are bound to use the powder room and notice it." Grayson's eyes twinkled. "I had a client in the south of France who kept a seventy-five-million-dollar Van Gogh above her bathtub. The insurance company didn't want to allow it, they were afraid it would warp. My client said if she paid that much for a painting, she wanted to hang it where she spent the most time." He looked at Sabrina thoughtfully. "Leo is expecting a tell-all, but that's not what I want to write. There will be some of that; I won't disappoint him. But isn't a memoir the only chance one has to teach something important?" He leaned forward. "I want to write about my own Christmas miracle."

"A Christmas miracle?" Sabrina repeated.

"Life is about three things: there's hard work. You can't be happy if you aren't passionate about what you do. But there's also luck. Luck can make the difference between leading a pleasant existence and having a life where every day is exciting and you can't wait to get out of bed."

"And the third thing?" Sabrina asked.

"That's the part a lot of people get wrong," he answered and a small cloud passed over his face. "Recognizing the luck when it arrives."

"It sounds interesting," Sabrina said doubtfully. She had to fill three hundred pages and it was easier to write about concrete names and places than nebulous ideas. But Grayson was paying her and she had to do what he said.

"It better be," Grayson chuckled. "Or people at the airport bookstore will pass over the book and buy the autobiography of that fellow who flips houses." He smiled at Sabrina and his face was almost boyish. "I believe my assistant discussed pay and accommodations. She booked you the Fitzgerald Suite, it's on the next floor."

"I don't need a suite!" Sabrina insisted.

"That's all that was available. And you can charge any food or drink at the hotel. You will be working over the holiday week and I don't want to seem like some kind of Scrooge."

Sabrina pictured eggs benedict and Belgian waffles for breakfast and lunches of French onion soup and the Plaza's famous burger and had to stop herself from blurting out that she'd work for free.

"That sounds fine," she said instead. "I brought a suitcase with a few clothes. I left them with the valet."

Thank God her best friend, Chloe, worked in fashion and regularly trolled the sample sales. Sabrina had begged to borrow Chloe's Vince sweater and Theory pantsuit.

"Excellent," he said, beaming. "And I promise we won't work all the time, if you might be meeting anyone."

Sabrina tried to remember the last time she'd had a date. It had been in August when a magazine writer had asked her to attend Shakespeare in the Park. Patrick had been as broke as she was, and even after pooling their resources, they could barely afford two hot dogs. He said he'd call after he got his next check but he never did.

"I don't have anyone to meet." Sabrina shook her head.

Grayson looked at Sabrina kindly and held out his hand. "Do we have a deal?"

For the first time since she'd entered, she allowed herself to glance around. The floors were parquet and there were gold upholstered armchairs and gray velvet sofas. The sideboard was set with blue-and-white china and there was a coffee table with a glass chess set. How could she pass up six nights at the Plaza and a paycheck that would allow her to pay the heating bill and get her hair cut in the same month?

Sabrina shook Grayson's hand and felt the same anticipation she experienced when she entered the Plaza's lobby: for a short time, her life could include paper-thin cucumber sandwiches at the Palm Court and holiday cocktails served in tinted glasses and topped with whipped cream.

"We have a deal."

They worked for an hour and then Grayson apologized that the combination of jet lag and old age was making him tired and he needed to lie down.

Sabrina took the elevator to the fifteenth floor and slipped the key into the door. There was a small salon with one wall of mirrors. An art deco desk stood by the window and stockings hung from a marble fireplace. The bookshelf held leather-bound books and a Christmas tree was decorated with glass ornaments.

In the bedroom, Sabrina discovered a four-poster bed and a bedside table with a Tiffany lamp. The welcome card detailed the 24-karat gold fixtures in the bathroom and the soaking tub that could be filled with a selection of bath salts. White-glove butler service was available twenty-four hours a day, and anything she needed was on the other end of the phone. But it was the bed itself—king-size with a padded headboard and white comforter as soft as fresh snow—that was the most inviting.

When was the last time she'd had a full night's sleep? She'd spent the last two weeks working twelve-hour days with an aging rock star until he decided he needed spiritual awakening before he could finish his memoir. The next day he'd flown off to Joshua Tree without paying her fee.

She peeled back the bedspread and rested her head on the pillow. She'd close her eyes for a few minutes and then she'd transcribe her notes.

When she woke up, the time on the bedside clock said 12:30 A.M. and for a moment she didn't remember where she was. She drew back the curtains and was stunned by the beauty of the night skyline. Fifth Avenue was a patchwork of colors far below. The Empire State Building was festooned with green and red Christmas lights, and Central Park shimmered as brightly as an airport runway.

Then she sank back on the bed and realized she was starving. The only thing she had eaten all day was a turkey sandwich that she had fished out of the bottom of her purse when she got off the subway. When she'd taken it out from under her laptop it was completely flat and the mayonnaise had leaked into the plastic bag. She'd taken two bites and tossed it in the garbage.

Grayson had said she could sign for whatever she liked, but she didn't feel like ordering room service. She changed into the Vince sweater and a pair of slacks and stepped into the hallway. The sleeves were a bit long but Sabrina was glad she'd brought it. At least if anyone saw her, they wouldn't think she'd snuck into the Plaza for the free hot chocolate.

The Palm Court was dark except for the light of a vacuum

cleaner being pushed across the floral rugs. The Champagne Bar had closed at midnight and there were only a few Christmas cookies left on the complimentary display in the lobby. Sabrina took the stairs down to the Rose Club, but the sleek walnut bar was empty. She was about to go back to her room when she noticed a man asleep on the sofa. He wore an expensive-looking gray suit and there was a silver tray and an empty glass on the coffee table.

The man stirred and sat up.

"I'm sorry, I didn't mean to wake you."

"What time is it?" He rubbed his eyes. He had dark wavy hair and spoke with a British accent.

"Almost one a.m.," Sabrina said after glancing at her phone.

"That's six a.m. London time," the man groaned. "I don't usually fall asleep in public places, but I've been awake for almost twenty-four hours. I'm surprised someone didn't wake me before." He glanced around for a bartender but there was no one there. He grinned at Sabrina. "For all I know, a housekeeper was here to vacuum but didn't want to disturb me. I'll have to apologize to the front desk."

"Did you just arrive?" she asked.

"Last night." He waved his hand and Sabrina noticed his gold cuff links. "It's all a bit of a blur. My stomach wanted breakfast but the clock said it was time for dinner."

"That's why I came downstairs," Sabrina said. "I took a nap and woke up starving. But everything is closed."

He pointed to the tray.

"You're welcome to share some of mine."

"I couldn't do that." Sabrina shook her head.

The man sat up straighter and ran his hands through his hair.

"Please. This caviar is four hundred dollars an ounce; it would be a shame for it to go to waste. And the lobster rolls are delicious, I can't imagine where the Plaza gets fresh lobster at Christmas."

"They partner with a lobster farm in Maine," Sabrina answered. "The lobster is put on a train every morning and delivered directly from Grand Central Station to the Plaza."

"How did you know that?" he asked.

Sabrina blushed and shrugged her shoulders. "It's the kind of thing some New Yorkers know."

"So you live in New York and are staying at the Plaza?"

Sabrina was quiet. One of the rules of being a ghostwriter was to never disclose anything about her work or the client.

"I'm staying here for a project," she said offhandedly. "It's too distracting to work from home."

"Then you must join me," he insisted. "This is only my second time in New York and you can give me some tips. You know, like when tourists come to London and they're disappointed because Prince William and Kate aren't at any of the nightclubs and no matter how many times they walk past Buckingham Palace, they never see the Queen coming out."

Sabrina laughed and glanced longingly at the tray: caviar in silver bowls and pink lobster on pumpernickel. Wedges of cheese that looked as soft and buttery as whole cream.

"If you're sure." She could barely pull her eyes away. "I'm Sabrina."

"Ian." He piled a plate with caviar and melba toast and handed it to her. "I thought only Californians were friendly," he said, when he had poured two glasses of sparkling water from the bottle on the table. "But I couldn't walk through the lobby without being asked what temperature I liked my suite and whether I preferred a silk robe or cashmere pajamas. I've never discussed how I sleep with another man before." He grinned and she noticed how his eyes crinkled at the corners. "He would be disappointed that I wear a T-shirt and flannel pajama pants."

"That's only at the Plaza." Sabrina smiled. "If you want to meet grouchy New Yorkers, you only have to walk down Fifth Avenue at Christmastime. You can't enter Macy's because of the tourists standing in front of the window displays, and there are so many people sledding in Central Park, it's as dangerous as schussing in the Alps."

"Londoners are the same. We insist that everyone who comes to London must see the Christmas lights in Piccadilly Circus, and then we're cross that there aren't any taxis."

"New York at Christmas is magical," Sabrina sighed, biting into melba toast. She'd never had caviar before and at first it tasted foreign. But she took a second bite and the crunchy toast and salty fish eggs were a perfect combination. "My parents brought me to New York when I was eight. They wanted to show me the Natural History Museum and the children's floor at Saks but all I wanted was to come to the Plaza Hotel and meet Eloise."

"Eloise?" Ian repeated.

"I guess you've never been an eight-year-old girl," Sabrina laughed. "Eloise was the most beloved guest of the Plaza Hotel. She was six years old and lived in a suite with her nanny and her dog, Weenie, and her turtle, Skipperdee. She got into all sorts of trouble but she always managed to make things right. I looked for her everywhere: at the Palm Court and in the Persian Room. I even cajoled a butler into opening the Royal Suite to see if she was there."

"You must have been irresistible if someone showed you the Royal Suite. That's reserved for kings and heads of state."

She suddenly felt embarrassed. She had never talked about

Eloise with a guy before. It was like admitting she liked rom-coms or preferred a Snickers bar to imported chocolate.

"I didn't find her because she lived in a book," Sabrina finished awkwardly.

"I've discovered some of my best friends in books," Ian rejoined. "Harry Potter of course, but also Pip in *Great Expectations*. I wanted to be like Pip: street smart but with a heart of gold."

"You read Dickens?"

"He was one of my favorite authors growing up, along with John le Carré and Ian Fleming," he admitted. "After I outgrew Pip, I spent a few years wishing I was James Bond."

Sabrina was about to say she had a copy of Dickens's *A Christmas Carol* in her room and stopped. She was at the Plaza to work, not to flirt with strangers. Besides, any man who could afford to stay at the Plaza probably dated corporate CEOs or high-powered attorneys.

The screen on her phone blinked 1:30 A.M. She had to get some sleep or she wouldn't be alert in the morning.

"I really should go." She stood up. "Thank you for the caviar."

"I'll go up with you," Ian suggested. "If I stay here I might fall asleep again and I'll be in pain for days. Eight hours twisted like a pretzel on the plane and then a sofa cushion for a neck pillow instead of the down pillows they have in the suite."

The lobby was deserted except for the concierge idling behind his desk. The Christmas tree glittered under white chandeliers, and Sabrina was reminded of the scene in *The Nutcracker* when everyone had gone to bed and the toys had woken up and become real.

"What floor are you on?" Ian asked when they stepped in the elevator.

"Fifteenth floor, please."

"It looks like we're neighbors," he said pleasantly.

Sabrina stood toward the back. The intimate mood in the Rose Club—the crushed velvet of the sofa under dimmed lighting, the novelty of eating melba toast and caviar—evaporated, and she felt self-conscious. What had she been thinking, sharing a meal with a stranger past midnight?

The elevator stopped and Ian took out his key. He turned to Sabrina and held out his hand. "It was nice meeting you, Sabrina."

"It was nice meeting you too," she answered. His hand was warm and smooth and she wondered if she would see him again. "I hope you enjoy your stay in New York."

Sabrina put the key in her door and it clicked open.

"Sabrina," Ian called from across the hall.

"Yes?"

"I think you're wrong about Eloise. I guarantee that you're the most delightful guest the Plaza has ever had."